Gods in Londinium

# Gods in Londinium

JOHN DRAKE

LUME BOOKS

LUME BOOKS

Published in 2022 by Lume Books

ISBN 978-1-83901-513-7

Typeset using Atomik ePublisher from Easypress Technologies

www.lumebooks.co.uk

*Dedicated to the valiant Ukrainian nation,*
*led by the heroic Volodymyr Zelenskyy.*

# CHAPTER 1

My dreams are always bad, and this one is even worse. I am on a beach, some miles from my city of Apollonis, and the monster – the Chimera – is mounted on a platform facing the sea. The Chimera is a machine. It is Greek engineering perverted, and – worst of all – it is *my* machine, since I designed it. It is my creation and it is a weapon of war.

It is a war machine, but no sort of artillery that warfare would recognise, because it has a furnace and a hot stench and men standing by to work it, while shaking in terror. Only two things are certain about the Chimera: it is the product of science, not magic, and it is wildly uncertain in operation. It is dreadful to the enemy, but likely to kill every man of its own crew.

So, I am wearing protective clothes: a robe and hood with boots and leggings, all of wool, since wool is slow to burn. All the crew are in wool, but I am the commanding officer, with more protection.

My junior officer comes forward with a shield. It is a Roman shield, the *scutum militaris*, a half-cylinder of laminated wood that is large, light and strong, and one of the few devices that the Romans invented all by themselves without a Greek to show them how. And they invented it very well, because even we – the men of Apollonis – voted to adopt the Roman shield in battle.

"Honoured sir," says the young man, "please take the shield."

"No," I say, "I will not take protection that the men cannot." I look at the crew. They cannot hide behind shields while working the machine, so they are terrified, and they are here only because they are criminals excused the death sentence for this duty. Once, the Chimera crews had been volunteers. But not anymore. Not now.

So I look round. Only soldiers are present. All the people have been kept away from this secret place. The young officer speaks again.

"Honoured sir," he says, "I must give you the shield. I am commanded by high authority."

I sigh. I take the shield. He bows low.

"Now get back," I say. "Get away from here."

"Will you not retreat yourself, honoured sir?"

"No. My duty is here."

He runs off. I ground the shield according to drill. I kneel behind it to take most protection, and prepare to duck low at the slightest need. Then I shout to the crew and they reply.

"Furnace man ready?"

"Ready!"

"Safety valve clear?"

"Clear!"

"Hose men ready?"

"Ready!"

"Torch man ready?"

"Ready!"

"Shoot!"

2

But then comes the explosion, which throws the crewmen burning and shrieking and only my shield saves me. Perhaps a valve stuck: who knows?

The dream shifts.

I am in the senate chamber of the city of Apollonis. Everything is white marble. A dome rises above me. The sun shines through the illuminating circular opening – the oculus – in the peak of the dome. One hundred senators sit in formal robes. Grey hair, white beards, dignity, soft echoes of conversation in the great stony hall. We are the governing body of Apollonite democracy. We sit in semi-circular ranks, each man in the marble chair incised with his name, rank and clan.

The speaker of the house lifts his voice and every man stares at me.

"I call upon Ikaros!" he says, "Ikaros, son of Cleon! Ikaros: grandson of Philippos of the Clan of the Horse! Ikaros: co-opted to the command of the Chimera!"

I stand. I go forward to the speaking place. I am given tongue by Apollo. My words flow with passion.

"The Chimera brings shame upon our city, our clans, and our gods! No man will work it willingly, it is disgrace to compel the unwilling, and even when it works, it inflicts such wounds upon the enemy as are beyond all civilised usages of war!"

"AYE!" say the senators in a united growl.

I continue. "If the Romans come, and if we must fight, then let us fight like men! Let us fight with honour, so that those who come after us may be proud!"

"AYE!"

I go on and on. Not one word is said against me. At last I sit down.

The speaker nods. "I congratulate Ikaros son of Cleon for his chosen words," he says.

The senators agree. "AYE!"

The speaker of the house continues. "The motion put before us by Ikaros son of Cleon, is that all works on Chimera shall cease, while it, and all records of its design, shall be destroyed."

"AYE!"

"All present will now stand, who wish to support the motion!"

A rustle and rumble as every senator stands.

Then, all of them are coming to me, in smiles and congratulation.

The dream shifts again.

Two years have passed.

Apollonis is burning. Fires roar, smoke rises, even as the Romans come over the walls from the great ramp built by their engineers. The long siege is ending in victory for Rome. Our men are stabbed by Roman swords, while the noblest of our women are dying by their own hands rather than be defiled or enslaved.

I am in my house. I am on my knees. My armour is hacked and dented, my helmet is thrown off, my sword hangs useless in its scabbard. I am holding my wife and children in my arms. They are dead and I am soaked in their blood. I am in agony because I know very well … I know without the slightest doubt … I know to the deep of my soul … that had I not spoken against the Chimera, and had we used it against the Romans, then our city would not have fallen, and my loved ones would still be alive.

# CHAPTER 2

But why was I suffering nightmares? Why nightmares in a comfortable bed in Roman Londinium, where I was living in safety and luxury? Some explanation is needed.

Londinium was in Britannia, at the extreme reach of Roman power, and Britannia was strange and violent, and could not be trusted with any shade of self-government. So it was an imperial province, directly owned by the emperor, ruled by a governor, and held by three legions plus auxiliaries and cavalry: the biggest army of occupation in the entire empire. So, what did the Romans want of this strange and violent province?

Britannia was valuable in terms of produce: gold, silver, lead, pearls and corn. Also, local manufacture delivered a range of goods, including even the technically complex Roman army shield. Thus the province attracted entrepreneurs from across the empire, provided they were bold enough to take the risk of ferocious native uprisings. There was indeed great wealth in Britannia. But the real reason the Romans took it and held it was as a message to their rivals outside the empire – whether German savage or Parthian sage – that Rome could conquer any one, or any thing, that Rome chose. So the Germans,

Parthians and others must make no hostile move against Rome, for fear that Rome will visit them with ten thousand pairs of boots, all tramping in perfect step.

So much for Britannia. What of myself? I was a Greek from the lost city of Apollonis: a tall man with a little of grey in my beard. I was pleasing to women and accustomed to the signs of their appreciation: a half-smile, then downcast eyes and a raised hand patting the hair in place. Also, I was a slave, but what kind of slave? Because – like everything else in the Roman world – slaves were ranked from high to low as defined by their cost. As the Romans say, *servus pretium scit*: the slave knows his price.

At the bottom were those condemned to the mines: criminal brutes, who were worked to death in a few years. Next came field slaves, worth more than pigs but less than horses. Then house slaves, who were valued according to skill: maids, footmen, cooks or even major domos of high price. Higher still came craftsmen: smiths, potters, carpenters, even locksmiths and jewellers and the like, who were semi-independent of their owners and might become so wealthy as to buy their freedom. At the top were the exotics: beautiful boys and girls whose prices were measured in millions, also educated Greeks recognised by the Romans as being superior in knowledge.

I was one of this latter group, having been captured when the Romans destroyed Apollonis. Beyond even that, there were other slaves of truly colossal value, as I shall explain later. But all slaves, of whatever kind, were property and not people. They were possessions, with no more legal rights than a mongrel dog or a priceless Chinese vase.

In my own city I had been a senator, an engineer and a surgeon. I was an officer of cavalry too, in wartime. So I was valued for these things, and for other skills that were my blessing and my curse. Thus everyone says that I am a very clever man. I suppose that I am, but I see no cleverness in myself: only the ability to make deductions, based on evidence, that seem obvious to me, even if obscure to others. Or perhaps I am too modest? Perhaps I am better at understanding evidence? How should I know?

The outstanding result of my supposed cleverness is my ability to know what men and women are thinking, and to tell truth from lies. The world calls this *mind-reading*, and the world is united in believing that I do it by magic. But I do not. In conversation I note facial expressions, posture and manner, and make judgement based on facts. Everyone does this to some degree, since everyone knows a smile from a frown, and everyone guesses that a man who picks up broken glass is thinking of cut fingers. So I insist that I do not work magic.

Conversely, my capacity to observe and make swift judgment is so greatly above that of everyone else, that perhaps I am indeed magic? How should I know, by hell, damnation and misery? Only the gods know. So I despair of explanation, and you the reader must decide for yourself.

Meanwhile, I have not explained why my gift is a curse. It is a curse because sometimes I look into the minds of those whom I respect, and like, or even love, and I do not like what I see, and disillusion is a great pain. That is probably why I drink.

# CHAPTER 3

Enough of my dreams, except to say that they were not messages from the gods, as is generally supposed. My dreams were caused by my sense of guilt for the loss of my family, and almost anything reminded me of that, even if I did something good.

I was in the great harbour of Londinium, just downstream of the bridge on a cold day under a grey Britannic sky. It was a two-cloak day, a thick puttees day, and I shivered and longed for the warmth of the Mediterranean. I was there with Morganus, first javelin of the Twentieth Legion: the senior of the legion's sixty centurions. We made a good pair, he and I. He personified the military might of Rome, and the Roman law that stood behind it, while I was a tall Greek, with the beard which Romans thought to be a sign of intellect. They especially thought that of a Greek, because Romans were nervous of Greek intellect and they were entirely correct to be nervous of mine, especially given my trick of 'mind-reading'.

I was therefore accorded special status. I had been purchased for the empire as an imperial slave, owned by the emperor himself. I thus became one of those very clever foreign slaves – mostly Greeks and Jews – who ran the imperial civil service. Who else would do it, after all? Romans are not clever enough to run their empire. Or perhaps I display Greek prejudice?

But I was a slave none the less, with Morganus standing *in loco Imperatoris*: in place of the emperor, as the Romans say. Thus I was obliged to live in his house and he was my owner in the emperor's name. If he had not been Morganus, that would have been humiliation for a man who had been a senator. But he was indeed Morganus, he was my dear friend, and his wife and daughters – in their gracious kindness – treated me as one their own. Therefore, despite all the troubles of my life – and one very great trouble in particular – thanks to Morganus and his family, my world was not entirely without sunshine and I bless them for it in Apollo's name.

And so to Morganus himself. I am tall but he is taller, especially when wearing the helmet of a first javelin with its transverse crest of swan feathers. The legions called him *the big man*, both for his height and the fact that he was a veteran of forty years' service, having joined up at fifteen and won every decoration that the Roman army had to give. His titles in full were Leionius Morganus Fortis Victrix: First Javelin, Hero of the Roman Army, Father of the Legion and Chief Priest of the Legion.

As regards the last title, note that a Roman chief priest is not a holy mystic rolling in the ecstasies of faith. He is an administrator, who maintains smooth relations with the gods in exactly the same way as the official in charge of aqueducts maintains a smooth flow of water. This is so because Romans see the gods as creatures like themselves, who deliver good fortune in return for ritual and sacrifice in a business-like exchange. That is the Roman way, and it works for them. After all, they rule the world, so the gods must be on their side. Even a Greek knows that.

So, there we stood on one of the main wharves of the port of Londinium, surrounded by ships large and small: some coming to anchor, some casting off, and all the busy noise of a sea port. I do love a sea port for the life-force of it: bold mariners, insolent dockers, arrogant merchants, and the arguing and calling, and the creak of ropes in blocks as cranes of all kinds heave goods out of the ships.

There we stood: the mind-reading Greek, too clever for his own good, the great and loyal soldier, and all that turbulent company took care not to bump or jostle us. They took care not just because of the formidable appearance of Morganus, but for the four huge Roman soldiers who stood like iron statues behind him. They were his bodyguard, found from the biggest men in the Twentieth Legion. They went with him everywhere – even to the latrine – and were as much a part of his equipment as the sword at his side or the boots on his feet. They were his insurance – and mine – that he could go anywhere in Britannia without watching his back in fear of dagger, and in those days in Britannia, that was useful.

It was also practical, since the Roman Empire had taken special note of the combination of Morganus and me. It did so because while Romans cannot invent anything, they are swift to grab any useful thing that they find by chance. Thus, the governor of Britannia was using myself and Morganus as detective agents in matters of high crime and politics. The governor did this because unlike my own city of Apollonis, the Romans had no police force: not even officers patrolling the streets to prevent crime, let alone detective inquisitors who investigated crime once committed.

But today we were not investigating crime or politics. We were in the port for other reasons.

"Ah!" said Morganus, "Here they come!"

A group of men shoved through the crowded dock. Shouts and complaints rose up all round, especially from the seamen who give no respect to any landman whatsoever. But the newcomers pushed, shoved and came forward. There was quite a company of them, with big slaves on the outside to clear the way for their masters— six well-dressed citizens— while a clump of superior slaves followed behind, clutching documents. But the dockyard folk grinned and yelled at the anxious looks on the citizens' faces as they approached Morganus.

"Been caught out?" said someone. "Had your hand in the strong-box?"

"Oooooooo!" said the crowd.

"Dirty buggers!" said someone else.

"Guilt written all over 'em!"

Then, the citizens and slaves stopped and bowed to Morganus. Or at least they did so eventually, but first there was an oddity that I had become used to on these occasions, because by normal Roman etiquette the citizens should have addressed Morganus and ignored me. They should have ignored me because I was a slave. Nobody greets a horse before its master, and it was the same with a slave. But Morganus was Morganus, and all Londinium knew that he was followed around by the magic Greek who read minds: the Greek who was dangerously clever. So, while the slaves entirely avoided looking at me, out of superstition, the citizens dithered and chewed their lips and glanced at each other, then gave a full bow to Morganus, and then a hesitant, awkward nod to me. It was amusing. I managed not to smile.

Then one of them spoke. "Honoured and illustrious Spear of the Twentieth," he said to Morganus with a glance at me, "I'm Grannix Calindo of Gaul and I'm the harbour master."

We nodded. We knew Grannix from previous investigations.

Grannix spoke on, introducing those he thought important enough to name. "These here, are Strabo, my assistant harbour master, and Secundus Ilyricus the shipmaster, and Timon the merchant who's buying the stuff, and his chief accountant, and all the clerks, and all the documents, all correct and legal, and in good order!"

"Yes!" said Strabo.

"All correct and legal!" said Secundus Ilyricus.

"All signed and witnessed!" said Timon the merchant.

"Good!" said Morganus. "In that case, later on in the harbour master's office, you will present all the documents for study by my comrade Ikaros of Apollonis." They all blinked at that and shuffled their feet. "But first you will take us to the ship *Lucky Home Bringer*, where my comrade will make inspection of the cargo, and pronounce upon its future."

"Ah … hmm …" said Grannix.

"Yes?" said Morganus.

"It really is all legal, your honour," said Grannix. He looked at Timon the merchant and added, "And it's big money, isn't it?"

The merchant nodded. "Over a million. My biggest purchase this year."

"None the less, we will go to the ship," said Morganus. "We will go now."

So we went along the quayside, followed by a grinning, chattering crowd, with more folk coming out of the warehouses and offices and the ships, for the fun of seeing the harbour master given orders and having to obey.

*Lucky Home Bringer* was a big Celtic merchantman, high-sided for ocean navigation, deep-bottomed, broad in the beam, and equipped with the usual twin rudders at the stern and a broad spread of sails.

It was a fine ship, which by the wonders of sea-faring could move a cargo of five hundred tons at the rate of a hundred miles per day, with only a dozen men to sail her. I never failed to be impressed by the comparison with moving such a cargo by land, because even with Roman roads, that would have required hundreds of wagons, beasts and men, in a stretched out procession which might cover only twenty miles per day.

The ship was made fast to the quayside by great cables, and her crew were lining the side, looking down on us as we approached with our noisy followers. I looked at them, and looked at the high masts, and the rigging and anchors, and the longboat astern on a rope that made me think of a dog's lead. But even before we went aboard, I knew what I would find. I knew it from the smell. It was a bad smell, with bad memories.

"Gangplank's here, honoured sirs," said Secundus Ilyricus, the shipmaster. "We've rigged hand lines, but you'd best take care going up, seeing as you ain't seamen."

He stepped back politely. Everyone did. They were making way for Morganus to go first. But the gangplank was indeed a plank. It was about two feet wide, with ropes dangling on each side for grasping, while the dirty, grey, rubbish-floating water of the port waited below, in the gap between ship and quayside. I looked at Morganus. He was in full armour. If he slipped and fell he would sink without hope.

"Huh!" he said, and grabbed the ropes. "Come on, Greek! You like ships, don't you?" And up he went. I followed with the bodyguards behind – gods help them – and then shipmaster, harbour master and the rest, and for a moment it was wonderful as I looked at the complex, cram-jammed tackles and gear of a ship, all madly confusing and yet neat and sensible. How I wished I had time to be a seaman!

But we cannot do everything in one life. Meanwhile we stood in a close group on the ship's main deck.

"Go on," said the harbour master to the shipmaster, "show his honour what we came to see!"

"Aye, aye," said the shipmaster, and beckoned to one of his crew. The man touched his brow and came forward with a small keg that reeked. "Put it there," he said, "in front of his honour the first javelin."

"No," said Morganus, "show it to the Greek gentleman."

"Aye, aye," said the shipmaster, and I was looking down into an open tub of naphtha, the rock oil that rises from the underground earth of those lands to the east of the Mediterranean. It has been known from ancient times and has a variety of colours and forms. The naphtha in this tub was reddish-brown in colour, while other naphthas are clear. But the smell is constant and unmistakable. I looked at Morganus and nodded.

"Naphtha?" he said.

"Yes," I said.

"Yes," said the harbour master and shipmaster both together.

"Yes!" said Timon the merchant. "Naphtha. Rock oil."

I pointed to the keg and spoke to the shipmaster. "And is this your cargo? Is it all like this?"

"Yes!" he said. "Why not? It's all bought and paid for, and all done proper! We've opened hatches so's you can see. Come and look."

I looked. The main hatch was open and I was looking down onto rows of densely-packed barrels: huge barrels, of the greatest size. Timon the merchant was beside me.

"It's naphtha," he said. "It's marvellous. It preserves timber, it cures the croup and the phlegm and the itch, and it's good on roofs, and it kills weeds, and all those millionaires that want fancy Egyptian embalmment – and there's plenty of them in Londinium – well, they need naphtha for that, don't they? And besides that ..."

I let him run on. According to him, naphtha would do anything and everything that mankind could ever imagine. I watched him as he gave his great and formidable list.

"Thank you, Timon the merchant," I said when he was done. "I am grateful for your explanation." I turned to Morganus. "Honoured sir," I said, "there will be no need to study the documents relating to this cargo."

"Ahhhhh!" said those around us, in a deep sigh.

"There will be no need," I said, "since it is clear that everything is in order, and is indeed correct and legal."

Indeed it was! Of course it was! I read that in their faces from the first instant that they claimed that *everything was correct and legal*. It leapt at me from their every twitch of expression.

"Ahhhhh!" they all said again, and in that happy moment, with them relaxed and unsuspecting, I asked another question. I asked with a smile, almost a laugh.

"Is there anything else that naphtha can do? Anything that Timon the merchant has not mentioned?"

They all smiled at that and shook their heads. Some even grinned in relief, because Timon the merchant had listed the properties of naphtha to the point of boredom and beyond.

"No," they said, and they said it with open and obvious truth. I looked very carefully. I looked at every face and I saw that none of them knew any more of naphtha than Timon the merchant. And that was good. It was very good indeed.

Then Morganus and I accepted cakes and wine in Grannix the harbour master's office. He had gone to efforts in that respect, with tables laid, pretty serving girls, special cakes brought in and some truly excellent wine. It was a further and useful opportunity to check that none of them had omitted anything concerning naphtha.

Finally, we left and started back towards the legionary fort. There were fewer people about now, since no more fun was to be had from the harbour master's discomfort. So Morganus and I walked on, with the bodyguards clanking behind. Morganus checked that nobody was near enough to listen.

"Well?" he said, "Was that *it*?"

I said nothing.

He persisted. "That was *it*, wasn't it? Naphtha? You said it had a smell like nothing else. Not like proper oil, from olives. Not sweet. You said it stung the nose, and that stuff did just that. So was it, or wasn't it? And what can it do? What can it do that you don't like?"

I still said nothing. Morganus was more than a friend. He was my comrade and my brother by sacred oath. So of all mankind I could never lie to him, and in any case I detest a lie, because lying is an affront to the gods. But how could I tell him the truth?

"Greek!" he said. "What's the matter with you?" He stopped, took my arm and turned me round. He stopped so suddenly that the boot-nails of the bodyguards skidded on the flagstones as they struggled not to run into us.

I was in distress. I could not bring myself to look Morganus in the eye. "Ikaros," he said, "speak to me! This isn't like you. Normally, you never stop you talking." He shook my arm. "Was that the stuff or was it not?"

The distress grew worse.

"It's hard," I said. "It's so hard … I can't … I …"

I was saved by a screaming and shouting. I looked and saw a clump of people by the quayside. A woman was howling and tearing her hair. Men were climbing out of a boat. One held the body of a child. The body was pale and limp, and other folk were starting towards them. The woman screamed and screamed, and fell on the child's body and kissed it and held it in agonies of emotion.

I ran. Morganus and the bodyguards followed. I pushed through the crowd. The child was on the planks of the jetty. He was naked. He was white. I knelt and touched him. He was cold. The woman howled and ignored me, and held hard to the child, and I fought to push her clear. Then the bodyguards and Morganus were there.

"Get her off!" I said. "Let me work!" They hauled away the woman by brute force, and then fought off the man that had brought the child from the water, and then kept back the rest.

"Leave it to him!" cried Morganus. "He's a Greek!"

I got the child face down over my knee. I thumped his back to clear away water. I laid him down. I cleared his mouth and tongue of weed. I followed the drill that every man or woman of Apollonis knew. I pinched the child's nostrils, drew breath and breathed into him. I saw his chest rise as I did so. Then I kept on doing the same. The drill is to continue until you drop, and never give up. I heard voices all the while.

"Little tinker was swimming, even in the cold."

"He loves the water, he does, but he was out too long."

"He was face down, when we found him. Not moving."

"And he's cold. No life in him."

Then, the distraught woman was speaking.

"He's my little lovely. Gods save him! Gods save him! Gods save him!"

"No use missus," said someone, "the poor little lad's gone."

There was much more sorrow and gloom. Very much more, and many tears, and I carried on and on, and on until my strength began to fail. But then – rapture and joy, because the child coughed and choked and opened his eyes, and I took him up and passed him into the arms of his mother, because it pleased the gods that he should live, and I was very happy indeed.

After that, there was hysteria. Very many people were around me, and they were bowing to me, and kneeling and kissing the hem of my cloak, and the father of the saved child was fallen at my feet, bowing and bobbing his head, and nervously jerking his fingers; the right hand tapping his left hand, then tapping his breast and brow. He was old and I supposed him to be afflicted with some tremor. He was pure Celt, but very well dressed, and wearing good jewellery.

Then, still kneeling at my feet, he spoke. He spoke good Latin.

"I beg to know your name, noble sir," he said. "So I can re-name this child, after your worshipful self."

"And we'll raise a statue of you," said the mother.

"We'll all put money to that," said a neighbour.

"What gods do you serve?" said another voice, "We'll raise an altar to all of 'em!"

But then the mood changed, and the voices became low and awe-struck.

"He's a god himself. He breathed life into that boy."

"We all saw him do it."

"Only the gods can do that."

So they all made the holy sign that Romans use in the presence of things mystic: arms stretched outward, bent up at the elbow with palms forward. They call it *sublatis armis*: raising the arms. I do it myself, having become Roman to that degree. And in any case, the gods are everywhere and it is wise to give respect. But it was profoundly disturbing to see arms raised to myself. It was both disturbing and profoundly unjustified, because any Apollonite could have done what I did. We were taught the mouth-to-mouth technique as children, in school. Of course, that was in the days before the siege, when our city still existed, and my own children still lived.

Hence my dream, in which I punished myself, winding fact around cruel distortion, but transmitting the message that although I saved a Celtic boy from death, I had caused the deaths of my own family with my arguments against the Chimera.

# CHAPTER 4

The dreams came later. Before that, I was received in triumph by Morganus's family.

As a senior centurion, Morganus was allowed to marry and maintain a house in the Twentieth Legion's fort just outside Londinium. His house was in the very heart of the fort, close by the Holy Temple of the Standards. It was a large house, well-appointed but amazingly, for the Roman world, there were no slaves, because the army has no slaves. With limitless manpower, and defaulters for dirty work, the army needs no slaves and wants no slaves, because slaves hear everything and pass it on to other slaves in gossip. So there can be no secrets where there are slaves, and the army has secrets to guard.

Morganus's wife, Morgana Callandra, was waiting outside the house, even in the cold, and her daughters were behind her. They were lesser images of their fine and comely mother, who was a dark-haired Britannic Celt of the Artrebates tribe, much younger than her husband, and who had long since become Roman in her ways and thoughts. Morgana stood beaming at her door as we approached and Morganus made formal greeting, though it was soon obvious that news had flown ahead of us.

"Hail to the-lady-my-wife," he said, "and to the children of our marriage."

"Hail to the-lord-my-husband," she said, "and hail to the magic Greek who breathes life into lost children."

There was a roar of foot stamping at that: foot stamping from the bodyguards and from a large number of legionaries gathered by Morganus's house. Foot stamping is the legion's sign of approval. Then they began to chant:

"Legionis … *pater*! Legionis … *pater!* Legionis … *pater!*" which meant 'father of the legion'. The soldiers were all grinning, but by Roman usage they congratulated my owner – Morganus – for his slave's achievement, which was perfectly normal when a slave did something clever. At least they did not raise hands in the *sublatis armis*. At least, not when I was looking.

Inside the house, with the bodyguards standing grinning, things were less formal. Morganus swept off his helmet, gave it to one of the bodyguards and threw his arms around Morgana, lifting her clear off her feet.

"Did you hear what he did?" he said. "It was pure magic and I won't be told different!"

I just shook my head, knowing when argument was useless.

"We know, we know," said Morgana and the girls together. Then Morgana put formal arms around me – she always treated me like a son, though I was ten years older than her – then she pretended a frown. "You've got mud on your cloak from kneeling," she said, "you never take care." And she brushed at the cloak with her hand, the girls clucking in pretend disapproval behind her.

"Well I had to kneel," I said. "As you know."

Everyone laughed. Then food was served and the bodyguards left, deeming Morganus to be safe once within the fort. Later still it was lamp time – which came early at that time of year – and Morgana and the girls lit the lamps themselves, which never ceased to amaze me, because lighting-up was a servile duty that no Roman matriarch ever did for herself. But this was an army house.

Afterwards, Morganus and I were left alone to talk. Even with lamps there was more darkness than light in the room, and I could barely see the nice new wall-paintings of chariot racing, done by one of the legion's painters. Morganus loved the races, as all Londinium did, with the new chariot racing stadium just outside the city. So we sat, in soft, comfortable indoor tunics, at a table with a wine flask and two goblets, and the house was warmed by the underground hypocaust: the whole house – note that – not just the bath chamber! That was a truly first javelin luxury. So we sat in companionship, and Morganus took his usual sips of wine and I took my usual gulps.

"Now then, Greek," he said, "you didn't answer my question."

"Which question?" I said.

"Don't be a clever Greek. You know which question."

I sniffed and drank a full goblet, then filled it again.

"Don't empty the flask all in one go," he said.

"Can I ask you a question first?" I said.

"Provided you answer mine afterwards," he said, and I nodded.

"You were under orders from the governor to inspect that ship," I said, "weren't you?"

"Yes," he said. "You know that already. Well … it wasn't the governor himself. It was orders from Petros of Athens."

I nodded again. Petros of Athens was the governor's personal secretary, holding a position of enormous power – and Petros was another clever Greek, another imperial slave. He was at least as clever as me, though in different ways, and that worried me.

"What did Petros know about that cargo?" I said. "What did he know about naphtha?"

Morganus shook his head. "Not much," he said, "I'll show you his letter." He got up, took a lamp to a cupboard and took out a letter-scroll. It had been sealed with the governor's seal, but was now open. He gave me the letter and I read it.

"Ah," I said. "Actually it's addressed to the legate Africanus, the legion's commanding officer."

"Of course," he said, "that's the usual chain of command. Governor to legate, legate to me. But look at the letter. All it says is that I am to inspect the ship *Lucky Home Bringer* ..."

I read out the rest aloud.

" ... *which ship bears a cargo of naphtha which substance has not previously seen in Britannia, and you are to seek best opinion in your accustomed way* ... "

"Which means taking *you* along," he said. I nodded and continued reading.

" ... *on the appropriateness, safety and propriety of introducing this exotic substance into the imperial province of Britannia.*"

"There you are," he said, "that's all there is to it. Nothing military."

"I see," I said.

"So *now* what are you worried about?" he said. "You've been muttering non-stop about naphtha."

"I have not!" I said.

"Yes, you have! You've been muttering about dreadful things, shameful things, and the Chimera, whatever that is."

I was shocked. I stood up. I gaped at him.

"I *never* said that! I *never* used those words!"

"Oh, really?" he said. "So, where did I hear the word Chimera?" He waved a hand at me in exasperation. "In the name of all the gods, Greek, just sit down and take some more wine. You don't know what you say sometimes. You're off in your dreams, and you talk to me as if I wasn't there."

I sat down. I did take some more wine– quite a lot– with him shaking his head.

"So, what did I say?"

"You said that your people had a weapon that was dreadful and shameful, and that it came out of naphtha."

"Did I say that?"

"Yes, you did!"

"Did I say any more? Did I talk about the machine?"

"So it was a machine, was it?"

"Yes."

"Right!" said Morganus. "Now then, Ikaros of Apollonis: Ikaros the magic Greek who reads minds." I started to protest but he raised a hand. "No," he said, "spare me the lecture. Just sit and listen for once because, by Jupiter, Juno and Minerva ... I'm going to read *your* mind!"

"Oh?" I said.

"Well don't look so surprised," he said. "You always say it's easy, and now it's my turn."

"Oh?" I said.

"Right!" he said. "Well, the first thing is that you don't want to talk about this weapon, do you?" I shook my head. "Right!" he said. "Second thing is that it's something very, different, isn't it? Not swords or slings or artillery? It's something different, and you think

24

it's something horrible…" He paused to let me think about that. "I'm right, aren't I?"

"Yes," I said.

"And it's powerful as well as horrible," he said, "am I right?"

"Yes," I said, "tremendously powerful."

"Of course it is!" he said. "You've been muttering about it ever since you heard the word naphtha. And, in case you're wondering, I didn't have to do any of your mind-reading magic because you've told me all this already, with all your muttering."

"Oh,"

"*Yes!* So, here comes the surprise. I don't want to know about this thing, this Chimera! Not what it does, or how you make it, or how you use it. I don't want to know anything, right?"

"Oh?" I said.

"Gods of Olympus!" he said. "Can't you say anything but *Oh*? Not when you're Ikaros the mind-reader? Ikaros who raised that little kiddie from the dead so all the docks think you're a god?" I said nothing. "Huh!" he said, "Now you just listen to me, Greek, because this is how it is, right? I'm an old soldier and I don't want new weapons and new rules, because we Romans are on top with Roman drill and Roman arms, and I don't want the dice thrown up in the air, to come down gods-know-how. D'you understand? What if you made this weapon and others copied it? They're not all savages out there. Not the Parthians, Dacians or the Chinese at the far end of the silk road!" He leaned forward and tapped my brow with a finger. "So you just keep the Chimera in there, and try to forget it."

Then he filled our cups, and leaned forward to link arms with me as he'd done once before, on a past occasion when I was in despair. So I could see that he was about to make the army's most sacred oath

25

between comrades. Something unthinkable between a free man and a slave. So we linked arms and raised our goblets.

"Brothers?" he said.

"Brothers!" I said, and we took wine on the oath, before all the gods.

"And we won't talk about this ever again," said Morganus.

"No," I said, and was content.

Which contentment lasted three days and half a night, with Morganus on his army duties, which were considerable, since a first javelin bore a heavy load of administration. Likewise the Twentieth Legion was constantly seeking my technical advice on such matters as the design of pumps, water clocks and surgical instruments. I even had my own office, with excused-armour legionaries as clerks.

But I had some private moments. Morganus's house had a garden, and there was a day with sunshine – cold but bright – and I sat in a chair, wrapped in a cloak with my box of letters: the cheap, Roman letter-tablets. Each was a pair of thin, smoothed sheets of wood the size of a man's hand, tied together and sealed shut, with address on the outside and message on the inside, written in ink with a pen. I had several of them, and I was totally absorbed in the latest, when someone spoke.

"Is she well?" It was Morgana. I tried to smile.

"Yes," I said, "and she prays blessings upon your house."

"She is very kind," said Morgana.

"She says that *you* are very kind," I said, "to me."

"He lets her write to you? Her master?"

"He *encourages* her!" I handed Morgana the letter. "Look," I said.

Morgana was an educated woman. She could read fluently. She sighed over the letter, then embraced me like a mother and I was much moved, because a man's emotions are deeply disturbed when he has lost his past loves and is denied his present love.

"Go and see her," said Morgana, "like the other times."

"I can't do it again," I said, "I can't bear it."

"Can you bear *not* to? I'll leave you to think about it."

She left and I hesitated, then took up some blank letter-sheets and my pen. Later, I took my letter to the legionary post office where I was received under privilege of Morganus's rank. So there was swift delivery, and the letter was in her hands within the hour, in the palatial house of Gentius Civilis Felemidus – Felemid to his friends – the Celtic merchant who was one of the richest men in Britannia. Her reply arrived later that day, since any post from Felemid was likewise swiftly delivered.

Thus, somewhat before the eighth hour of the next day I stood in the vestibule of Morganus's house, with Morgana adjusting my cloak, having checked that my hair was brushed and that I was properly bathed and sweet, while Morganus and the bodyguards stood behind her.

"Give her this," said Morgana, handing me a small pot of brightly-coloured winter flowers, "and do take care."

"Don't worry, lady-my-wife," said Morganus, "he won't be alone."

"Thank you," I said, because two of the bodyguards were not in armour, but cloaks and tunics like any harmless civilians, except that their swords were hidden under the cloaks.

"Now then, you two!" said Morganus, looking at them.

"Honoured sir?" they said.

"If he doesn't come back in one piece," he said, "then the gods might forgive you, but I won't!"

"Yes, honoured sir!"

Later, I was walking through the dense crowds of the Londinium forum, one of the busiest and most populous places in the western empire, since Londinium was the capital city of Britannia and there was no bigger city than between here and Rome. It was dry-goods market day, and stalls were ranked in rows, filling the forum from end to end, and selling absolutely everything, as was loudly proclaimed by the stall holders.

"Finest pots and dishes! Red samian! Gaulish samian! Finest tableware!"

"Best cloth! Straight from Italia! Get it here, don't take no other rubbish!"

"Planes and chisels, hammers and nails!"

"Pens and ink! Pens and ink!"

The noise was intense, with every stall-holder out-bellowing the last, and it wasn't in Latin only, because every shade of humanity filled the market, from black Africans to pale Germans, and there were men, women and children, freedmen, slaves and dogs. So I heard Greek, Aramaic, German and of course Celtic, since Londinium was a tremendous focus of trade in those days, pulling in the bold and active of the empire.

So I pressed through the crowd, taking care to keep a grasp of my purse for fear of the pick-pockets, even though the crowd parted before me, since the market folk were too sharp to miss the two big, grim-faced men who followed behind me, trying hard not to look like soldiers.

"Ah!" I said finally, seeing the big golden cat that was the trade sign of my destination. Market days were harvest time for the wine shops and restaurants that lined the forum, and there was a busy trade of customers, visible within the open doors. The Golden Cat wine shop was on the prestigious, south-facing side of the forum, but not in the centre, since it catered for slaves. That is to say, it catered for the senior and wealthy class of slaves: for them but not for citizens. The citizens walked past with their noses in the air and did not enter. This had the amusing result that my two bodyguards – both Roman citizens – hung back in doubt, not wishing to stain their reputations. But I was used to that.

"Wait outside," I said, "I won't be long."

"Yes, your worship," they said, and hovered by the door, much relieved and trying to be inconspicuous. In fact, it was all pretence: they were a signal that I was not to be touched, because everyone knew what they were, and what the legion would do if I was harmed.

So I went inside, where everything was clean and neat, and the tables in rows, and conversations fading as everyone looking at me, and nudged one another, because I was well known and easily recognised. Then I was greeted by a bowing, sycophantic waiter with a long apron.

"Your worship! Your worship! Best table for you! Only the best! I can …"

"Never mind," I said, and pointed, "I'll sit there."

I sighed as I saw her. I saw her and I saw *her* bodyguards, because she too had come in company. There were four of them: big men with the look of farm boys. Heavy muscles and rough faces. But none of them dared look me in the eye. Slaves are like that. They think I'm magic. But they'd cleared a separate, nearby table for her and nobody else was with her. So I sat down, and attempted to enjoy the company of the woman I loved, in this ludicrous insult to privacy which was the best that could be contrived.

I looked at her and was consumed with emotion. She was so lovely. Such fresh, pale skin. Such deep green eyes. Such red hair. And so dainty.

So fine in figure. So expressive in grace and bearing. She was my lady and I longed to reach out and touch her, but I knew I must not. She was Allicanda, an exotic like me. A top class slave valued in millions, and now the exclusive property of Felemid the merchant, who knew me very well and wanted things from me that I could never give.

"My poor, sad man," she said, guessing my thoughts, "how are you?" She smiled and the smile was joy and sunshine.

"Well enough," I said, and gave her the flowers. She smiled again.

"Thank you," she said. "I love them."

"How long can you stay?" I said.

"Not long," she said, and nodded at the farm boys. "They're watching."

"I know," I said.

"He wants us to meet," she said.

"Felemid?"

"Yes. He wants us to meet, to keep hope alive." She paused. "He says he wants … *to keep passion burning…* that's what he says."

"He talks to you?" I said.

"He does. Often."

"Does he …" I faltered, because I could not ask the question.

"No," she said, "he never touches me. You know that. He likes men."

"Yes," I said.

"And what of you?" she said. "Women like you. They always do. So have you been close to anyone, when all those women like you?"

By the curse of my gift I saw the ugly jealousy in her, because women do like me, and I had certainly received approaches. But I had taken no advantage, and told her so. So she smiled But my gift looked behind the smile, and punished me with the knowledge that she did not quite believe me.

"I like *you* most of all," I said, and she shrugged.

"And *he* likes you most of all," she said. "Felemid: he says … *your passion for the Greek, it is nothing as compared with my passion for him* … that's what he says. He wants you physically, and he says his offer is always open, such that if you become his lover, then you may have … *access* … to me."

I nodded. I knew that already. As an imperial slave, richly rewarded for past services, I was wealthy enough to buy Allicanda. But Felemid would never sell her. Not to me or anyone else. I knew all that, but there was something else.

She continued. "The gossip says that he wants more."

That gripped my attention – gripped it hard – because Allicanda was leading me into a gold mine of knowledge, since what she called *the gossip* was everything that slaves hear and see in a slave-owning society. I have already said that the Roman army has no slaves, to avoid leakage of secrets, but otherwise slaves are everywhere, and although the master and mistress do not even notice them – indeed *because* the master and mistress do not notice them – then slaves notice everything, from the bribes passed by the master to win elections, to the wind passed by the mistress at dinner parties. Then the slaves gossip with other slaves, in the market place, the wine shops and the household, and Allicanda was the supreme high mistress of slave gossip, because she was charming and welcoming, and all the other slaves of the house liked her and confided in her, while she – being an acutely intelligent woman– would analyse carefully, and separate truth from fantasy.

"It's not just *as a man* that he wants you," she said, "It's political. You're close to Petros the Athenian, aren't you?" I nodded. "Well," she said, "Petros is close to the governor of the province of Britannia, and Felemid sees you, Ikaros the Greek, as the pathway to Petros, and then the governor and then to politics in Rome itself, because Felemid has dreams beyond this province."

After that we spent as long as we dared together, urged on by the farm boys pretending to cough, then shuffling their feet. The most I dared before I left was to touch the back of her hand, and see the tears in her eyes. It was bad. Very bad.

# CHAPTER 5

But life goes on, and life continued its normal routine for three days and half a night, until I was roused from sleep by loud voices outside Morganus's house, then by Morganus himself, entering my bedroom in a nightrobe, holding a lamp.

"Get up, Greek," he said. "It's Petros!"

"What is it?" I said.

"Don't know," he said, "but it's urgent."

So we dressed in haste and went out into the dark cold, where the bodyguards and an escort were waiting with flaring torches. The escort was large and splendid, because no Roman of status did anything alone: not if it was important, not when a first javelin was summoned to Government House in the dead of night.

The first century of the first cohort was waiting for us, drawn up in ranks. The elite, double-strength first century: one hundred and sixty legionaries led by two men, holding eight-foot shafts with silver discs and other shiny emblems, which were the cohort standard, and the century standard. These two men wore wolf-skins over their helmets and armour.

But front and centre the legionary standard bearer stood forth, holding the Sacred Eagle of the Twentieth, and he wore a lion skin with a mane, and two long teeth, on the brim of his helmet.

Romans, Romans, Romans! They love their drills and their parades, because there were even more of them– two buglers, the optio in command and two sub-optios. Then off we went at quick march with halts, challenges and passwords, at fort gates and city gates, then deep into Londinium, beyond the forum and basilica, to the north and Government House, where a century of the governor's guard were waiting, lit by their own torch men, standing in ranks behind their aristocratic officers.

"Look at 'em," said Morganus as we approached, "see their lovely legs? Their mothers must be so proud!" He said it aloud, and everyone sniggered, because the Twentieth thought the governor's guard – who never took the field – were just pretty boys in fancy dress, trying to look like the heroes of olden times. They had antique bronze armour and spears, bright red cloaks, and short kilts to show off their thighs, even here in frozen Britannia.

"Escort to first javelin … *HALT!*" yelled our optio, and the tribune commanding the guard, yelled out in reply.

"Company … *PRESENT ARMS!*" he cried. He had mirror-polished armour, a fortune in silk drapery, gold-laced boots, and a powerful waft of perfume. At least he had a big voice. Then, there was much yelling between him and our optio, and a great show of the tribune consulting written orders handed to him by a minion, and then frowning, and demanding details of our purpose and duties, even though all present recognised Morganus, and the tribune and escort had been turned out to greet him. But eventually the guardsmen stood aside, and we marched up the steps and into Government House through massive bronze-plated, elaborately decorated doors, where, our escort waited, while the tribune led Morganus, me and the bodyguards, into the building.

Government House was plain outside but lavish within; with an enormous entrance hall that had flooring of black-and-white marble slabs, lined with alabaster columns with statues between them. In the hall, silver, multi-flame lamps hung on silver chains, suspended from rings held in the mouths of silver lions.

Even at this time of night, clerks and officials were running about, whispering to one another, and it was obvious that something was going on. They bowed at Morganus and stared at me– just like the folk in the Golden Cat. They even nudged each other, and whispered of my well-known oddities. Meanwhile, the tribune gave up his posturing, and I saw his dear-little, young-little face peering out from his helmet, gaping at Morganus in awe of so famous a soldier.

"O Father of the Twentieth and Hero of the Roman Army," he said, bowing low, "would you be so graciously kind as to follow me? I am commanded to convey you to his honour, Petros of Athens, who is secretary to his grace the governor."

"Gods save his grace!" said Morganus instantly.

"Gods save him!" cried the bodyguards.

"Hmm," I said.

So we went down dark corridors, past sentries, and finally into a big office bright with lamplight, and Petros of Athens was rising from his chair, and coming forward, round an enormous desk, to greet us.

He was pure Athenian in dress, accent and bearing: a man in his forties, with a sharp-featured face, neatly trimmed beard and moustache, and hair receding at the temples, leaving a peak over the brow. His hair had once been black, but the strain of his duties had painted him with streaks of grey.

He was an imperial slave like me, but had risen high in the service of his master the Governor of Britannia – Marcus Ostorious Cerealis Teutonius– and Petros was hugely valued by Rome for his administrative talents. He was a dedicated career bureaucrat who was remarkable in being a tremendously *efficient* bureaucrat. In pursuit of that efficiency he kept a special team of slaves of the highest quality: men of intellect, memory and diligence and armed with note-books, pens and abacuses. Petros had six of them, all Greeks, with shaven heads and dressed in the uniform tunics of the House Teutonius. He kept them in attendance as his library, ledger, prompt, record book and calculating engine.

That was Petros, and being Petros he nodded first to me, before bowing to Morganus, because Petros knew me very well. Indeed, it was Petros who first realised how useful Morganus and I could be to the empire. Then he plunged straight into business. No cakes, no wine, no distractions.

"Mind-reader that you are, O Ikaros of Apollonis," he said, "you will now tell me why you have been summoned here in the middle of the night."

I bowed. I had expected that. I hardly needed to think.

"Something bad has happened," I said, and he could not help but give a tiny nod. "Something public. Something that can't be covered up." That was obvious. If the matter had been secret, he would not have discussed it in front of the bodyguards and the shaven-heads. "Something public and bad, involving somebody important." That was also obvious, because nothing moves under Rome without someone important being involved. I saw dismay in his eyes. "Something very bad indeed!" I said. "A death!" He nodded, and I studied his face. His expression was wrong for natural causes, but right for some outrage.

So I made a guess. "Murder?" No, it wasn't murder, not quite. I could not read him to that degree of precision. But his eyes flicked to the floor and mosaic of a chariot race. Such images were everywhere in Londinium, and the centrepiece of this one was a victorious driver, holding palm leaves of victory. "It's one of the racing drivers, isn't it?" I said. "He's been killed and you want Morganus and me to find out who killed him."

"Ahhh!' said the shaven-heads, looking at one another. Being clever, they were wondering how I did such a clever thing.

"Ahhh!" said the bodyguards, not wondering at all, because they thought I was magic. Unfortunately, so did Morganus, who stared at me with that puzzled expression that he gives on such occasions, and which depresses me. But what can I do?

Petros smiled.

"Well done, Ikaros of Apollonis," he said. "I am surprised that you cannot not give me the man's name."

But then I saw – I only *just* saw, because he attempted to hide it – his lips moving. So – out of vanity – I practised a small trick of deception.

"I can't read the name," I said, "because you are reciting the Holy Prayer to Athena." I raised hands in respect of the patron goddess of Petros's city. "You do that when you don't want me to read what is hidden behind the prayer."

He laughed. But he believed it and so did everyone else.

"It's Zephyrix," he said. "Zephyrix the Celt." And Morganus and the bodyguards gasped.

"Zephyrix the Great?" said Morganus, "He's a *thousander*. He's won a thousand races, usually coming from behind at the last moment."

"Yeah!" said the bodyguards. They were close to weeping and even the shaven-heads looked miserable.

"Him!" said Petros. "Now listen and pay attention. Listen well! Zephyrix was brought to Britannia in the name of his grace the governor.

"Gods save his grace!" said Morganus and the bodyguards.

"Hmm," I said.

"Gods save him!" said Petros. "All the world knows that his grace has been rewarded for his excellent governorship of Britannia ..."

I sneered and Petros frowned. *Excellent governorship*? I thought. I remembered certain near-disasters under Teutonius, which Morganus and I had prevented.

"Bah!" said Petros. "His grace is to be rewarded," he said, trudging onward, "by promotion to the exalted rank of governor of Italia – homeland of the Roman people – which is a post second in honour only to that of the emperor himself!"

"Gods save his imperial majesty!" said almost everyone.

"If they must," said I, and Morganus frowned.

"Meanwhile," said Petros, "all the world also knows such a great promotion depends upon the balance of power within the senate and imperial household, and any disturbance in that balance might result in my illustrious master losing his promotion. Do you understand, Ikaros of Apollonis? And you, Morganus of the Twentieth?"

"Yes," I said.

"Yes," said Morganus.

"So what do you want us to do?" I said.

"You will investigate this unfortunate death," said Petros.

He beckoned and one of the shaven-heads came forward, bowed to Morganus and gave him a book-tablet and a sealed scroll.

"So," said Petros, "these documents give details of this regrettable event, together with written authority to act in *my*," he corrected

38

himself, "that is to say, in *his grace's* name, to go forth and make all things smooth."

I frowned.

"To *make things smooth*?" I said. "May I ask what that means?"

"Do you not know?"

"No."

"I am amazed to hear that form the mind-reader," said Petros, and he looked at Morganus, "But I am sure that you know, first javelin."

Morganus drew breath and sighed. He shook his head.

"Oh yes," he said. "I most certainly do!"

"Good," said Petros, "Then explain to your comrade … and then make all things smooth."

Later, Morganus spoke to me as we marched back to the fort through black-dark, sleeping Londinium with frost on the paving stones and the cold stinging my nose. A rhythmic tramping echoed back from the locked buildings as the escort stepped out, with a white steam of breathing rising over them in the torchlight. They made a lot of noise, because in Britannia the Roman army wore hob-nailed boots, and the optio rapped vine staff on shield to give time, and yelled out a steady, loud chant, copied by the sub-optios.

"*Left! Left! Left-right-left!*" I suspect it was more for swagger more than time-keeping, but with all the tramping and noise, Morganus hardly had to whisper so that nobody heard. But he did anyway, and did so fiercely.

"What's wrong with you?" he said. "Why can't you give respect to his grace and his majesty?"

"If I must," I said, "gods save them both."

He sighed. "Didn't you see Petros looking at you?" he said, "and you muttered something when Petros said his grace was rewarded for excellent work!"

"No I didn't!"

*"Yes you did!"*

"So what?" I said. "His grace is a clod-brain, dim-wit. You know that."

Morganus frowned. "His grace is a Roman nobleman of excellent family."

"True, but Petros controls him and tells him what to do. You know that too. Petros *owns* Teutonius!"

Morganus fell silent. He looked away.

"Oh never mind," I said, "So, some chariot driver has been killed and we have to make everything smooth. What does that mean?"

"*Some* chariot driver?" said Morganus. "*Some?*" He looked at me in disbelief. "You don't know a thing about the races, do you?" I shrugged. "Zephyrix is – was – champion of champions. He's been winning in the Circus Maximus these last fifteen years. He's famous from one end of the empire to the other." He paused. "You have heard of the Circus Maximus, haven't you?"

"Yes," I said. "Biggest stadium in the world. Three hundred thousand people."

"More!" he said. "Half a million."

"Unbelievable," I said.

"Believe!" he said. "I've seen it! It's the money the drivers make that's unbelievable. Zephyrix has won thirty-six million sesterces, which is equal to two-and-a-half tons of gold!"

"That much?" I said.

"Yes! And that much money is political. It buys power, so ..."

But the optio shouted. He roared like a bull.

"First-century-first-cohort … *Halt!* Forrrrm … *Square!*"

They stopped so fast, I skidded on the pavement. They stopped and stamped, then changed formation with boots thumping up and down, and the column became a square with men facing outward and standards in the middle. *Crunch-crunch* they stamped, as the job was done.

The optio yelled again. "On the comannnnd … *Draw!*"

"Hi … *HO!*" cried the legionaries, as blades flashed and they leaned forward in battle stance, awaiting the onrush of the enemy– which was farcical because there was no enemy, just three Roman soldiers running towards us from far up the Via Principalis, holding torches and shouting and waving. The optio was just showing off the men's drill for Morganus to see.

So Morganus – being Roman – looked at the human square, which to me seemed perfect, and he frowned.

"Lines aren't straight," he said. "It'll have to be better next time!"

"Yes, honoured sir!" said the optio. "What do we say lads?"

"YES! HONOURED SIR!"

It was comical. I should have laughed. But then I remembered that while we Greeks invented art, science, medicine, philosophy and everything else that was magnificent, the Romans invented just military drill and conquered us with it. Then, the three running soldiers came up and stopped in front of us. One was a centurion in sideways-crest helmet. The other two held torches.

"O honoured Morganus!" said the centurion, gasping from his run. "O pride of all the legions! I greet you this night, with respect and in hope." He said that, then stood to attention and saluted with right arm stretched out, palm down. He was elderly, and gasping heavily. Morganus knew him.

"Artifax!" he said, "Tertius Filius Artifax: commander of the walls!
Take your time, old comrade. Catch your breath." He frowned. "Why
are you running when there are young men to do that?"

"Heard you were out, honoured sir," said Artifax, then nodded at
me. "With *him*." He paused and his eyes flicked from me to Morganus.
"With the Greek … er … gentleman." He managed not to call me
the Greek *boy*. I was special but still a slave, and all slaves were *boy*
to a free man.

"And so?" said Morganus.

"Something funny is going on, honoured sir," said Artifax. "Been
going on for a while, in the dark hours. Normally I wouldn't bother
you, honoured sir, but seeing as you was out," he looked at me again,
"and with the Greek gentleman, honoured sir, I've took this chance!"

He saluted again, and stood silent. Morganus glanced at me. I
think he was about to say that we had duties that could not wait. But:
"It's about, *them*, honoured sir," said Artifax, "*them!*" and he raised
his arms in awe of the unknown.

The two men with him did the same. They were afraid, even
though we were an armed and armoured company with swords
drawn. They were afraid even in this pacified, Romanised city,
surrounded by buildings and statues, with water mains and sewers
beneath our feet. But it was a cold, dark night and we were in
Britannia – far out on the rim of the world – and Britannia was
emphatically not civilised: not all of it, because very much indeed
of it was wild and tribal, and strange gods ruled who were not the
gods of Rome.

"Shut up!" yelled the optio, because some of the men were
muttering. It was a strange moment – an uncanny moment – and
I was fascinated. So Zephyrix the charioteer went clear out of my

mind, since I had never even heard of him and I was bored by Roman politics. But the uncanny fascinates me and it fascinates me especially when it involves something that Artifax did not even name, or rather some *people*. It was the druids: the priestly caste of the Celtic folk. It had to be them because – in all of Britannia – only the druids made the Romans uneasy: uneasy and afraid.

So druids were forbidden under Roman law and subject to instant execution if discovered. This was partly because their faith included human sacrifice, which abominates Rome, and partly because druids were the intellectual power of the Celtic people: their spiritual masters, who forever incited them against Rome.

All of which is a powerful list, but for the legionaries around me that night – mostly peasant farmers, before they joined up – there was also the hideous barrack room rumour that druids used magic to fetch away a Roman soldier in the night, such that he woke up hanging naked from a tree, while the druids skinned him alive from the feet upwards, with razor-sharp knives and hideous slowness.

Morganus knew all that better than I did. He looked at Artifax, then looked at me and raised his eyebrows. I read the question and gave answer.

"Honoured sir?" I said, "Perhaps we might find time to investigate? Because if it troubles so senior an officer as this," I bowed to Artifax, "it must be serious."

I was carefully polite to Arifax, because he was ashamed of his fear, and was not telling everything. But a little reassurance eases the tongue.

"Gods bless you, your worship!" he said to me, and stood straight and smiled. "We was hoping to have your worship there, because the sods can't do their magic on you, can they? Everyone knows that! So if *you're* there, then the sods can't put a curse on us, can they? And you might even frighten them off."

"Yeah!" said his two men, and they nodded to each other.

Perhaps I should have been flattered, but I was not. Not when I saw that Morganus was also nodding. As I have said a thousand times, superstition is a soft, warm bed– ever cosy, ever welcoming– while rationality is a hard, uphill climb in the wind and the cold and the rain.

But Morganus was looking at me, and he knew my moods.

"If the Greek gentleman thinks this is serious," he said, "then yes, Tertius Filius Artifax, I would be happy to see what's going on."

"Blessings upon you, honoured sir!" said Artifax, "Blessings in the names of Jupiter, Juno and Minerva. If you'd follow me, I'll show you."

44

# CHAPTER 6

Morganus and I, and the bodyguards, followed Artifax up the stairs to the city walls. leaving our escort below. As we climbed I looked around, and with a thin moon and the stars, I could see that Londinium's defences were excellent, as indeed they had to be given the appalling fire and slaughter that Boudicca's Iceni tribe had inflicted on the city just forty years ago. So the present defences were built excellently strong, to deter any other tribe from attempting to imitate Boudicca.

Thus the city was enclosed within lines of earthworks forty feet high, bearing a fighting platform defended by a timber palisade with crenelations. Beyond that that there was a double row of deep 'V' ditches, to turn an enemy's charge into chaos. There were artillery towers at twenty-yard intervals, each mounting a heavy ballista manned by a crew of four: one shooter, two winders and a loader. Also, there was a night guard of bowmen on the ramparts, with more men in barracks down below.

I shivered as we reached the top. I hate the cold of Britannia. It stabs my bones and it was worse on the walls, with a wind blowing over the wet ground that surrounded the broad Londinium river – the Thames – to the south of the city.

"This way, honoured sir," said Artifax. "You can see it from one of the towers." He paused. "That's if they do it."

The artillery crew stamped to attention as Morganus approached, but he waved a hand.

"Quiet!" he said.

"Yes, honoured sir!" they said, and stamped again anyway. Morganus sighed.

"This way, your honours," said Artifax, beckoning myself and Morganus to the palisade. So we joined him, and waited. And waited. And waited. And nothing happened.

"Well?" said Morganus, after a while.

"I don't know," said Artifax. "Maybe they won't come tonight."

We waited some more, and the cold got through my cloak. So I looked at the artillery machine, to take my mind off the cold. It was one of the latest type: entirely metallic, strong and light, with the torsion springs enclosed in steel cylinders. It stood on a universal mount, capable of swivelling up or down in any direction.

Artifax saw me looking.

"It's a two-span," he said, "shoots a two-span bolt. That's ..."

"Two of these," I said, indicating the distance between my elbow and finger tip: a *span,* the ancient unit used to measure the length of ballista bolts.

"That's right, your worship," he said, "it shoots a two-span bolt five hundred yards, and straight through any armour or shield." He blinked, remembering my reputation. "But then you'd know that, being a Greek engineer, before ..."

"Sir! Honoured Artifax!" said one of the artillerymen. "They're out there."

"Look! Look!" said Artifax.

So we did, and beyond the walls and ditches, everything was dark shadows with low hills and a few trees, but mostly marshland and bushes, all dark, dark, dark. Up on the walls, behind our palisade, some dozens of us looked out into the wilderness of Britannia, where strange things lurked which were beyond the grasp of Roman civilisation.

"See?" said Artifax, "There they are! Just like I said. Listen to the buggers!"

Out in the darkness, torches were flaring– they came out of nowhere, just appeared, and then there was a moaning singing of some native song that shivered the spine. Although I know the languages of scholarship – Hebrew, Greek and Latin of course, and others too – I am weak in the Celtic tongues and could not follow the chanting. But I saw Morganus shudder and raise his right hand, fist clenched, with the first and small fingers outstretched. That was the bull sign of Mithras, god of the legions. It was the sign that soldiers made to defend themselves against evil.

Then a figure appeared, out in the dark. He just appeared, and began to rise up. He was all in white, with long hair and a crown of green leaves, and he stretched his arms towards us and chanted and groaned and rose higher, till he was floating more than man's height above ground. Then, more torches flared, and his voice rose up, and all the Romans shivered in fright, as another and another white figure appeared and began to rise, and as they rose they joined in with the chant.

"See?" said Artifax. "It's druids, gods save us, it's druids! Listen to the sods!"

I looked at Morganus. He spoke the Celtic tongue fluently, having learned it from his wife.

"What are they saying?" I said.

"It's a curse," he said, "they're calling down plague on our heads."

"And the sods are flying," said Artifax. "It's sodding magic!" He was so disturbed that he grabbed my arm and shook it, in his fright. "You're the clever Greek!" he said. "Can you stop the dirty sods, can you stop 'em from …" His voice faltered, and I guessed what he feared.

"Stop them from skinning you alive in the night?" I said, and he gasped and joined the legion of those who believe that I read minds by magic. "Listen to me!" I said, and pointed at the white-robed figures, "If you saw *that* in the theatre – men rising out of the ground – you'd know it was done by machines: by ropes and pulleys, yes? Your Roman theatres are full of machines for special effects, aren't they?"

"But they're soddin' savages," he said, "they haven't got machines!"

"They don't need them," I said. "A few men could lift another on a wickerwork hurdle, and if they were all dressed in black, you'd never notice them. Not at night."

"Ah," he said.

"Ah," said everyone else.

"I never thought of that," he said.

"And if those are druids out there," I said, "and I think they are…" I reached out and touched the ballista. "Then why don't you shoot them? They're all under sentence of death!"

"Ah, ah," he said, "we're forbidden to …" he stumbled over the formal words, "to … *commence hostilities in the absence of authorisation from chain of command.*"

I turned to Morganus.

"Honoured sir?" I said, "may we *commence hostilities*?"

He paused, considering the risk of shedding blood in this notoriously dangerous province, full of warrior tribes that hated Rome. Would we be throwing a torch into a dry haystack?

"That's a druidic curse they're chanting," he said, finally, "so they're druids." He turned to Artifax, "are your men trained in shooting at night?"

"Yes, honoured sir. Everything looks closer, so they'll allow for that."

"Good! Then this is what we'll do."

He gave swift orders, which cheered up the rest wonderfully. Romans are like that. Once they have a plan, they work together like cogs in a corn mill. So there was running of messages up and down the wall, and busy hands winding ballistas, and slapping bolts on to the shooting slides.

"Quick! Quick! Quick!" cried Artifax. "While the buggers are still there!"

He need not have worried. The chanting continued steadily, until Artifax saluted Morganus with outstretched arm.

"Ready, honoured sir!" he said.

"Then give the word," said Morganus, and Artifax cried out in a big voice.

"Three ... two ... one ... *shoot!*"

A dozen ballistas twanged like giant harps and the night was split with the most atrocious howling, such that it was the druids' turn to be afraid, since – by Morganus's orders – a dozen shrieker bolts shot out into the night. They were ingenious projectiles, flute-like and partly hollow behind the steel tip. They were designed to frighten the enemy– and they did. The chanting stopped, the torches wavered and – to a great cheer from our ramparts – one of the druids fell right off whatever platform it was that he was lifted on.

"Give 'em another!" cried Artifax. "Shoot, shoot, shoot!"

The artillerymen cheered again, and nearly burst themselves in a fury of re-winding, re-loading and sending out another volley, this time of standard bolts that flew faster and hit harder than the shriekers.

The crews were skilful, so the machines shot fast: one bolt after another, the volleys stopped whatever it was that the druids were trying to do. Then, out in the night, there was yelling and shouting, and the sound of men running, and finally hoof-beats as the druids and their accomplices mounted up and fled.

"Cease shooting!" said Morganus. "They've gone."

"Cease shooting!" cried Artifax, then he roared, "Legionis…?"

"PATER!" cried all present, in joyful response.

"Legionis…?"

"PATER!"

"Legionis…?"

"PATER!"

"Hail to the big 'un!" said Artifax, and all was smiling and beaming, and admiration of Morganus. Which was no more than his due, though it would have been pleasant if Artifax – or anyone else – had mentioned who it was that had crushed fear of the occult, and suggested that we use the artillery. But that was only one of the many burdens a philosopher must bear.

Then, when the cheering was over, Morganus gave further orders. "Send out some men, as soon as it's light," he said. "See if there's anything out there, and report to me."

"Yes, honoured sir!" said Artifax.

"And if you find anything, *don't* touch it," said Morganus. "Because the Greek gentleman will want to examine it."

That pleased me. At least Morganus knew that I was there.

Afterwards, we marched back to the fort with our escort, and I managed a few hours' sleep in Morganus's house before dawn. Then it was bright morning, and breakfast of eggs, porridge and honey, with mulled wine against the cold. It was served by Morganus's wife and daughters, while I read through the scroll and book-tablet concerning the death of Zephyrix. I had the tablet and scroll on the table as I ate, and I must have got porridge on the scroll, because Morgana looked at me reprovingly, and wiped clean the scroll with a cloth.

Then the bodyguards arrived, and were buckling Morganus into his armour as I finished reading.

"So," said Morganus, taking his helmet from one of the bodyguards, "what now, Greek?"

"The scroll is our written authority, signed by his grace the governor."

"Gods save his grace!" cried Morganus and the bodyguards, stamping hard.

"Hmmm," I said, "it's our authority to investigate at any level, questioning any person of any rank, and in the name of…" I paused, "in the name of *Teutonius*," I said, and Morganus frowned as he guessed why I had avoided the word *governor*.

"And the book?" he said.

"Details of where Zephyrix was found," I said, "and who found him. It was a garden slave. The body was in a pool in the garden of the procurator's new house up by the north-west wall."

"The procurator?" said Morganus, "The fiscal procurator? Quintus Varanius Scapula?"

"Yes," I said, "him: Scapula, the third-ranking man in the province!"

Which he was, because in power and prestige the first man in Britannia was the governor, Teutonius, who ran the army, the government and relations with the tribes. Next came the lord chief justice, who was a senatorial nobleman like the governor, and he ran the law: that massive body of regulation which was so ponderously logical as to be a reflection of Rome itself. Indeed, it was a wonder the words did not march in step to the tap of an optio's stick.

After these two senatorial luminaries, there was a mere *equestrian*, a Roman knight – The fiscal procurator who ran the treasury, taxation and expenditure, and was responsible for checking up on the governor and chief justice to guard against fraud. Though of course, each of the three were supposed to check the others for fraud, which meant that they must spy on one another.

That was the Roman system, and through clenched teeth I admit that it was a good system, because each man knew that two others were looking over his shoulder, so it was hard for any of them to get away with anything seriously corrupt. Which is yet another reason why Rome rules the world. But Morganus was frowning.

"A new house?" he said. "Scapula? I didn't know he had one."

I smiled. "You should talk to the-lady-your-wife," I said. "She knows all the latest fashions, and building by the north-west wall is the latest. If you're rich, that is. North-west is upwind of the city smoke. That's where the luxury houses are, these days."

This time we marched more discretely from the fort and through the city: Morganus, me, the bodyguards with a mere half-century of red shields to clear the street pavements. Thus we passed through crowds of townsfolk on their early morning business with a cacophony of noise, and groaning barrow loads of provisions. They chattered and stared while free-born boys on their way to school, pointed and gasped in recognition of the heroic Morganus. They recognised me, too, and I confess that I had grown so used to my status – Morganus's reflected status – that I feared the day when I might lose it and become merely a common slave. It was yet another burden on the soul of a philosopher.

Scapula's house was large and splendid. It occupied the whole of a city block – an *insula*– in an exclusive part of the city where other rich men were building Mediterranean-style dwellings under the grey skies of Britannia. It was ludicrous. Meanwhile, we were expected, and a company stood before the doors to receive us, including a guard of legionaries, and a centurion who stamped and saluted on sight of Morganus.

"Gods give you greeting, O spear of Rome!" said this officer. He was a junior centurion, sent on a task that in my city would have been the work of the police. But of course, Romans have no police.

"I greet you in return," said Morganus. "And who stands with you?"

He looked at three men just behind the centurion. One was a citizen, in formal mourning, with ashes in his hair and the costly material of his toga prominently torn at the hem. The other two were slaves of highest quality: shaven-skull Greeks in tunics bearing the emblem of the procurator. They were like those who attended Petros, the governor's secretary.

"O father of the Twentieth," said the centurion, "may I present his honour Marcus Ligarus Basilus, an equestrian knight who holds the post of deputy fiscal procurator."

"I greet you with respect, Marcus Ligarus Basilus," said Morganus, "and may the gods support this house in its time of affliction."

Basilus dithered, and tugged at his toga as if to adjust it. He was young, pimple-faced, new to the province, and wondering how to conduct himself. Note well, incidentally, that nobody bothered to introduce the two shaven-skulls. They were like me; just slaves.

"We are here, me and Ikaros of Apollonis," said Morganus, "under high authority to investigate the death of Zephyrix the Thousander. I ask that you lead us into the house."

Morganus was impatient and wanted to get on with the work.

"Oh, oh …" said Basilus, and dithered some more. "I'll take you to his honour the fiscal procurator. It's his house. It's his house … and his responsibility."

That was clear enough. If there was politics in the death of Zephyrix, then young Basilus was keeping well clear of it.

So in we went, leaving the red shields outside. Basilus and Morganus led, followed by me and the two shaven-skulls, with the bodyguards behind. The house was luxurious and full of slaves, as are the houses of all Roman billionaires. We passed through several large and excellent rooms, with slaves bowing low, and a whispered conversation got under way – in Greek – between myself and the shaven-skulls.

"I am Ikaros of Apollonis," I said. "Benedictions upon you! May I know your names and duties?"

"Benedictions!" said one. "I am Aetius of Athens, senior attendant to his honour the procurator." He was an impressive man: a classic Greek, with high intelligence and dignity of bearing.

"Benedictions," said the other. "I am Myron of Thebes, attendant to his honour."

"What has happened here?" I said.

"Zephyrus the Thousander was killed," said Aeitius.

"Murdered!" said Myron.

"Who did it?"

"Only the gods know," said Aetius.

"How was it done?"

"Thrown to the lampreys," said Aetius, and frowned. "Who would believe it?"

I said nothing. I was amazed. Lampreys? I recalled the famous tale of Vedius Pollio, a friend of the Emperor Augustus a hundred years ago, who was in the habit of throwing his slaves to the lampreys if they displeased him. Lampreys are huge fish like eels, kept by the rich in garden pools as a delicacy for eating. But they have rasping teeth that inflict horrible death on anyone thrown into the pool, since the lampreys take hold and, being slippery, cannot be thrown off.

In the story, a slave broke a valuable glass dish, and Pollio would have thrown him to the lampreys, but Augustus was so disgusted that he pardoned the slave, had the lamprey pool filled in, and ordered Pollio's entire collection of glassware to be smashed before his eyes.

So, surely nobody kept a lamprey pool for such purpose? Not now? Or did they? I had no chance to ask, since we were swiftly shown into the procurator Scapula's private study. It was richly decorated with Greek pottery, book-cases, and exquisite little marble statues of the gods. Scapula himself was reclining on a couch, looking nervous. He was thin, middle-aged, and had lost most of his hair and some of his teeth, making him embarrassed to open his mouth. He had a large wine flask and goblet on a table in front of him, and his eyes were watery from drink.

He too had a rent in his toga and ashes in his hair, and he was attended by four more shaven-skulls. Aetius and Myron silently joined them, Aetius standing to the fore. They bowed as Morganus approached and young Basilius– cautious fellow – stayed out of the room.

Morganus and I knew Scapula well, having met him on a previous investigation. He was honest, efficient and a sound administrator with a depth of learning which – unfortunately – he constantly displayed by quoting the classical authors. It was irritating and pompous. Thus:

"Virgil tells us," he said, "that *the gates of Hell are open night and day; smooth the descent and easy the way.* So forgive me, first javelin, if I don't rise, because I am weak and unwell. *We are but dust and shadow*, as Horace says."

"I offer condolence, O Quintus Veranius Scapula," said Morganus, "Since I and my Greek comrade" – Scapula's eyebrows twitched at the word comrade– "are here to investigate the blow that has fallen on your house. So I ask that Ikaros of Apollonis, might speak directly to you. I ask in the governor's name."

"Gods save his grace!" said everyone.

Then I bowed and spoke.

"Blessings upon your honour, in this time of trouble," I said. I spoke with deep respect, because I try set a mood of reassurance on such occasions, and by this means to stimulate a response of expression and gesture that enables me to do what the world calls mind-reading. I do it by that means, and also by deductions from any information I can dig up, scrape up, catch, trap or steal by whatever means, just so long as it bears on the case. It is not even difficult. Not for me. It is instinctive.

So I studied him, and saw a man deeply troubled by fear. He was wondering what would happen to him, with the world's most famous racing driver killed in his house. He was wondering what power shifts might follow, back in Rome. So he was afraid– not just for his post as procurator, but for his very life. I saw all that, but not a trace of guilt. Whoever had murdered Zephyrix, it was nothing to do with Scapula. But I questioned him anyway. I already had much detail in the book-tablet from Petros, but I wanted to test it on Scapula.

"Honoured and knightly sir," I said, "I believe it was yourself – at the request of our governor – who brought Zephyrix to Britannia together with his companions, and that you have paid all costs and lodged them in this house."

I bowed again in reassurance, but he trembled– and it was shocking to see the fear that seized hold of a man who was basically decent and honest. His hands shook. His voice faltered.

"They'll blame me," he said, "and I did nothing. Zephyrix was safe that evening – we all saw him – but he was found in the pool next morning. Dead in the pool while all the house slept, so it'll be poison or the dagger for me." Then he sighed, thinking of things even worse. "My eldest boy's on the Rhine with the legions, he's a tribune in the Eighth Augusta, and the other two are here with me and their mother. I can only hope they'll be spared … her too … if the worst happens."

"Have no fear, honoured sir," said Aetius of Athens, leaning forward. "You are immaculate in innocence. You acted for the good of the province and the empire. In addition to all else, you were to pay for the races to celebrate his grace's promotion."

"Yes!" said Scapula. "A hundred thousand in gold for the champion – who would surely have been Zephyrix– and a crown and diadem too. All at my expense." He looked at Aetius "They'll remember that in Rome, won't they?"

"Of course, honoured sir!" said Aetius.

"Of course!" said the shaven-heads.

But Scapula wasn't the only one afraid. These privileged slaves were wondering if they, personally, would survive the fall of their master. None the less, I saw no guilt in any of them and I wanted to seek evidence elsewhere.

"Knightly sir," I said, "I will trouble you no more in your distress, but I ask that I might be taken to those who came here with Zephyrix, and also to examine his body."

Scapula gulped. He was terrified that I might find something to incriminate him even though he had done no wrong. Sadly, this is a common fear among the innocent and I have seen it many times in my criminal investigations. So, Scapula said nothing. But again Aetius leaned forward.

"Honoured sir," he said to Scapula, but looking at me and Morganus, "these men come with authority from his grace the governor."

"Gods save his grace," muttered Scapula.

"And it would therefore be wise, honoured sir," said Aeitius, "to show such open readiness to assist them, as shall proclaim your innocence to all the world."

"Yes, yes," said Scapula, "take them. Take them where they ask. Show them everything." Then, a better thought came to him. He sat up, clenched his few teeth and pointed at me. "Take him to *the followers*," he said. "Take this cunning Greek to Zephyrix's followers – dirty-minded scum that they are – for it will surely be one of them that killed him! I swear it by all the gods of Rome!"

That was interesting. Very interesting indeed.

"Honoured sir," I said, "can you say more? Do you know who killed Zephyrix?"

But he shrivelled again, looked away from me and said nothing. He just shook his head. At the same time, Aeitius glanced at me, and twitched his head towards the door. He had something to say, but not in his master's presence. He bowed to Scapula.

"As you commanded, honoured sir," he said, "I will take the first spear and his comrade wherever they wish in this house."

"Do it!' said Scapula. "Get on with it!" And he waved a hand, in sorrow and in misery, as if to brush away his troubles.

So we left him with his flask of wine – not one drop of which was offered to me – and followed Aetius to the followers, and then to the body of Zephyrix.

# CHAPTER 7

By protocol, it should have been Morganus who was led forward by Aetius, but Morganus knew my methods. So he hung back and I walked beside the senior shaven-head as, once again, we passed through room after room of grovelling slaves. Aetius spoke to me in Greek. He spoke carefully, knowing that Morganus was listening.

"In his wisdom," he said, "does the first spear speak our language?"

"No," I said, "so speak without restraint. Speak as one Greek to another."

"Ah!" he said. "First: know that Scapula is free of blame, as are my colleagues and I. This I swear on the gods of my city and the souls of my children."

"I see," I said, and I believed him. He was a classic Athenian in speech and manner, and I judged him to be both pious and honest.

"So where does blame lie?" I said.

"Where Scapula placed it! Among the followers. There is poison among them. They say Zephyrix was a drunkard with filthy habits."

"Such as what?"

"He would not use the latrines. He passed his motions in the garden."

"Why?"

"It's the custom of his folk: ignorant peasants from Gaul."

"You just said *first*," I said, "so what else should I know?"

"Know that some men are not here now, who *were* here when Zephyrix was killed."

"Who?"

"The *broad stripes*!" he said, meaning men of senatorial rank with broad purple stripes in their togas.

"Who were they?"

"Horatius, some of his friends, and Felemid the Celt," he said.

Horatius– in his full name Marcus Ostorius Cerealis Horatius Teutonius– was vice governor of the province, and the governor's nephew. He was a man tremendously high in rank, but – to express it kindly – he was as limited in intellect as his dim-wit uncle. He was someone I already knew, as was Felemid the billionaire – may the gods drag him screaming down to Hades – because Felemid was the owner of my beautiful lady Allicanda, held as bait for my corruption.

"So, where are they now?" I said. "The broad stripes?"

"Can you not guess?" he said. "They are senatorial! They stayed the night to sleep off their wine, and in the morning when we found the body, they walked past the legionaries on the doors. Who'd dare stop them? They passed in regal glory." He looked at me. "And it is not only they who are missing."

"Who else?" I said.

"Blephyrix," he said, "Zephyrix's slave. His slave and personal attendant."

"How did Blephyrix get past the guards?"

"He did not have to. He was already gone when we called in the army."

"You mean he ran away?"

Aeitius shook his head. "He left before doors were locked for the night."

Then we arrived at a pair of large, cedar wood doors, where a pair of legionaries and a sub-optio were on duty. They stamped to attention and Morganus pointed at the doors.

"Open!" he said, and the doors were flung apart.

We entered a south-facing summer room, with lovely wall-paintings of idyllic Mediterranean scenes: blue skies, blue seas, and glorious sunshine over olive groves and pines, all drawn with such wonderful perspective as to draw the eye into tranquillity. Hating the cold of Britannia as I do, I sighed in sorrow as I saw all that I missed of my homeland.

But there was no other tranquillity in the room, just six persons who all jumped to their feet at once. There were five men dressed in gaudy robes, and one in a toga who stood to the front. He was a thick built, aggressive man, deeply confident in himself, while the rest treated him with profound deference

"I am Quintus Cassius Veronius," he said, in the authentic accent of the city of Rome. "I am Veronius! Veronius, impresario of races, whose name is famous throughout the world, and intimate even of the emperor himself."

"Gods save the emperor!" cried all present.

"Indeed!" he said, and stared me hard in the eye, because – by Apollo the Great, Hermes the Swift and Athena the Wise – this was a man of colossal self-esteem, and he was not done yet. "I have come to this damnation of a province," he said, "under promise of protection from highest authority. I have come here bringing racing drivers," he waved a hand at the men standing behind him, "each one of them worth four million sesterces, as well as Zephyrix the Thousander, who was owned by an alliance of high nobility, and priced at twenty million. Twenty million, I say! Thus I ask you – in the name of that high alliance – who will cover the loss and make all things right?"

There was much more, as he ranted on, pointing at me and Morganus in accusation. It was a nasty moment: very nasty indeed. I am adept at human nature and the physical sciences, but profoundly ignorant of Roman politics– except for knowing that it can be violent and deadly. I had only to consider the fear that had fallen on Scapula to know that.

Also, I was taking note of the fact that these world famous racing drivers were not free men, but slaves. They were at the very pinnacle of exotic slavery, and valued at eye-blinding cost, but they were mere property under Roman law, and they were owned by men at the heart of Rome: men who I feared might over-rule even Teutonius, the governor of Britannia.

I looked to Morganus in this political moment, and saw his eyebrows raise and a tiny smile on his face. Nobody else saw that, but I did, and I was encouraged. On the other hand, I glanced at the bodyguards and saw the fear on the faces of these big, armoured men. That was Roman politics. So I took a deep breath, wishing that in all reality I was as magical as everyone believed, because it was up to me to placate Veronius and those in Rome whom he represented.

So when he ended his rant, I simply kept silent. I kept silent, gave a small bow and looked at him with an expression of enquiry, as if I were puzzled over something. I did so because I have found this to be a powerful means of persuading someone to divulge more than they had intended, since the urge to fill silence is very great. And so…

"It's not my fault," he said. "I can't be up all night watching." Then he clamped shut his mouth.

So I seized the opportunity.

"If Blephyrix fled in the night," I said, "why did you not say so? Is it because you think he killed Zephyrix? Are you afraid that guilt attaches to you, since you brought Blephyrix here?"

"Ah! Ah!" he said, in alarm; but he did not collapse. "Blephyrix is not mine. He is the property of Zephyrix. A slave may own slaves."

"None the less, it was you that brough Blephyrix here, so you would be guilty of ..."

But Veronius interrupted as anger swept over him.

"I know you!" he said. "You are the mind-reading Greek owned by the first javelin. You are a slave yourself ... *boy* ... and I don't answer to slaves!"

Leaving aside the insult of calling me *boy*, I wondered who had told him about me. Meanwhile he spouted more abuse, with the men behind her nodding their heads off as they hid behind him. Finally, he ended with a threat.

"I shall write to Rome," she said, "seeking justice for my employers – my *powerful* employers – and seeking punishment for those who are holding me here against my will!"

"Do as you please," I said, "but be aware that punishment will fall on those who are accessories to murder."

He had strength for one more outburst, which I summarise.

"Outrage ... insult .... disgrace!" He affected anger, but some of the fire had gone out of him, and his followers were looking at one another and muttering.

When he was done, I bowed and spoke.

"You will stay in this house while I complete my investigations," I said, "because I shall want to speak to each of you individually. And now, I give you good day and may the grace of the gods fall upon you!"

I forgave them for not responding with a polite '*and upon you*', and turned to the doors which were shut, leading to a considerable difficulty of Roman protocol. On formal occasions, doors are opened and closed only by the lowest-ranking slaves. Morganus and the bodyguards could never perform this servile duty, and I certainly was not going to do it in front of Veronius. So I looked at Aetius, who saw the problem and made a swift decision. He stepped forward and opened the doors. As a shaven-headed exotic it was probably the first time he had ever done such a thing. But I respected him for it, seeing that he was a man used to taking initiative.

Outside, Morganus looked at me.

"What now, Greek?" he said. I looked around. There were too many people present. There were slaves in every corner, standing with bowed heads but with ears at the ready, as slave ears always are.

"Can we go into the garden?" I said to Aetius. "I want to see the lamprey pool."

"Of course," he said, still sighing from opening doors. But he led the way, and again, we conversed in Greek as we went.

"What manner of man is Blephyrix?" I said.

"Broad and strong. But introverted. He spoke little. He was quiet."

"What relationship did he have with Zephyrix?"

"Zephyrix mocked him for his size. Blephyrix dreamed of being a racing driver but was too big. Zephyrix mocked him for it, and so did the other drivers."

"So what Blephyrix do, if he was not a driver?"

Aetius laughed at that. "He was here to make right after Zephyrix."

"Meaning what?

"He paid off those whom his Zephyrix wounded."

"Wounded?"

"Raped."

"You mean Blephyrix paid off the girls Zephyrix raped?"

"And boys," said Aeitius. "Blephyrix followed behind with a purse of gold."

Then we were in the garden which, like the house, was trying forlornly to be in the Mediterranean. It had fountains and a little stream for coolness: coolness, in Britannia! But the gardeners had done their best, and planted whatever it is that thrives under grey skies and plentiful rain. So there were artfully-trimmed bushes and even some flowers, and patterns of smooth, round marble stones, artistically scattered. It was a pleasant place.

"Aetius," I said, "will you take his honour and myself to the pool and then leave us to talk?"

He did, and Morganus and I looked at the lamprey pool, which was deep, square and twenty feet across. It was stone-flagged all round, planted with water lilies, lined with lead sheet and surrounded by iron railings four feet high. There was a gate in the railings and the gate was locked. So I had a very good look at the railings, then looked behind some of the flower beds, kneeling on the ground for a closer look, smiled at what I found, and stood up.

"Well," said Morganus, pointing to the railings, "nobody's going to fall in by accident, are they?"

"No," I said. Then: "Ugh! Look at them!" The water was suddenly heaving with long, black serpentine creatures, thick in the body, glistening slimy, and evil of mouth.

"They think it's dinner time," said Morganus, "and we're the dinner!"

"I doubt they can actually kill a man," I said, "they haven't got teeth like sharks."

"What do they do then?" he said.

"Hang on to a man who is exhausted and can't get out of the pond," I said.

Morganus nodded. "Then they dig into him and suck his blood," he said, "and he can't pull them off because they're slippery." He shook his head. "Nasty," he said, very nasty." He looked at me. "So, what now, Greek? What did we learn in there with that racing peacock?"

He grinned, which surprised me, then I told him everything and asked his opinion, which was exceedingly useful because – being Roman – he knew something that I did not.

"These powerful men back in Rome?" he said. "Those who owned Zephyrix, and are employing Veronius?"

"Yes?" I said.

"They're only knights!" he said.

"How do you know that? And what if they are?"

"Well, they must be knights because – in Rome – it's the knights who run the big businesses: corn, shipping, oil and so on. The senatorial noblemen don't do that because it's beneath their dignity: their *Roman dignity*." He so much believed in these words that I may have sniggered, because he frowned. "Don't laugh," he said. "Can't you just listen? I'm trying to tell you something."

"I apologise," I said. "Please continue."

"Well," he said, "those who owned Zephyrix are only knights, while we have the authority of his grace the governor."

"Gods bless him!" I said, and he paused, wondering if I spoke in mockery.

"Bah!" he said. "Teutonius is senatorial, and they're only knights, so we out-rank them."

"But if they're rich, very rich," I said, "wouldn't they have power over senators?"

66

He smiled at that.

"No!" he said. "Because all knights want to be senators, and they won't become senators if they don't give respect to the existing senators. So the knights are expert crawlers: they know their place!"

"Like all Romans," I said, and he sighed.

"Why do you say these things?" he said. "What's wrong with you?" He took a breath and continued. "So, Veronius won't be writing to Rome. He'd be wasting his time and he knows it."

"Good!" I said, much relieved.

I looked along the garden and saw Aetius waiting at a discreet distance. He gave a small bow, which I returned fully. I could see that he was still smarting over the door opening, and I needed his cooperation.

"So," I said, "let's go and see the famous Thousander."

So we did. The house slaves had taken him from the pool, pulled the lampreys off him and – on Aeitius's orders – laid the body in a small side room that served as a library. It had a large table, some chairs, a number of book cabinets and good light through glazed windows. Also it was unheated and cold: a good place to lay out a corpse.

This time, Aetius had found a minion for the door, and he fell back as the rest of us entered. Instantly, Morganus and the bodyguards raised arms in respect, then removed helmets and bowed to the body of the world's most famous racing driver. I too raised arms, for the gods are everywhere, and then there was a murmur of incantation as we gave prayers for the dead: myself to Apollo, Morganus and the bodyguards to Mithras.

And now, since truth is invincible and virtuous, I confess the unseemly fascination that fell upon me. By then I knew that feeling well, and had been anticipating the pleasure of it even by the lamprey pool. It was the consuming delight of investigation. I love puzzles of all kinds, but none are so sweet as reading the signs, signals and traces that are left at the place of a crime. So I fell upon the task with the delight of a glutton at a feast.

Zephyrix the Thousander was laid on his back, fully dressed in expensive clothes, still damp from the pool. So the first thing I did, with the help of the bodyguards, was remove all his clothes, examine them carefully, and then examine every inch of the body for wounds and marks of any kind. The rigor of death was upon him, especially in the face and limbs, and I judged the time of death to be perhaps a day and half ago.

He was a man of thin stature, wiry and muscular, about thirty years old and exceptionally well groomed; even the hair of his armpits and pubis had been plucked, as was common for those who use the public baths. I knew at once that there were deeper investigations, which I could not perform here, but I completed this first examination, noting a crunching of broken bone to the back of the head and several odd, round wounds which I took to be the work of the lampreys. Also, there were small cuts to the buttocks– barely visible, but present.

But even before that, an oddity leapt out at me. Zephyrix had been wearing three expensive tunics, in fine wool of harmonious colours, one on top of the other, as was common in cold Britannia, and also puttees bound around his lower legs. But beneath all I took note of the under-garment, the *cingulum*. It was made of priceless silk, but otherwise was of the usual form: a roughly triangular garment, that was put on by a man standing with the cingulum behind him, then drawing two loose ends in front where they are knotted to comfortable tightness, then the third end is passed between up between the legs, pulled under the tied-together ends, and finally draped in front as decorative wear. Gladiators and athletes wear the cingulum with nothing else, to display their muscular bodies, but in some form or other, it is usual wear for all but the poorest.

The oddity that I noticed, as we undressed the corpse, was that the cingulum, as draped in front, bore an embroidered monogram, in large bold letters in actual gold thread. Thus, three letters were entwined together– Z M I– but at first I could not recognise them, until I realised they were the wrong way round, like mirror images.

"Z M I?" I said. "What can that mean?"

"Huh!" said Morganus, and the bodyguards looked at each other in amazement.

"It stands for Zephyrix the Magnificent and Invincible!" said Morganus. "Everyone knows that– except you."

"Yeah," said the bodyguards. They couldn't help it. They got a scowl from Morganus for speaking without permission, but I could see that he agreed with them. I shrugged. There was much about Romans that I would never learn. It is the same with their religious festivals. I never know when they are coming.

That made me think of Morgana, because she always warned me when a festival was imminent. So there was something I had to do.

"I'll need to wash," I said. "The deceased stinks of fish and weed." I looked at Morganus, "I cannot enter your house smelling of fish. It would be an insult to the-lady-your-wife.

Morganus moved close to me and sniffed. "You stink of worse than fish," he said, "and you've got mud on your tunic. She won't like that, either."

I nodded. "Then we must get the body to the fort," I said. "We'll need a cart, and something to cover it, for decency."

Morganus frowned. "Why must we move him?" he said. "Haven't you had a good look at him already, begging his pardon?" He bowed to the body again and raised arms. The bodyguards did the same.

"Yes," I said, "but there is more to be done, much more."

"What do you mean?" said Morganus. I told him— and he did not like it and there was a considerable argument between us, but I reminded him that we had the full authority of the governor in this matter, and the obligation *to make all smooth*.

Finally, having washed and cleaned myself, and with the assistance of Aetius and the house slaves, we took the body of Zephyrix to the legionary hospital in the fort. We took it on a large hand-cart pulled by a pair of slaves, and we covered the body in cloaks conscripted from lesser slaves. These unfortunates could never again wear such luck-cursed garments, so I insisted that Aetius provide them with new ones. It was only fair.

And so to business: fascinating business. At least, I thought so.

# CHAPTER 8

One of the bodyguards fell over like a statue hauled from its plinth. He went down with a crash of armour, and his helmet came off and rolled away. He had fainted, and his three companions looked ready to follow him, being sickly grey in the face with beads of sweat running down their cheeks.

"Get him out!" said Morganus, "and stay outside with him. You're no use to me, any one of you! What sort of men are you for soldiers? Get out!"

"Yes, honoured sir!" they said, and heaved their comrade up – groaning and gasping as he was – and hauled him out. Then one came back for the helmet and scuttled out fast.

I was not greatly surprised. Nor was I surprised that the one who fainted first was the biggest and toughest: the arm-wrestling champion of the Twentieth Legion. But no blame attaches, since people often react like that when attending a post mortem. Indeed, in my medical training I had seen students faint even as the teacher takes up his knife, let alone plunges it into the subject. But what really sent the bodyguard reeling was the first incision: the cut that runs from the sternum to the pubic symphysis, laying open all the slimy viscera that the gods have crammed into a human belly.

So I exchanged smiles with the hospital's surgeons and dressers – eight of them – who had begged to be present out of professional interest. So we smiled at each other, and shook our heads at the frailties of first-timers. But I was pleased to see Morganus stand square as a pyramid, at least in the anatomical sense, because he still had legalistic doubts.

"What do we say if we're accused of desecration?" he said, pointing to the slit-open body of Zephyrix.

"We shall say what these learned gentlemen have told me," I said, and looked at the surgeons and dressers. "Which is that when some important deceased is returned to Rome for burial, it is normal to disembowel the body, then pack it in salt, so that it might reach Rome un-decayed."

The learned men nodded.

"Though sometimes we send the viscera with the body," said one. "In sealed jars."

"For those who follow the Egyptian cults," said another.

"Yes," they said.

"Thank you, learned sirs," I said, and since I was standing by a slab bearing a subject, and since I was wearing a surgical apron, with instruments laid out beside me and a dresser to had them to me, then for a moment I was again a surgeon of Apollonis addressing a class. But first – having learned Roman ways – I raised hands.

"With the permission of the gods," I said.

"With the permission of the gods," they all said, raising hands.

"So," I said, "we have here the body of Zephyrix the Thousander who, we are told, was a drunkard, and who by implication was so drunk that he fell into a pond and drowned. Therefore we shall now examine the stomach for wine, and the lungs for water."

"Very poetic," said Morganus.

"Very necessary," I said, and the audience nodded. "A drunkard carries a cargo of wine within him, and any man has water in his lungs if he drowns. So these are vital signs in establishing the cause of death."

"I see," said Morganus.

"Retractors please," I said to the dresser, "and could I have assistance?"

Two men stepped forward, each took up a double-hook retractor, took hold of the sides of the deep cut and pulled hard on the triple layer of white flesh, red muscle and yellow fat, to expose the viscera in full and easy gaze. After that, it was slippery work to find my way through the tangled masses to locate the stomach and lungs. In preparation for this, my torso and arms were unclothed apart from the apron, so that I might easily pass hands and arms through the organs, and then clean myself afterwards.

It was absorbing. Very absorbing. Time fled in an eye-blink.

When all was done I left the surgeons and dressers to eviscerate, sew up, and await formal identification by Veronius, so that the remains of Zephyrix the Thousander might be placed in a salt-filled coffin, and shipped back to Rome. But that would be days later.

Meanwhile, once I was washed and dressed, Morganus and I sat in the hospital refectory to talk.

It was miserable little room, just benches and tables and there was a constant clatter and chatter from the next-door kitchen, coming through the serving hatch. But we had it to ourselves, since there was just one door to the outside, with the huts and buildings of the fort beyond, and the bodyguards to keep everyone else out. They kept themselves out too, on Morganus's orders.

"I don't want any of you in here," he said. "Fainting like girlies? I'm not pleased. Out!"

"Yes, honoured sir."

"So, what have we learned, Greek?" said Morganus, who may not entirely have enjoyed the autopsy, since for once he took a good gulp of wine and not his usual sip. Of course, I joined him. I had bread and cheese too, but he did not.

"We know how he died," I said. "He did not drown, and the lampreys did not kill him."

"But I saw their marks on the body," he said. "Those round marks."

"Trivial," I said. "Neither mortal nor serious. They were just taking their dinner, as you said."

"Ugh!" he said.

"Quite!" I said. "So it was not lampreys, and he did not drown and was not drunk. There was little or no wine in the stomach and no water at all in the lungs. A drowning man breathes water into his lungs."

"What killed him, then?"

"A massive blow to the back of the head. Someone hit him with a big stone: a marble stone. The garden is full of them. I found it among the bushes. It had hair on it, and blood. Did I not show it to you?"

"No," he said, "you were on your knees digging the earth with your hands, and muttering to yourself."

"Oh," I said. "Well, I found the stone, and I found his motions, too."

"His what?"

"His faeces."

"By the gods! I said you smelt of something worse than fish!"

"Well I'm clean now," I said, "and it was necessary to the investigation. I think someone who knew Zephyrix very well, followed him out when he went to relieve himself, then hit him with the stone and threw him into the pond. There were threads of his tunics on the railings, which means whoever killed him did not have a key to the gate, and had to throw him over the railings, which is the work of several men, or one strong man. And I found something else."

"If you say so. Go on."

"His buttocks were shaved. It was done with a razor."

Morganus gasped.

"What?" he said "Zephyrix? Zephyrix the Magnificent? Never!"

I shrugged. "His buttocks were shaved. I state that as fact."

"Oh no," he said. He was horrified. He looked as if he had lost a loved one.

"Morganus?" I said. "What's wrong?"

He sighed and told me.

"Well, those that prefer men to women," he said, "they like everything smooth, so the professionals shave their backsides."

"You mean male courtesans?"

He closed his eyes. He could not speak, and I finally realised what was troubling him. It was the sexual morality of Romans, and a very strange morality it was too, since they accepted – just as we Greeks do – that men may desire men, and women may desire women. That is the way of the world. It is how the gods made us. But Romans differed from Greeks in believing that while a virile man could have coitus with any person he chose, whether male or female, he remained virile only if he were the penetrator. Thus, it was huge disgrace for a Roman man to receive penetration, and a thousand times greater disgrace to receive it for payment.

So Morganus was indeed bereaved: bereaved at the death of a hero's honour.

"I'm glad they're not here," he said, looking out at the bodyguards.

"I wouldn't want those lads to hear that. Nor anyone else, really. So we won't tell them just yet."

"But we have to tell the truth," I said, "because truth …"

"Is invincible," he said. "I know. You always say that. But we'll wait till we know it's the truth, right?"

I hesitated to reply, but the look on my friend's face was so painful that I nodded in agreement, and then a runner came in, and there was no more discussion.

We heard his feet pounding, even over the kitchen noise, and even saw him as he ran down the Via Preatoria – the east–west road – towards the hospital. He was a young man in a legionary's tunic, but bare-headed and unarmoured, and he carried a messenger's rod, which he held aloft as he ran.

"Look!" said Morganus, "signal coming in!"

The runner came straight to the refectory door, where he was stopped by the bodyguards. He stood panting and gasping. Then he drew breath and shouted: "Message for his gracious and reverend honour the first javelin, from his honour Tertius Filius Artifax, commander of the Londinium walls!"

Soon after that, we were riding out from one of the Londinium gates, with a cavalry escort of twenty men, and Artifax leading. For me, it was pure joy to be on horseback, since I come of the horse clan among my own people and was first put on horseback at the age of three. Morganus, Artifax and the bodyguards rode like infantrymen, bumping in the saddle and so much feeling the pain that the cavalrymen – mad Batavians – would have laughed if they had dared, since Batavians were born in the saddle.

So we rode on, over wide open ground with rising hills in the far distance. Everything was green with thick tufts of grass, and bushes, and lumpy little mounds all around, and the damp wind of Britannia ever blowing. But for once I never felt the cold, being entirely content to be on a horse.

Artifax raised arm to bring us to a halt when we were about two hundred yards from the ramparts and ditches, and I leaned forward to pat my mount on the neck, to tell her that I was grateful for her efforts. I did so because a rider should always be kind to his horse, and may the fiends of hell fall upon those who are cruel. Meanwhile, Morganus looked around in surprise.

"Is this it, Artifax?" he said, "We've not come far. We could have walked!"

Artifax disagreed. "Can't be too careful, your honour," he said. "If any of the buggers are about, I want to get you back inside those walls as fast as possible."

We all looked round as he said that. This was Britannia after all, and who knew what might be hiding behind the lumpy little mounds?

"Anyway," said Artifax, "there they are, the buggers that I told you about. Them and some of their rubbish. We left everything as we found it, so the Greek gentleman can see it and work his … I mean do his job." He stumbled over his words, just about managing not to say that I would *work his magic*.

But what can I do? There is no arguing with ignorance. So I looked round. A few paces from where I sat upon my horse, I saw two dead men and some wickerwork hurdles: intertwined fencing, each one two yards square. Also there were a few native axes and clubs, and a Roman household shrine– a tiny house of pottery, no more than a foot square, brightly painted and with small images of the *lares*: beneficent gods of somebody's home. Every Roman home had a *lararium*, as it was called, and the paterfamilias would lead prayers before it every day. But this one was dumped on its roof and had been deliberately battered and abused.

"Look at that!" said Artifax. "Filthy animals! Who'd do that to the gods of someone's home?"

Morganus and the bodyguards growled in anger. Even the Batavians were frowning, though they had gods of their own. But I was more interested other things. So I dismounted, gave my reins to one of the Batavians to hold, and knelt down beside the two dead men. Morganus got down beside me, much to the alarm of Artifax.

"Don't you want to stay mounted, your honour," he said. "The buggers might still be about!"

"You just keep watch," said Morganus, "and let the Greek gentleman do his work."

So I did my work, which once again was absorbing and fascinating. The two men had been shot with artillery bolts. They were obviously native Britannic Celts. Their clothes, jewellery and long hair proclaimed that.

They were young men in the flower of youth, and like all rural peasants their faces were tanned and roughened by the outdoors. They were unbathed, with black fingernails and an animal smell. One had been hit in the thigh, the bolt passing straight through the limb and beyond. This man had bled to death from the severing of blood vessels within, and his lower garments were thick with dried blood. The other had been hit twice, once half way down his back, with the bolt still embedded in the bones of his spine, surely causing paralysis of the lower limbs, while another bolt had struck in the region of the kidney, then tumbled and shattered as high velocity projectiles sometimes do. It had left a huge and gaping wound in his side, all stuck with splinters of the bolt.

I searched the bodies for possessions or evidence of any kind, and found only simple things: a fire-maker with flint, steel and tinder, and small knives, combs and toothpicks. Neither had a sword, so perhaps they had carried axes or clubs? Each wore a pouch at the neck, and each pouch contained a carving of three little men in hooded cloaks standing together. The carvings were about the size of my thumb, and differed slightly in style, but the subject was identical in each. I assumed they were sacred objects, and raised arms in respect, since you can never be too wary of the gods.

Then I stood and looked over the two young men generally where they lay, noting that one had an arm around the other. That caused me to look at his hand, then the hand of the other. Also, I noted marks on the ground. But most of all I was struck by the differences between the men, because one was squat and dark, while the other looked almost Greek, but with blue eyes. The tribes of Britannia were almost different races, and had their own particular features, so I turned to Morganus.

"They come of different tribes," I said, "don't they?"

"Yes," he said. "The dark one's Silure, and the one with the straight nose is Dumnonii. Their homelands are way over to the west," he looked at me. "and they hate one another, the Silures and Dumnonii. They're tribal enemies since forever. They hate each other more than us! But here they are together."

"More than that," I said, "because the one shot in the leg, took hold of the one shot in the spine, and dragged him about twenty yards. The marks are there in the grass. I think he was pulling a comrade clear of the battle. He died trying to do that. Gods rest his brave soul!"

"But they're tribal enemies," said Morganus.

"Well, someone has brought them together," I said. And I paused, seeing the nervousness of Artifax, and the bodyguards. They could guess where this was leading and did not like it. They were already making the bull sign. But I pressed on, looking at Morganus.

"Who could that be?" I said.

"Druids," he said. "We know they were here, and who else could make a Silure love a Domonius?"

Also, Morganus and I knew from past investigations that although the druidic faith had been extinguished at the point of the sword wherever the legions trod, it still flourished in the tribal heartlands, holding great power over the rural folk – and the rural folk were the vast majority in Britannia. But that was a state secret, and not to be spoken aloud.

"So is this a druid sign?" I said, pointing to the left hand of the Silure, then the left hand of the Dumonius. "Look at the junction of thumb and forefinger. They've each got three black dots tattooed into the skin. What does that mean?"

I looked to him for guidance, he that had a Celtic wife and spoke their language.

"I don't know," he said, "I've never seen that before."

"Well I think that I may have," I said. "Do you remember that child I saved?"

"Who could forget?" he said.

"His father was constantly touching his left hand with his right hand then tapping the right hand to his brow and heart. I'm not sure, but I think he may have had three black dots on his hand like these two."

"We'd better talk to him," said Morganus. Then he went to the despoiled lararium, set it upright, stood to attention and invoked the blessing of Mithras upon it. Then he spoke.

"Artifax?" he said.

"Honoured sir?"

"I'm not as honoured as *this!*" he said, bowing to the little shrine. "Take it back into the city, and find where it came from, because it must have been stolen. Find who was robbed of it, then take it home. Do it with proper respect."

"Of course, honoured sir!" said Artifax. "I'll turn out the guard, and we'll march it home with standards raised and trumpets sounding."

"Good," said Morganus, then looked at me. "You were right about the hurdles," he said, "hazelwood plaited hurdles. There's several left lying around. That's what they lifted the druids on."

"It was not hard to guess," I said.

"Not for you," he said, then spoke to Artifax: "Clear up here. Get the bodies buried, and put everything else in store in case we need it again. Also, warn me at once if there is any more of this midnight nonsense."

Afterwards, Morganus and I talked as we rode back into the city. Artifax and the bodyguards kept their distance, and the Batavians hardly spoke Latin. They merely understood commands. Morganus began with his usual question.

"What now, Greek?"

"I'm intrigued by the three dots and the three little men," I said.

"Me too," he said. "All the tribes wear sacred pouches round the neck, but what's in them varies from tribe to tribe: wheel of Beltranos for the Brigantes, black stones of Mol for the Artrebates and so on. And now here's a Silure and a Doumonius, both with three little men in hoods!" He turned to me. "But this'll have to wait. What about Zephyrix? We're under orders to find the killer: *governor's* orders! So gods bless his grace."

"And gods bless Petros the Athenian," I said, "who rules over his grace."

"Holy Jupiter!" he said. "Can you not guard your tongue?"

"Yes," I said, "because we still have to find out what happened, and the first, obvious person to interrogate is brother Blephyrix, who has run off with a bag of gold."

"Ah!" he said, seizing on my words. "Blephyrix paid off the victims, didn't he?"

"Yes," I said.

"So," he said, "if there *were* victims, and if Zephyrix was a rapist, then he couldn't have been a …"

But he saw the doom of such reasoning and cursed violently. "Pluto, Charon and Styx!" he said, and fell silent. So did I, because before all else what Petros the Athenian really wanted was not so much to find the killer of Zephyrix, but *to keep all smooth* in the body politic. But so far our investigations had revealed two things. First that the druids – supposedly suppressed and driven deep into the rural wastes – were active around the very walls of Londinium and second that Zephyrix – beloved world champion of the races – was one kind or another of sexual deviant, if not both.

# CHAPTER 9

The sun was down by the time we got back to the fort and Morganus's house. That gave me all night to attempt sleep— and fail, as so often I did. At least I had the excuse that I was considering the investigation and planning the next step.

"Felemid," I said to Morganus at breakfast. "Gentius Civilis Felemidus, we'll see him next."

"Not that that's his real name," said Morganus, "it's just his Roman name."

Behind him the four bodyguards sneered like vinegar. They stood waiting to start the day, and they did not like Felemid: not him, nor any of the other Britannic Celts who had grown so fabulously rich as to buy their way into Roman citizenship and high rank.

"He's really Felemids ap Dinidomen," said Morganus. "It means *man who came from the dunghill.*" The bodyguards grinned. "Well," he said, "it's praise, really. It means he made good after a bad start."

"I see," I said, because everyone knew that Felemid was raised among the tribes of the far north east of Britannia, but had climbed to great heights by his own talents and effort.

"What about Blephyrix," said Morganus, "and the father of the boy you saved? What about them?"

"We don't know where they are," I said, "we'll have to make inquiries. But we know where Felemid is, and he will know if there is anything political in Zephyrix's death."

Morganus nodded. Felemid was deep in Britannic politics. He was consul of the Britannic Council: a fake senate, talking shop set up by the Romans to keep the Celtic billionaires happy. It had all the trappings of a real parliament, including an assembly house in Londinium, but was meant to have no real power, except that the billionaires were constantly pushing and contriving to get power.

"We'll see Felemid first," I said.

"Whatever you think best," said Morganus, "because I always back your judgement, seeing as it's magic judgement."

I was about to become annoyed, but I saw the bodyguards grin.

"But whatever you do today," he said, "you'll have to do it with Sylvanus."

That puzzled me and I frowned. Then he likewise frowned.

"You've forgotten, haven't you?" he said. "Today is the first day of the cycle of the bull, and I shall be needed as chief priest at the Holy Temple of the Standards. We're blessing the standards in the name of Mithras."

He raised fist in the bull sign. So did the bodyguards.

"Gods bless the holy standards!" they said.

"Ah," I said, "of course. Blessings on the standards in Apollo's name."

I had been deep in thought, and noticed only then that the bodyguards were not holding Morganus's weapons, armour and helmet. They had a toga and a wreath of laurels instead. "Of course," I said, "I shall make do with centurion Sylvanus, today."

"Not just today," said Morganus. "The ceremony lasts all night, and for two more nights of vigilance. That's three days. But I've given an extraordinary licence of absence to Sylvanus and his team, so that you can continue with the investigation, and I've told them that – at your command – they act in my name."

"Of course," I said. "Thank you."

"Here," he said, handing me a small writing tablet, "these are the passwords for the next three days. Everyone knows you, but the fort guards won't let anyone through without passwords, even me!"

"Of course," I said.

"Huh!" he said. So did Morgana and the daughters.

So he left, and I did make do with Sylvanus. In fact, Morganus and I would have gone to him in any case, for what we needed now. Sylvanus was the officer in charge of a company – fifteen of them – of excused-armour clerks in the legionary headquarters, who were on special duties to me. As pen-pushing office workers, they were plump by army standards – Roman soldiers were typically lean and wiry – but they were highly intelligent and were fluent in Latin and Greek, and not just 'boot-fillers' like most legionaries. So, considering the work this team of men was doing for me, and considering how far they had come from being mere clerks, then in my city of Apollonis we would have called them officers of police. But Rome had no police. That was Rome.

I went to their office in the headquarters building, and they all stood up from their desks as I entered. They stood with a scrape and a rumble, and I suppose I was pleased. It was flattering, considering the fact that they were citizens and I was a slave. The office was a typical Roman army office: immaculate, swept, whitewashed, everything in lines – desks, filing boxes, scroll cases and stools – with large windows filled with precisely-carpentered wooden grids. It was bright, light, busy and cold. I shivered in my cloak. But I was bred up for warmth and sunshine, not Britannia.

Sylvanus sat at a high desk at one side of the room, facing the door. He nodded politely.

"Good day to you Sylvanus," I said. "Good day, men of the Twentieth." I felt like a schoolmaster coming into a class.

"How can we serve your worship?" said Sylvanus.

I explained what I wanted, and he thought briefly then replied.

"Felemid is easy, your worship," he said, and pointed to one of his men, "You!" he said, "get a message run to the house of Felemid, in the name of his honour the first javelin, seeking earliest possible appointment for Ikaros of Apollonis."

"Yes, honoured sir!" The legionary bowed, and headed for the door.

"At the double!" said Sylvanus, so the man ran. "And you," he pointed to another, "pick five men and go round the docks, asking for the Celt whose child got raised from the dead by his worship!"

I let that pass. What point was there in arguing?

"The rest of you, gather round. We're going to think where Blephyrix could have gone, even with all his money, and we're going to ask after him: ask at the gates, the port, the tart shops, cooks' shops, and anywhere else we can think of. I want a plan drawn up, of who's looking where, and I want it done fast – 'cos it's for the big man, Morganus."

I was impressed. As I have said, Sylvanus was intelligent, and I could not have organised a better plan myself. But plans do not always work as intended. Thus, there was no swift reply from Felemid, not even to a message in Morganus's name, because Felemid was out of the city, having gone to his country villa. On the other hand, we had almost instant success in finding the father of the child I had saved.

"He's called Denmultid the Writer," said one of Sylvanus's men, returned within an hour from his task in the docks. "He's famous among the dock people. Everyone knows about the magic Greek bringing his kid back from the dead." He looked at me and bowed. His companions did the same "He has a little shop by one of the quays so we went there. It was easy. He's a scribe who writes letters, fills in forms, does a bit of lawyer work. He deals with the port authorities for those who can't do it themselves."

"Have you told him I want to speak to him?" I asked.

"Yes, your worship, of course, your worship."

"And?" I said. The soldier sniffed and thought He was puzzled. He tried to make sense of what he had seen.

"He got a bit funny: Denmutid," he said. "He sent his slaves out – he has two slaves – and then he said, he said … *I will see the Greek. I must see him. The holy gods are upon me to see him. I must pay my debt. His life is on it.*"

"My life is on it?" I said, "Did he actually say that?"

"Yes, your worship, he did. And then he said … *But I ask a favour* … he was very humble, your worship, bent over double and holding his hands up like he was praying."

"Go on," I said. "What was this favour?"

So the soldier told me, and I decided to grant it. But I was able to do so only because Morganus was not there. Even Sylvanus argued as hard as he dared. But he did not have the authority to stop me. Finally, he gave up.

"In that case, your worship," he said, "I'm coming with you, I'm taking some of the lads, and we're going armed."

"So be it," I said, "but no shields, no armour, no helmets."

"Yes, your worship. He'd run off if he saw any of that."

"Good!" I said, and showed him the tablet Morganus had given me. "Will these passwords get us into the docks?"

Sylvanus looked at the writing. "No," he said, "the docks are guarded night and day, with auxiliaries on the gates." He pointed to the tablet. "These here are military passwords, and the auxiliaries don't like us regulars anyway. What you want is Port of Londinium Council passwords."

"Can you get them?" I said. "Aren't they restricted?"

He just smiled.

Later, at the end of the short winter day, I was inside the harbour palisade, walking in the dark with Sylvanus and five men. It was an uneasy place at night: not entirely empty of life, since the anchored ships had men aboard, and we could hear distant voices aboard the dark, high-sided vessels. There was even someone playing a flute, while ships eased up and down on creaking cables, and the river hissed and gurgled as the tide rolled out, around the timber piles supporting the wharves.

In any case we trod carefully, because there were trip hazards everywhere: heavy ring bolts for securing ships, dark rows of planks, barrels and urns, and every imaginable form of slippery waste underfoot: fish, oil, and grease. Then Sylvanus spoke.

"There, your worship! See the cranes? You want the middle one. The one with the big barrel hanging. That's to show which one, 'cos that's where he'll be."

The cranes stood like obelisks in the night: black shadows rising high up from their swivelling bases to the narrowing, pointed tips. The Londinium dock cranes were giants of their kind: entirely planked-in and powered by a pair of huge treadmills at the bottom, such that teams of men could walk the wheels round, winding a cable on the rotation axis, such that the cable hauled mightily on the block-and-tackle gear at the top of the machine. These cranes could easily lift loads of many tons, swaying them in and out of ships.

"You must wait here," I said to Sylvanus, but he looked around in the dark night. There were shapes and shadows, and things half seen, all around us.

"Anyone could be hiding here," he said, and his men were likewise looking round and muttering.

"I must go alone," I said, "or he'll run off."

"At least take this," said Sylvanus, reaching for his sword.

"I can't," I said. "I'm a slave. I may not bear arms. That's imperial law."

"Take it anyway," he said, "and damn the law."

"No," I said. "You could lose citizenship just for *offering* me a sword."

"What will the big man say if you come to harm?"

"Tell him I take responsibility. I say that before all of you."

"Then gods be with you, your worship."

So I went forward. I went forward alone, feeling extremely alone and wishing that I had taken the sword after all, and reflecting that I could – of course – have taken a staff or a cudgel, which would have been better than nothing, and which were not regarded as weapons by imperial law. But everyone is wise after the event, even a philosopher.

So I crept towards the middle crane, and when I got to within about a dozen steps from it, the door in the base opened – it opened with a loud creak – and a man stepped out, heavily wrapped against the cold. He could have been anyone, and the hairs stood up sharp on the back of my neck and I wished ten times over for Sylvanus's sword. But not only did he make no threatening move, but he bowed at the waist and spread his arms to show that he carried no weapon.

"Your honour," he said. "Your magic and divine honour. You that gave me back my boy, and who I can never bless enough, or thank enough, not in a thousand years."

89

He went on after this fashion, and I was embarrassed because in offering what we of Apollonis called *first aid*, I had done no more than any man or woman of my people would have done.

Then he stopped talking, looked every way and beckoned me. "Here, here, your honour," he said. "I have a duty, two duties, and I am in agony."

He sobbed and I should have known my danger even then, but my gift betrayed me. I was so enwrapped in my attempt to read inside his head, that I did not look around me. It was fascinating. I saw the wringing of one hand by another, I guessed rather than saw the twisting of his face. Then the gods gave me a small light. The moon danced out from a cloud and I got first proper look at the horror of his face – mouth gaping wide – as he gave an upward glance … and his right hand jerked in an odd motion, and then he shrieked, and lunged toward me pushing with both hands out in front, and sending me staggering back.

He thereby saved my life, as the great barrel at the tip of the crane came whirring down like the thunderbolt of Zeus. It came down precisely on the spot where I had been standing; and instead of killing me, it smashed the life instantly out of Denmultid the Writer. It broke his body and bones so utterly and completely that his blood spattered all over my clothes and my limbs, and one stave of the shattered barrel struck my shins as native beer gushed in all directions, splashing and foaming and stinking.

Then Sylvanus and his men were rushing up in a clumping of boots.

"Light! Light!" cried Sylvanus, and two of his men came from behind, puffing and blowing and running carefully, being burdened with lanterns kept with the shutters closed. "Light! Here!" said

Sylvanus, and by all the gods in that nasty moment, I felt a fool for acting without Morganus and the bodyguards, and wishing for their presence right now rather than these overweight clerks, who would be little use in a fight.

Which was an ungrateful thought on my behalf, considering how excellent Sylvanus's men were in other ways. Meanwhile, I was looking at the remains of Denmultid, distorted and ruined as they were. Yes: indeed he did have the three spots on his left hand, and yes indeed he had something clutched in his right hand. It was a length of strong line, thin but very tough. I followed it back towards the crane. It ran in through the door.

"Lantern!" I said.

"Bring a light!" said Sylvanus, "Here, let me!" He grabbed a lantern and followed me. Inside the crane, there were the two big winding wheels and tackles and gears of all kinds. The thin line ran around a pulley, then to the end of a lever. Sylvanus brought the lantern close and we peered at the mechanism.

"Look, your worship," he said, "there's a bit broken here."

He was right. Someone had broken a safety check that should have prevented a brake lever from being thrown accidentally. It was no accident, because the safety check was of thick iron, and had been forced out of place with a powerful tool such as a crowbar.

"Yes," I said, "someone has rigged the drum brake so that it can be released." I looked up to the tackles overhead. "So, just one pull on that line would let go the load at the top of the crane."

"The line was in his fist," said Sylvanus. "Denmultid wanted to kill you!"

"But he did not," I said. "He changed his mind at the last moment. I saw it happen."

Shortly after that there was a blowing of whistles and running of feet as auxiliary guards ran up to investigate, since the crash of the barrel had been heard from end to end of the docks. Likewise, on the bulwarks of the nearby ships, here were lanterns held up and men peering, there was much shouting, and gaping at the dead body by the auxiliaries.

Fortunately, the auxiliary optio recognised me, and knew that he and his men were out-ranked by Sylvanus and his men, who were citizens and legionaries. So we came away free from the site of this tragedy, with our feet soaked in beer, and myself holding the little image of three men in hoods, that I had taken from the pouch around the neck of Denmultid the Writer.

We left his body for whatever formalities the Port of Londinium Council might require, and for whatever rites, before whatever gods, that were proper to his family. It was a mistake not to sequester the body for the legion. But I was soaked in blood as well as beer, and perhaps not quite myself, as I trudged back to the fort with Sylvanus and the rest.

At least I had the sense not to return to Morganus's house in my disgusting state. I could not face the wrath of Morgana, who never failed to chastise and then fall into tears at my carelessness. As I have said, despite my being older than her, she treated me as a wayward son. So I cleaned myself in the legionary bath house, and Sylvanus found fresh clothes. But I should not have bothered.

"Where is your blue cloak?" said Morgana as I entered Morganus's house. She was waiting for me: waiting with a lamp. "That is a cheap army cloak! Where is your blue cloak?"

I was tired; I cannot lie, because I detest lies, and I have not the skills of a liar. So I told the truth, and provoked just such reaction as I had feared, with the daughters roused from their beds and joining in.

"It's your fault!" she cried, "you never take care! Just wait till the-lord-my-husband returns! He'll throw you from this house! I can't bear this anymore!"

Then, finally, she sank into a chair, weeping, with the daughters folding her in their arms, and myself apologising.

"I will not do it again … I shall take more care … never again on my own …"

It was bad, very bad. I had upset them deeply.

But in the morning it was worse.

# CHAPTER 10

On a good day, Morganus's house awoke at dawn, to the sound of the Twentieth Legion's bugle calls rousing the men from sleep. So it was a bad day when the house was roused by Morganus himself coming into the house from outside, and shouting my name.

"Ikaros! Ikaros!" he cried. "Get up!"

I heard him from my bedroom– and then he was next to my bed in the grey light, with deep concern on his face. He wore a plain tunic, and the laurel wreath of a priest, but he had thrown off his toga. "Up! Up!" he said. "We've got work to do."

"What is it?" I said. "What about the ceremony? Blessing the standards?"

"Broken!" he said, "Spoiled! I was called from it. Shame and disgrace!"

"What's happening?" I said. "Tell me!"

"Not here," he said. "I'll tell you as we go."

The bedroom door was open, and I saw Morgana and the daughters, in night clothes with blankets thrown over. I saw the bodyguards looking grim, and this time they were indeed holding Morganus's arms, armour and helmet. I got dressed fast as they buckled him into his gear.

"Stand firm, lady-my-wife," he said. "We'll deal with this. Me and the Greek."

"Deal with what, lord-my-husband?"

"Can't say." She nodded as a Roman wife should, gathered her daughters behind her and they all bowed to Morganus.

"Gods be with you, lord-my-husband," she said.

"Gods be with you, lord-my-father," said the girls.

Then we were outside. I was shivering in the cold, a miserable Britannic sun was heaving its miserable self over the fort ramparts, and a company of Batavian cavalrymen was waiting with horses for me, Morganus and the bodyguards. There was a legionary, too. He was sitting on his horse with useless legs dangling, and not gripping as a horseman should. He looked like death. He looked like horror.

"Come!" said Morganus, as the bodyguards heaved him into the saddle. They then got up themselves with much effort, while I vaulted on to my horse, as I'd learned as a boy. The Batavians liked that. They grinned. Then we were riding. We rode through the camp, past gates and sentries, and towards the walls of Londinium but without seeking to enter the town. We rode over the ever-green grass of Britannia, and out past deep entrenchments, high ramparts and round artillery towers.

Then we crossed the Great South Road, with morning traffic carts and peasants bringing in produce, then a turn down another line of entrenchments, ramparts and artillery, until I recognised the ground where we had found the Silure and the Dumonius, and the despoiled household shrine. All this, and still Morganus said nothing.

There were more horsemen waiting. Another company of Batavians and a legionary, all mounted. The legionary was Artifax, commander of the walls, and he raised a hand in formal salute— but we were closing at a fast canter and I could see what was waiting for us, in the exact same place that we had found the two Celts.

It was an ugly sight, the ugliest I ever saw in all my years, including years of warfare. So we reined in, looked down, and the poor horses sniffed and tossed heads in dismay, and shuffled their poor feet in as much distress as their human riders.

Someone had erected three crosses, such as were used by the Romans to execute the worst kind of criminal. The crosses stood about six feet high, and the least frightful of them bore the armour of a legionary trooper: plumed helmet, scarf, cuirass and military belt, and even a pair of boots nailed to the woodwork. A sword and dirk hung by their straps.

It is hard to say which of the next two was the worst, because – on one – a *thing* was hanging that I strained to recognise. Then disgust overwhelmed me as I saw that it was the skin of a human being– the skin of a man– thick, limp, heavy and pale, and hanging in folds.

The third cross bore the body of a man: a body that had been flayed of skin, displaying naked red muscle and sinew that dripped with blood, but which some evil monster had left still with the face intact, so that the man might be recognised.

Everyone groaned at the sight. Everyone called on his gods, raised hands, raised a fist in the bull sign and ground teeth in anger. One of the Batavians of our company even fell from the saddle, retching in helpless spasm.

"Knock 'em down!" yelled Morganus at utmost strength of voice. "Knock down those filthy things, and give honour to that man! Get him off that cross and cover him decently and take him for burial – burial like a Roman – and burn everything else. Burn it all in the name of Jupiter, Juno and Minerva. Burn it! Do it now!"

"Honoured sir," I said. "Please, Morganus, comrade and brother, let me look first. I must look. We must know what this means."

"I know what it means," he said. "It's disgrace and dishonour on Rome and the gods of Rome, and done by the druids!"

"Please?" I said. "Let me look first."

"Gods damn you if you must," he said. "Get it done! Be quick."

So I did. I looked at everything. I looked very carefully. Then the dead man was decently covered and returned to the fort, and a great bonfire built, with oil and wood brought out from the city.

Much later, Morganus and I entered the centurions' hall in the fort: a high-ceilinged dining chamber with polished furniture, mosaic floor, wall paintings, and service of food and drink at whatever time pleased the centurions. It was so senior a place that the bodyguards must wait outside, but there were several centurions at table, all of whom rose and saluted Morganus. Their faces told me that they already knew what we had seen outside the city walls, and the most senior of them spoke.

"Honoured, esteemed, and victorious sir," he said, "we shall withdraw to leave you in reflection with your Greek, and may the Lord Mithras be with you."

Morganus nodded. "And with you, and with our legion," he said.

"Gods save the emperor!" they all said, and such is the vanity of mankind that even in such a moment I noted that I had been mentioned only as a possession: *Morganus's* Greek.

Then we sat over a flask of wine – a large flask – and Morganus took more than ever I saw him take before or since. So did I, but that was not remarkable.

"That fire will burn for ten days," he said, "to purify the ground."

I nodded. He took another gulp, then took refuge in routine.

"What now, Greek?" he said. "What have we learned?"

"First, what happened to *you*?" I said. "You were at the ceremony of the standards."

"Yes," he said, "then Artifax found that ... that *disgrace* ... outside the walls and sent a messenger at once, and I stopped the ceremony." He shook his head. "Shameful," he said. "Shameful!"

Then he looked at me. "Go on," he said, "you looked at everything. What did you find?"

"It was done quickly and in haste," I said. "They cut his throat, then hacked off the skin. It wasn't done slowly and he was dead when they did it."

"Thank the gods!" he said. "Everyone's afraid of being skinned alive."

"Where did that come from," I said, "that tale about being skinned by druids?"

"I don't know," he said, "but it's new. Not traditional. Go on, what else did you find?"

"There were horses there, and lots of men, and they left these everywhere." I handed him some oak leaves, from my pocket-pouch. They were old and dried, from last year's season.

"Yes, yes," he said. "Oak leaves! So we know it was druids that did it. The oak is sacred to them."

"It must have been revenge," I said. "Revenge for our shooting at them."

He nodded. "Yes," he said, "they're sending us a message. Getting bold."

"We must find out who he was, the one they skinned." I said.

"No need," he said. "He was Sub-Optio Publius Junius Cabo, second century, fourth cohort. Recently promoted, and now dead."

"You recognised him?"

"I gave him his badge of office, just a month ago."

"We need to find out how they caught him."

"And make sure it never happens again," he said. "In case something's going on."

His words made me think. They made me think about Denmultid the Writer, who had two duties, and who decided at the last moment, not to kill me. What duties? One was presumably gratitude for my saving his child, but what was the other? Why did he want to kill me? What was, indeed, going on?

So I told Morganus about Denmultid, and had to endure another storm of outrage.

"Can you not be trusted?" he cried. "Could you not have waited for me and the lads? You're not a soldier anymore. You can't wear a sword. You don't even look where you're going …"

And so on, and so on, and so on. His voice failed in the end, and he shook his head, and the service staff stood and gaped.

"I'm sorry," I said, finally, "and before all else I beg you not to blame Sylvanus, who was only doing what I told him, and I promise I won't do it again."

"Yes you will," he said, and emptied the flask into our goblets. "You'll never change. The lady-my-wife says so."

"She has spoken to me already," I said, and he laughed at that, and began to forgive me. I took a drink and thought some more.

"If something is going on, something caused by the druids," I said, "then we need to know if it's just here in Londinium or elsewhere. We know they're active in the tribal regions. What about the other towns and the legionary forts?"

"Good question," he said. "I'll find out. I'll send letters via the army lightning post."

"And we need to tell Petros what we've found," I said.

"Yes," he said, "it's all bad news, but we can't keep this quiet."

Morganus got us to see Petros in Government House later that day. We were taken to the same large office, and Petros was there, behind his desk, with his six shaven-heads around him, and others besides who had the appearance of tradesmen, all of them burdened with notes, tablets and pens. The desk was covered with documents, scrolls, maps and writing materials, but dominated by a magnificent scale model of the Londinium racing stadium, in bright colours, with tiny horses, chariots and spectators. Petros sighed as we entered, looked hard at me and judged my expression. He sighed again.

"Out!" he said, waved a hand, and all but the six shaven-heads bowed and left the room.

"You will be brief, Ikaros of Apollonis," he said. "There is much to do and little time to do it." I hesitated and looked at the shaven-heads. "Proceed," he said, "I keep no secrets from these *living tools*."

The living tools bowed in response. So I told him everything. Him and them. He paused, closed his eyes, thought briefly then spoke. He was most remarkable administrator: capable of swift decisions, and giving clear instruction, except in one respect.

"In order of importance," he said, pointing to the scale model, "the celebratory races must proceed. The entire population of this province is expecting the races. Rome is expecting them, Rome is watching. The celebratory races are deeply political and their success may affect his grace's promotion."

"Gods save his grace," said the shaven-heads.

"Quite," said Petros. "And therefore, the murder of Zephyrix will be kept silent, and some explanation given of an innocent death."

100

He looked over his shoulder to the shaven-heads and raised his eyebrows in question.

"Oysters?" said one. "Food poisoning?"

"Good choice," said another.

"There have been several cases in the city," said a third.

"Oysters, then," said Petros. "I shall send messages of reassurance to all concerned: to Scapula, Veronius, and the other drivers who will – all of them – be delighted to be liberated from guilt."

"What about our investigation?" I asked. "I still need to speak to the racing drivers. I want to know what went on between them."

"By all means talk to them," he said, "you must leave nothing loose: nothing that can rattle and bang, and disturb the races. And find Blephyrix! He's obviously the killer, so bring him back and I will arrange appropriate punishment."

"And the man that was skinned?" I said. "And the druids?"

"More complex," said Petros, hesitating. "We tread a narrow line where the druids are concerned."

"Are they not forbidden?" I said. "Under sentence of death?"

He smiled. "You know the truth of that," he said, "both of you."

I looked at Morganus and he nodded.

"We do know," said Morganus. "The army knows. We tolerate the druids in the tribal kingdoms: the client kingdoms that pay tribute to Rome."

"Yes," said Petros, "because the alternative is constant war with the tribes, and constant slaughter of the young men of the tribes who do the farming and craft work, and without them, we'd get nothing out of this province: not a grain of corn or a shard of pot. We can't keep killing the young men who do all the work."

"Assuming it's *them* that get killed, not *us*!" said Morganus.

Petros smiled again. "Is that lack of confidence, O Morganus Fortis Victrix?" he said.

"Listen to me, O Petros of Athens," said Morganus. "If one or two of the tribes takes the field, then the army will win. Even against three we might win. But if they all rose together ... who knows?"

"I leave all such matters to the army," said Petros. "Meanwhile, since many people will have seen the crosses, and that which was on them, we shall give out that it was the work of bandits."

He turned to the shaven-heads and raised eyebrows again.

"Possible," said one, "but whose band?"

"Brandos One-Eye's?" said another.

"Too old," said a third. "His band is full of cripples, these days."

"Trax the Brigantian, then," said the first shaven-head.

"Trax the Brigantian," said Petros. "Agreed! Pass the word to the official street-criers." He turned back to me and Morganus. "You will need to interview – interrogate, if you wish – Felemid the *Celt*," he sneered at the word, "the noble senator! The consul of the Britannic Council!"

I could see his contempt for a man whom he regarded as an uppity native. I saw it and was disappointed that a Greek should display Roman prejudice.

"Speak to Felemid as you wish," he said. "Frighten him! Bite his ankles! Because as regards the death of Zephyrix I do not want Felemid to give out any story other than the oysters. His influence would be far greater than that of anyone else in this business."

Then – though not entirely to my surprise – he turned away from me and stared at a wall painting. It represented the goddess Vesta, enthroned in laurels.

"I shall now concentrate on this lovely image," he said. "I shall do so, as I mention two final things: first, that Felemid may be able to advise you on the druids, and second, that some pretence must be made of your reporting all these matters to his grace. You will hear from me in that respect, and this meeting is now closed."

With that he began to recite aloud the holy hymn to Vesta, and the six shaven-heads raised arms and joined him.

They were still chanting as Morganus and I got up and left. We bowed politely, but Petros was absorbed in the prayer and ignored us.

"He was shutting you out, wasn't he?" said Morganus as we made our way through Government House with the bodyguards behind us.

"Yes," I said. "He does it when he has something in mind that he doesn't want me to know."

"Does it work?" he said.

"Yes," I said. "I've told you a thousand times that I don't work magic."

"So what is it then, that he doesn't want you to know?"

"I don't know, do I? He shut me out!"

"Then be my clever Greek … guess!"

"Something about contacting the druids," I said. "I think Petros is in touch with them, even though that's supposed to carry the death penalty. Let's go and see Felemid, and find out."

So we did, with results that were both informative and painful: at least for me.

# CHAPTER 11

While his team searched for Blephyrix – still of unknown whereabouts – Sylvanus arranged the appointment with Felemid. Thus, we received a magnificent letter-scroll, bound around a gold-leafed rod with crystal finials, and decorated with silk tassels and a red seal. It was drafted in superb calligraphy, by some expensive scribe. So Felemid was making a statement of wealth and status.

I still have the letter, and I present it as a statement of the perverse Roman system of year-dating, which does not number the years, but labels them with the names of those who served as consuls of the Roman senate during each year. Nor do Romans number the days of the month from start to finish, but by the number of days before the *ides* – or middle – of each month and then by the number of days before the *kalends* – or beginning – of the next month. They do all that, yet use no marks of punctuation. None the less, this bizarre system was natural and easy for Romans to use. It was natural and easy because there was always a Greek slave ready to explain it to them.

And so:

*To Leonius Morganus Fortis Victrix*

*At the fortress of Legio XX*
*III days before the kalends of February*
*In the year of the consuls LA Albus and MJ Homulus*

*Greetings to the Heroic First Spear of Legio XX.*

*In receipt of your deeply honoured solicitation of a meeting*
*it would be greatest pleasure to welcome you to the Villa*
*Felemidus, close by the Great West Road at noon on the*
*falling of the kalends, always assuming that such time and*
*date shall please your honour.*

*Your honour might be pleased to bring such advisors as your*
*honour chooses.*

*One such advisor who is commonly seen in the shadow of your*
*honour might thereby profit in knowledge.*

*In delighted anticipation of the pleasure of your visit,*
*Gentius Civilis Felemidus*
*Citizen senator and consul*

The letter was addressed to Morganus, and I was not mentioned by
name. But his so-called *advisor* was obviously myself, and I worried
over Felemid's words. Indeed, I spent sleepless nights wondering what
he meant by *profit in knowledge.*

Fortunately I felt better – as ever – once we were on horseback
making for the Great West Road. I do love a parade of cavalry, and
since this was a formal visit to a man who ranked as a consul, Morganus

the bodyguards and I rode with a full first javelin's escort. There were twenty-five troopers, with a centurion, two optios and four buglers, led by a standard bearer with a dragon banner.

The banner was a fine piece of swagger on a long shaft: a gleaming bronze head that grimaced with great teeth and gaping mouth, while trailing a long silken tube in bright colours that filled with the wind of our onrush, and lashed like a monster's tail. Every man wore parade armour and helmets, and every man gleamed and shone. As we passed through Londinium with hoofbeats pounding and bugles blowing, all the street crowds gazed up at us in awe, the men and boys cheered, and the maidens giggled and waved. So did their mothers, for that matter, because we made a fine show.

"There," said Morganus, once we were out of the city and well on our way. "That's better, isn't it? It has put a smile on your miserable face. He's bound to bring out that girl of yours, to show her off. So at least you'll see her."

He meant it kindly, but I fear it plunged me down again. *Show her off!* That's exactly what Felemid would do– and I was dreading it.

The ride was a long one, with stops for watering and feeding the horses, and the men taking opportunity to polish off the road dust. Then, just before noon, we sighted Felemid's villa. It lay in idyllic countryside, shaven and mowed by grazing sheep. There was a stream, artfully engineered to half surround the buildings, and beyond that there were many acres of the best farmland in the province: rich black soil to deliver fat crops, which today shone under such sunshine as Britannia occasionally delivers.

Thus we approached the villa buildings, with well fed, well dressed field slaves stopping work and bowing heads as we passed. It all looked very lovely, as did the villa buildings themselves. There was a neat cluster of them, around a main building that had a dome above, and a pillared pediment at the entrance, with broad steps leading up like those of a temple. Everything was white-plastered, then painted with thin red lines, to give the impression of a construction of massive stone blocks. There was real glass in the windows, and smoke curling from the chimneys of the main house, and what looked like a substantial bathing hall. And above all else, there were slaves by the hundreds, always bowing, always respectful.

Even as we clattered onto the paving slabs of a broad courtyard, Felemid himself appeared at the main gates of the house. He wore his broad-stripe toga, and he was accompanied by a staff of at least a dozen, who stood behind him in order of rank, including three citizens in togas and the senior house slaves in robes. Behind even them there were men in household tunics, who stood in a row with large hunting knives in sheaths hanging from their belts. They stood to attention like soldiers and they were hard, fit men. Thus Morganus frowned, because although the knives were the sort used to despatch a wounded stag or boar, they were nearly the size of swords, and only the army and the governor were allowed to deploy armed men.

But Felemid's show was not done yet. He smiled, spread arms then clapped hands loudly three times, causing doors to open, and men and girls in tunics bearing Felemid's crest to run out, bearing bowls and towels, and small cups of wine for the men, and fodder for the horses.

Thus there was a considerable process of bowing and scraping, and of formal hand-washing, and the offering up of toasts to the gods, and taking libation. Then our Batavian centurion, bowed to Morganus, who waved in acknowledgement, as his men were led off to be entertained and fussed over, and only then could Morganus be formally received by Felemid, who came forward down his steps with his retinue behind him, before bowing gracefully, and speaking with a bold, clear voice.

"This house is blessed," he cried, "to be so honoured by your illustrious presence, O father of the legions!"

Knowing my status as a slave, he spoke to Morganus, ignoring me, and Morganus replied with equal formality.

"I give you good day in the name of the gods, O senator and consul," he said, and everyone behind Felemid sighed with pleasure to see their master thus recognised by so prestigious a Roman as Morganus.

It was an interesting piece of theatre. I had known Felemid in his early days, when he struggled with Latin and spoke like a rural peasant. But not anymore. He had taken lessons in deportment and elocution and bore himself almost like a Roman: almost– but not quite, because he did not have the sneer of a true patrician. He had not been bred up – like a Roman – to believe himself chosen by the gods as ruler of all mankind. Instead, Felemid smiled, and smiled and smiled. He was quite young, not yet thirty, and he was slim with almost child-like stature, a high bony nose with heavy brow ridges, thin lips and a yellowish-white skin typical of the Brigantes tribe of the north west.

Then Felemid was making introductions, turning to the men in togas.

"Might your honour be pleased to meet these respected citizens?" he said to Morganus. "These citizens who, by chance, are guests of this house."

Morganus bowed, and Felemid introduced two broad-stripes.

"Here stands Pacuvius Sextus Novus and Marcus Longus Gallus," he said. "Senators of the provincial assembly."

They were Celts, like Felemid, Celts who had climbed the slippery slope of Roman advancement and adopted Roman names. They were his men, his friends and his supporters. I could see it in their eyes. Then, he introduced one actual Roman, complete with unsmiling Roman dignitas and the narrow-stripe toga of a knight.

"Here stands Casca Lucius Gaius," said Felemid, "my esteemed lawyer, who is here on business matters." Felemid bowed, this time to me, and smiled. "These honoured guests are in my house purely by chance," he repeated, smiling and smiling, and I presume he told so obvious and blatant a lie merely to emphasise that he had taken the precaution of having witnesses present, for any conversation with Morganus and myself.

After these introductions we were led inside, into a Celtic billion-aire's version of a Roman atrium: beautifully designed – probably by Greeks – with marble, bronze, lustrous pottery and an all-dominating statue of Emperor Trajan. Everyone bowed to the statue, then serving girls came forward with more bowls for hand-washing, and more cups of wine: tiny gold cups that barely wetted the mouth.

I am sorry to say that, during our progress into the atrium, Felemid – despite all his affectation of Roman dignity – could not control his erotic fascination with myself. He managed to walk beside me, and gaze up at me like a dog that wants its belly rubbed. It was embarrassing and frightening all at once, because he was far more wolf than dog, and an exceedingly clever wolf at that. How else could a rural peasant have risen to such power and wealth?

Finally, standing in the atrium, under the dome – freshly painted with the inevitable and fashionable scenes of chariot racing – a consid-erable number of us stood assembled and silent. We were almost a crowd: me, Morganus and the bodyguards, Felemid with his senators and lawyer, and the senior house slaves and ranks of lesser slaves. I could see that Morganus was utterly and entirely fed up with the formalities, so I looked at him, and he nodded, then laid down the rules of procedure for Felemid and the rest.

"Honoured and illustrious senators and citizens," he said, "I am here in the name of his grace the governor ..."

"Gods save his grace!" said all present.

"And I now stand back," said Morganus, "to give speech to Ikaros of Apollonis, who likewise acts in my name, and in the name of his grace, and in the name of Rome."

"Yeah!" murmured the bodyguards and they stamped to attention.

So everyone looked at me. Felemid especially looked at me, and I studied him with all my might, which caused him to gasp, because such is the perversity of mankind that Felemid – despite so many and tremendous talents – was a man who enjoyed humiliation. That is to say, he enjoyed humiliation if it was performed upon him in privacy by beautiful men. It was therefore my misfortune that he found me physically attractive, and was fascinated by my supposed power to strip naked his mind and read all that lay within.

So I studied him, and awaited his response which – as expected – was an unconscious glance at Morganus and the bodyguards. I nodded and he gasped again in the belief that I had read his thoughts.

"Honoured sir," I said to Morganus, "perhaps I might speak alone with the honourable Felemid?"

Morganus and I had already discussed this on the journey, knowing that Felemid would never speak confidentially to me with Morganus present. So Morganus nodded.

"I will now fall back and leave all matters to my comrade," he said, and this time it was the two broad-stripes and the lawyer who gasped. I may have been an imperial slave, but I was still a slave, and they cherished their status and dignity. None the less

Morganus and the bodyguards marched out, leaving me facing Felemid.

So now it was my turn. I looked at Felemid's slaves, and at the toga-clad citizens, and shook my head. This time, Felemid frowned. The clever part of him wanted his witnesses present. So I shook my head again, and he blinked and made a decision.

"Esteemed and honoured sirs," he said to the three togas, "it is my wish to speak alone with Ikaros of Apollonis, and …"

Being Celts, and not bred up to hide emotion like Romans, the two senators glared at me with open malice, clutched at Felemid's arm, and drew him aside muttering and whispering in his ear, while the lawyer blinked and pondered and dithered.

None the less, after so much preamble I was soon following Felemid through the building and outside to a most beautiful garden, with colonnades and such a lovely view over the countryside, and such lovely winter flowers, as made the garden of Scapula the procurator seem dull and miserable. There was even a bit of warmth in the sun, and I hardly shivered as we left the shelter of the house, and walked together while the birds sang around us.

"Here," said Felemid, indicating a sculpted wooden bench with arm rests. So we sat and he looked at me. "So?" he said, "What do you want?"

He was excited. The perverse part of him was in the ascendant. He gazed at me.

"What do you know about the death of Zephyrix?" I asked.

"Nothing," he said. "He was alive in the evening, and dead in the morning." Felemid was telling the truth. I could see it.

"What about Blephyrix?" I said. "What of him?"

Felemid shrugged. "The quiet one?" he said. "The big one? He followed behind his little master." He shrugged again. "What else should I know?"

He was telling the truth again. I asked more questions and found out nothing– because Felemid knew nothing, and neither, he said, did any of the other broad-stripes who had been in Scapula's house. He knew nothing of the murder, but I soon saw that there were other things inside his mind, which he was hiding. So I ceased asking questions, and looked at him, hoping he would fill the silence. Which indeed he did.

He leaned close and put a hand on mine. "You should not worry about this death," he said, "when greater matters are in hand."

"Such as what?" I said.

He smiled. "There could be a great place for you in my service," he said, and again I stayed silent. "In my personal service, and my political service," he said.

"Oh?" I said.

"I have risen to my limits here in Britannia," he said, "and have plans for Rome itself. So if you were in my service, you could leave Britannia – which I know that you detest – and bask in the warmth and civilisation of the world's greatest city."

I must admit, to my shame, that I was fascinated by that. The sunshine alone would be wonderful. So I wanted to know more.

"What plans for Rome?" I said, but even as I asked I felt that he was hiding something. He was concentrating furiously on these plans for Rome – whatever they were – and something was behind them.

I thought of Petros reciting prayers to shut me out; Felemid was doing the same.

"What plans?" I said again, and he poured out words about shifting gold to Rome, and making alliances, and exchanging letters with powerful families. So I tried to crack him open.

"And what else?" I said. "What else is there?"

He closed his eyes, redoubled his account of contacting the powerful in Rome, but he released just one unintended phrase.

" ... and I am compelled to act," he said, "in view of the great peril ..." Then he stopped, took a hard grip of himself, and was back to listing his political connections in Rome.

"What peril? Peril of druids?" I said, and he closed his eyes in the strain of hiding his thoughts, then he smiled, and squeezed my hand and blocked my inquisition with a shield that I could never penetrate.

"She is here," he said. "Allicanda... and you may speak to her."

That hit me as a squall hits a ship at sea, and drove all else from my mind.

"Ahhhh!" he said, seeing my expression. He pointed towards another part of the garden where there was a tall hedge, close-cropped and shaped with an arch in the middle, and a gate in the arch. "She is in there," he said. "I brought her here on purpose. She is waiting for you. Will you not go to see her?"

I did go to see her. What else could I do? I am a human man. I am not a magic Greek and my need was great. I ran to the gate in the hedge. I swung it open, and she was there: standing up from a bench, and there was nobody there than ourselves, and so I embraced her, and swung her off her feet and kissed her, which I had never done before, with our love so distant and flawed in the past, and with so many wrong steps by myself. It was wonderful and painful because it could not last, but for an instant I was enveloped in the scent of her and the feel of her hair, and her smile and even her tears.

So we sat and talked, and talked.

"Are you safe?" I asked before all else.

"For the moment, yes," she said. "And you? My poor, sad man with so many troubles."

I answered, and there was much more of lovers' talk, which is nonsensical to all others than the loved ones. But by stages we spoke of the world.

"Everyone says you are investigating the death of Zephyrix," she said, "although he died of bad oysters."

"He did not," I said, and told her everything, because I could hide nothing from her, even Zephyrix's odd sexuality. But she smiled at that.

"Shaved?" she said.

"Yes," I said. "His buttocks were shaved."

"Then someone did that to him," she said.

"Why?"

"Because that's *not* what they do, the men of that persuasion."

"Then what *do* they do?"

"They go to the baths for waxing, as ladies do."

"Waxing?"

"Hot wax on a cloth. The cloth on the body, and then ripped off, taking all the hair."

"Gods of Olympus! Doesn't it hurt?"

"Not really. Not when you're used to it."

I laughed at that. "So that means Zephyrix was only a rapist!" I said.

"Not necessarily," she said.

"Why?"

"Well," she said, "these heroes of sport, the drivers and gladiators, they're made almost into gods. They're so famous that women – even great ladies – fawn on them and offer themselves, such that the athletes don't know that a woman might say *no*, and mean it."

"I see," I said, and since we were discussing practical matters of investigation, I asked about Felemid, and whatever he might be hiding.

"What does he want from me?" I said.

"He wants you, as you," she said.

"I know that. But he wants more."

"He wants you as his magic man," she said, "to read what politicians are thinking. He believes that will help him rise up the ladder in Rome."

"But I'm *not* magic," I said.

"Are you sure of that?" she said, and I sighed. I was losing even the will to argue.

"He mentioned a great peril," I said, "do you know what that means?"

She thought hard. "He deals with the tribes," she said. "You know that, don't you?"

"Yes," I said, "some of his trade depends on furs and skins from the north of Britannia."

"And mining," she said. "He buys gold, silver and lead from the tribes. And he's become nervous of the tribes … well not the tribes … but *them*…"

"Druids?" I said, and she raised arms in fear.

"Yes," she said.

"How do you know this? How do you know he's afraid?"

"Slave gossip," she said. "The slaves see and hear."

Then perhaps I am indeed magic, because I made a connection. I took an object from my pouch and rested it in the palm of my hand. It was one of the small carvings of three hooded men, one of those I took from the men shot with artillery bolts.

"Do you know what this is?" I said.

She looked at it and raised hands again. "This is the holy trinity of Dagda, Danu and Cernunnos," she said, so I raised hands too. "The Danuic trinity," she added. "Dagda the father, Danu the mother and Cernunnos of fertility who is sometimes known as the child."

I looked at the little figures. "But they're all men," I said.

"No," she said, and pointed. "Look! These two have beards, this one does not. The beardless one is Danu the holy mother."

I looked, and indeed she was correct. I should have noticed that. "It's a trinity for women as well as men. The blessed holy mother is important to women. She binds together the father and child." She raised arms.

"A trinity!" I said. "Trinities are important among the gods. Rome has Jupiter, Juno and Minerva, and the new Jewish faith has father, son and mother goddess, just like this." I looked at the three little figures, then at her. "Who follows this trinity?" I said. "I have never heard of it."

"They are new gods," she said, "newly arisen, but powerful among the tribes outside the cities."

"How do you know this?" I said.

"Slave gossip," she said, "and ..." She paused.

"And what?" I said.

"I think Felemid may be a follower. I have heard that he has a statue like this." She looked at the three little figures. "It's in his private rooms, where only he and his boys are allowed."

"Boys?" I said.

"He has four Greek boys for his personal pleasure: very smooth, very pretty."

"I should like to talk to them," I said.

"He'd never allow it," she said, "but they gossip. Like all slaves."

We spoke some more, before I realised I had stayed too long. What would Morganus think? So, with sorrow, I stood and made to leave, but she took my hand and held it fast.

"I have something to say," she said.

"Then speak," I said.

So she did, and stabbed my heart as if with a spear.

116

# CHAPTER 12

Morganus was angrier than I was. In fact, I was so horrified that I could not be angry. I wish that I could have been, because it would have been more bearable. Even the ride home in perfect weather did not raise me up: not even the delight of being among a splendid company of horse.

"Listen here, Greek," said Morganus, riding close so nobody else should hear, even though they did, because his voice was not gentle. "Listen here, if he does *that*, then I'll find a reason – and that line of pretend soldiers with hunting knives will do very nicely – I'll find a reason and take a good company of men to that gods-damned villa and I will personally take hold of him, and ... "

"No, no, no!" I said. "He'd break you if you did that. He's a powerful man, and his lawyers would break you because ... what he said ... said he'd do ... it's perfectly legal."

"It can't be," he said. "Even slaves have some rights. No master can condemn a slave to the beasts in the arena, and no master can sell a slave to the brothels. Everyone knows that. It's against Roman law!"

"He's not threatening to *sell* her," I said, "He's threatening to put her out on loan: on loan at no cost, to friends who own the cheapest brothels in the city. The cheapest! So every beggar in the gutter can ..."

Words died in my mouth. I could not speak.

"The bastard!" said Morganus, on one of the very few occasions I ever heard him swear. "We'll get the legion's lawyers on it. It can't be legal."

But it was. The legion's lawyers confirmed it. So now, not only was Felemid holding Allicanda as bait, but he was adding the threat that should I ever do anything to displease him, or damage him, then he would take revenge not on me, but on her.

That was what she meant when I asked if she was safe, and she replied, "For the moment, yes."

*For the moment.*

Therefore, where Felemid was concerned, I was walking barefoot across a floor of spikes. So it was good for my sanity that such was the pressure of events over the next few days, that I did not have time to worry: except that I did worry. I worried whenever I was alone.

The first event was a series of replies that came down the army's lines of communication by high speed gallopers on the Roman roads. The first of these arrived the day after our return from Felemid's villa. In fact, it had arrived in the night, and Sylvanus presented it to Morganus before morning parade, and the daily meeting of centurions. Morganus sent one of the bodyguards to fetch me, and I found him in Sylvanus's office, with four army letter-tablets open on a desk in front of him. He looked grim, and so did Sylvanus.

"Look at this, Greek!" said Morganus, as I entered. He tapped a finger on each of the tablets. "This one from Isca Dumnoniorum in the far west. This one from Lindum in the east. This from Luguvalium in the north. This one from the hot springs of Aquae Sulis. That's end to end of Britannia, and they're all saying the same thing!"

"Which is?" I said.

118

"Druids!" he said, and everyone made the bull sign.. "They're active in the night outside all the forts, and two men – one at Aquae Sulis and one at Luguvalium – have been killed and skinned, and left hanging outside the forts just as we saw ourselves!"

"That's bad," I said.

"It's worse!" he said, "They're all asking for reinforcements, and the commander of the smallest fort – the one held by a single Cohort at Luguvalium– wants to withdraw his men to the main Legionary fort for safety. He says the local tribe, the Carvetii, are forming war bands with the Brigantes tribe to the south, and those two don't get on. Or never did before." He stood straight and rested one hand on his sword pommel. "It's the same as we found here."

"Yes," I said. "Silure and Dumnonii working together, and now it's two more of the big tribes." Then I thought of something else. "Did you ask about the carvings: the three little figures?"

"Yes," he said, "and they're everywhere. All the tribes are wearing them round the neck. It's a new religion. Look here." He handed me one of the tablets. "This one's from the Aquae Sulis: that's the bath-city where hot water comes up from the gods below."

"I know," I said. "We've been there."

"Yes," he said, "and the garrison commander is a good man. I know him. See what he says." I read the letter, which included the following:

*The hot spring was holy to the Belgae. It was a wild place in a swamp where they threw offerings. They hate us for building over it to make a bath-house. They are seized by the new trinity. Even some of our auxiliaries have three spots on the hand. They are arrested and await judgement.*

"See?" said Morganus, "It's as bad as that! The Belgae as well! That makes five tribes, and the druids are getting at the auxiliaries, which ought to be impossible. It's death to have traffic with the druids, and soldiers of all people should know that."

"It may have come from the local women," I said. "Soldiers are not allowed marriage, but they all have local girls, don't they? The girls will be Belgae, and the druids could be preaching to them." I thought of Allicanda and sighed, "We know that they preach to women as well as men."

"This is serious," said Morganus, "deadly serious. We need to speak to Petros and the legate Africanus."

We did. That same morning we were back in Government House, facing Petros and his six shaven-heads, but this time the legate Africanus was beside him, with a staff of tribunes and a pair of note-takers.

This time we were all standing, since the legate outranked Petros, and it was therefore an army meeting, and army meetings were held standing up. Petros's furniture had been neatly pushed aside to make room, and the office shone with polished armour: the legate and tribunes wore muscled cuirasses and scarlet cloaks, and held red-plume helmets, while Morganus's armour was always brilliant, and the four bodyguards stood behind him, likewise shining. Even the army clerks with pens and tablets were bright polished, and Petros and I were eclipsed into dullness in our plain robes.

It was all very army because Africanus– under only the governor himself – was commander of all Roman troops in Britannia. His full name was Nonius Julius Sabinus, and Africanus was a nickname that had sprung from his dark skin and tightly-curled hair. He was a senatorial nobleman, over eighty years old and afflicted with cataracts, which caused him to peer fiercely at everything, in order to discipline his eyes to their duty. He was a career soldier of great reputation, still sharp-edged and swift in mind.

When Morganus had finished a full report of all that we knew, Africanus responded with a single question.

"And what are your proposed actions, Leonius Morganus Felix Victrix?" he said, and Morganus was ready.

"May it please your noble honour," he said, "all leave cancelled. All formations to be on war-time readiness. All small detachments recalled to main forts. All ranks searched for three dots on the left hand."

"Good," said Africanus, and turned to his tribunes. "Give the necessary orders in my name." The tribunes stamped feet in response, and the clerks scribbled. Then Africanus peered hard at me. "And what will you do, O mind-reading son of Apollonis?" he said. "What will the clever Greek do?"

He knew me well and he valued me as a useful asset. But he valued me like a clever monkey that climbed trees to bring down fruit. It was yet another burden upon a philosopher. But I was as ready as Morganus with my reply.

"Noble sir," I said, "I shall cease investigation into the death of Zephyrix in the face of this serious danger to the province. I shall concentrate on this new religion of the trinity, and I shall question any persons found to have three dots on the left hand."

"*You* shall concentrate?" he said. "A *Greek* shall decide? A Greek shall do *this* and a Greek shall do *that*?"

"Yes, noble sir," I said. "Because sometimes a Greek knows better than a Roman."

Perhaps these words were ill chosen, but there is only so much that a philosopher can bear. There was a gasp from all present, and everyone looked to Africanus, who stood a second in thought. Then he laughed, and pressed on to practical matters.

"Soldiers of Rome with three dots?" he said. "My personal judgement would have been to send them to the torturers for interrogation. But you can have them. You will find out more … you with your magic!"

So the matter was almost decided, but Petros intervened. "Noble sir," he said, "there is another voice to consider."

"Ah!" said Africanus. "Of course. His grace."

"Gods save his grace," said all the Romans.

"Quite," said Petros.

"Indeed," I said.

"Ah …" said Africanus. He was Governor Teutonius's man. He owed his post to Teutonius and he looked to Teutonius for future advancement. But he knew the limitations of Teutonius's intellect, and was therefore uneasy. "And what would be the voice of our governor?" he said.

Petros gave an expressive gesture of the hands. He was helpless. "His grace has become convinced," said Petros, "that the killer of Zephyrix must be found and punished."

"But are we not saying it was oysters?" said Africanus.

"His grace knows the full story," said Petros, "and insists on meeting Ikaros of Apollonis, to give personal commands."

Everyone looked at everyone else. With the possible exception of the dimmest of the four bodyguards, everyone knew that Teutonius was led by Petros, as a dog is led by a master.

"Surely this can be managed?" said Africanus.

"No," said Petros. "In this matter, his grace is adamant."

"Adamant?"

"Yes!" said Petros. "He adores the races and held Zephyrix in extreme reverence. He has therefore commanded that Ikaros of Apollonis and Morganus Fortis Victrix should be brought to him at the racing stadium today, where he plans to consecrate an altar to the late Zephyrix." He looked at me and added, "I'd best come with you."

Within the hour we were on horseback, though as we mounted – after checking that Petros could not hear – Morganus growled at me.

"Can you not guard your mouth?" he said. "*A Greek knows better than a Roman*? You'll get us both crucified one day."

"I'm sorry," I said.

"No you're not," he said, and in all truth he was correct.

Meanwhile Petros proved to be an accomplished horseman and we rode out, beyond the city, to a natural fold in the land – a small valley – which had been engineered as only Romans can, into an enormous racing stadium 450 yards long and 150 yards wide, including seating, and a track designed for a maximum of twelve chariots to race at once. We entered at the southernmost end, past the timber starting boxes with their spring-loaded gates, where the drivers and chariots stood waiting before races.

We paused and looked up and down the enormous, echoing stadium, with a chill Britannic wind blowing and the sound of voices from workmen, and the thump and groan of tools, as everything was constantly kept proper and neat. We looked up at the rows and rows of wooden seats, and looked along the spina – the dividing line – that ran down the middle of the track. It was long and thin, raised up thirty feet on stonework above the sandy track, and decorated down the entire length with shrines and temples paid for by the guilds of enthusiasts who followed the races. Huge amounts of money had been lavished on these shrines, which was not surprising since the races were the most popular spectacle in the Roman world: far more so that the gladiators.

Thus, when the starting gates opened, the chariots would race down one side of the spina, with a ferocious turn at the northern end, where the most popular seats were, since they gave best view of the inevitable crashes, the so-called *shipwrecks*. Then the chariots came back up the other side of the spina to complete one lap, each lap being marked by the dipping down of one of a row of giant, gold-leafed dolphins at one end of the spina.

"There," said Morganus, pointing, at a troop of cavalry half way down the spina. They were stationary in neat ranks, with banners and musicians. "That's a governor's escort," he said. "So his grace will be close by." So we rode towards the governor's escort. "Pretty boys again," said Morganus, since the escort – like the governor's guard – was never risked in war, and its officers were precious young aristocrats. "All paid for by their mummies and daddies," said Morganus, looking at their gilded armour and bright robes.

The officer in command rode forward and saluted.

"Greetings upon you, honoured sir!" he said to Morganus. "I'm afraid you've missed the dedication but the reception is still on, and you are expected. Your honoured self is expected…" He looked at me. "And him."

"Ikaros of Apollonis is my respected colleague," said Morganus, "so we'll go up, if that's the staircase, just there?"

It was and we did. We went up with the bodyguards behind. The spina proved to be a jumble of construction, with one shrine crammed next to another, and a zig-zag of pathways between. The latest one, just raised by Teutonius, was by far the biggest. It was chiselled in stone, shining in precious metal, elaborately decorated with scenes of chariot racing, and a portrait statue of Zephyrix stood front and centre within laurel wreaths. The statue was formulaic and noble, and nothing like the man himself. But that is how Romans remember their heroes.

There was a cleared area in front of the shrine, where stood a group of men in togas and ladies in robes, and I could not fail to notice – no man could fail to notice – a woman of stunning beauty who stood prominent among the ladies, and was fawned upon by all present. She was the lady Secunda Julia Domitius, whom Teutonius, governor of Britannia, had married after the death of his first wife. Secunda had once been his slave, acquired during his military career in Germany. But she had been made free, and legally adopted as daughter of Domitius, lord justice of Britannia, which raised her sufficiently in rank to be a suitable bride for Teutonius.

She was quite young and had the fabulous golden hair that is unique to the German peoples. She was wonderfully lovely, and was accompanied by a small child – a boy – dressed in a miniature toga, and who clung to her robe with a tiny fist. He was the son she had given Teutonius, to his eternal joy. He was the only child present and he was there as a statement of dynasty to the elite of Britannia.

Like all the men present, the child had a fold of toga draped over the head, as Romans do on holy occasions. So Petros and I covered our heads, while Morganus and the bodyguards stamped to attention and bowed towards the shrine. The company turned to look at us, and I saw Veronius and his drivers, all in their best but off to one side, as the lesser beings that they were. More painfully, I saw Felemid among the togas. He was close to the governor and smiling at me.

125

"Ah-ha!" said Governor Marcus Ostorious Cerealis Teutonius, and advanced upon us. He was a man in the prime of life: athletic, handsome and with the authentic bearing of a nobleman. His speech was beautiful and he could switch with ease from the finest Latin to purest Greek. He had a true soldier's reputation and his nickname Teutonius had been earned by his command of a legion that had inflicted defeats on the barbarians beyond the Rhine.

He made a fine pair with the young man who followed in his wake. This was Horatius, Teutonius's nephew. He too had the bearing of a nobleman, he too was handsome and spoke with a lovely voice, but unlike Teutonius, Horatius was honest in manner and bearing since he invariably wore so vapid a smile on his face, that his inner stupidity was proclaimed to the world. By contrast, those who conversed with Teutonius were at first deeply impressed, and only by stages realised to their dismay, that he was dull as a blunt knife and had risen in the world entirely through the talents of his slave, Petros of Athens.

"Ah-ha!" Teutonius said to Morganus. "You are here auspiciously, first javelin."

"I am honoured to be here, your grace," said Morganus.

"See the tribute freely given at this altar, by these noble persons!" said Teutonius, waving a hand at the togas and ladies, "See how willingly the great and good of the province have contributed to the memory of Zephyrix the Great!" I saw Felemid smile again at that. "Zephyrix the Magnificent," said Teutonius, "who began racing at the age of fifteen … "

With these words Teutonius began a lifetime account of the career of Zephyrix, listing horses, races, winnings, betting odds and more, until even the marble Zephyrix was bored. Teutonius went on, and on, until Petros saved us.

"Noble and senatorial sir," he said, when Teutonius paused for breath. "If I may?" He leaned forward and whispered to Teutonius, and looking at their faces – even without hearing Petros's whispering – I read a sharp command given by slave to master. *Slave to master!*

I have often wondered what Petros said, but it was powerfully effective.

"Ah! Ah-ha!" said Teutonius and nodded, and stood straight. "It is my wish," he said, "that you, Morganus, and you, Ikaros, should immediately continue your investigations," he looked at Petros, "as guided by my advisor-in-chief."

"Oh?" said Horatius, tugging at Teutonius's toga. "Shall you not say more, noble sir? More on the life of Zephyrix?"

Petros stepped in and bowed to Horatius. "Of course, O noble and senatorial sir," he said. "His grace will do so at length."

"Oh good!" said Horatius, and fixed his smile upon uncle Teutonius.

"But Morganus and Ikaros are ordered immediately to their duties," said Teutonius, so Petros backed away, beckoning Morganus and me to follow.

Petros knew the layout of the spina, and led us down stairs and along a corridor to a long room, which was a dining chamber with fine Athenian furniture, and balconies giving a view of the track on each side. It was a place where the most privileged of spectators could enjoy the show, and eat and drink as they watched. Slaves bowed as we entered, and came forward with wine, goblets and cakes, but Petros waved them off and we sat down together, with the bodyguards at discreet distance.

"Now, listen to me," said Petros. "Despite greater and more urgent matters, you will have to pursue the Zephyrix investigation because

I am on my limits of what I can do with *him*. So get on with it!" He was annoyed with himself: furious that for once he could not entirely control Teutonius. "What will you do next?" he said.

"First," I said, "does Horatius know anything about the murder? He was in the house when it was done."

"Horatius?" said Petros. "That one? He doesn't know how to wipe his own arse without a slave to do it."

I took that as *no*, and continued. "We're still searching for Blephyrix," I said.

"So find him!" said Petros.

"And," I said, "since Veronius and his drivers are here. I'll speak to them."

"I'll have them sent down here," said Petros. "Do you want them together, or one at a time?"

"One at a time, starting with Veronius," I said.

So we spent some hours, Morganus and I, facing Veronius and the rest. It was tedious, and repetitive, because they *knew* very little so we *learned* very little, except as regards the character of the drivers, and why Veronius was now smiling.

We discussed this as we rode back to the fort in the dusk. It was very cold by then, and I huddled in my cloak and pressed knees to my mount for the warmth of his body.

"Felemid," I said, "made the biggest contribution to that altar, and he paid the twenty million, to cover Veronius's loss and keep him sweet, so there won't be rumours to spoil the governor's races."

"Has Felemid got that much money?" said Morganus.

"Felemid's got billions," I said, "and he's crawling round Teutonius for favours."

128

"What about those drivers?" said Morganus. "I wouldn't have any one of them in my house!"

"Louts!" I said. "Vulgar louts. They're nearly as stupid as Horatius, their conversation is full of oaths, they think rape is a joke and that Zephyrix never did anything wrong."

Morganus smiled at that. "Better still," he said, "they said he never did anything at all! They said he was timid with women, and that Blephyrix went round with the purse, to *pretend* he was dangerous with women, in the hope that the other drivers would respect him."

"That's a strange way to get respect!" I said.

"It's better than being a rapist," he said.

"And what about Blephyrix?" said Morganus. "Do you think he did the murder?"

"He's certainly violent," I said. "The other drivers said that when Zephyrix mocked him for being so big, Blephyrix would find someone to beat up!"

"But he never turned on Zephyrix?"

"No," I said, "the drivers said he never did that. He just got angry."

"So did he do the murder?"

"I don't know," I said. "We need to see him."

"If Sylvanus can find him."

Which he did, leading to still further bloodshed, but this time at sea.

# CHAPTER 13

We were in the Londinium docks again, and again at night. But this time, the docks were alive. The first century, first cohort were out, with torches blazing and steel gleaming, as orders were shouted and men of the Classis Britannicus – the Roman navy's provincial fleet – were turned out of their barrack house, close by the navy's wharf.

There was a great rumble of feet and blowing of bugles, and all the crews of the merchant ships alongside or anchored were up on deck peering down at the clamour. There were even civilians and slaves about: those whose duties gave them living accommodation in the dockyards. These few pointed and chattered, wrapped in their blankets against the cold.

Morganus, the bodyguards and I stood talking with Sylvanus and some of his men, together with the harbour master and his clerks, outside the revenue and taxation building.

"Are you sure it's him?" I said to Sylvanus.

"Yes, your worship," he said, looking at one of his men. "Tell his worship!" he said.

The soldier saluted with right arm, and spoke.

"Honoured sir," he said, "he was a thick, heavy man with a Gaulish accent, plenty of money to spend, and he was hiding out over there," he pointed to a warehouse, "which is supposed to be for oil and fish sauce, but which is a knocking shop, honoured sir!"

He saluted again and stamped foot. We all looked at the harbour master, who spread arms in apology.

"What's wrong with a knocking shop?" he said. "They pay their taxes, they make no trouble, and the sailors have to go somewhere."

"In the docks?" said Morganus. "Inside the palisade?"

"Of course," said the harbour master. "So they can't get out with anything stolen off the ships."

"It doesn't matter," I said. "What matters is that Blephyrix has bribed his way on to a ship, outbound for Gaul, *Good Wife Carata*, and that ship got under way on the midnight tide, two hours ago."

"That's right," said the harbour master, "and why not? That ship was all correct from stem to stern, and keel to main-truck! All dues paid and all documents signed. Nothing wrong there!"

"Yeah!" said all his clerks. Then a naval officer ran up, a centurion followed by two marines. We turned to look. He stamped and saluted and so did the marines. He was in tunic and cloak, with a badge of rank. He wore a sword but no helmet or armour. But the marines were equipped like legionaries, and I wondered at their courage, being encased in steel which would drag them down to death if they fell overboard.

"Honoured sir," said the centurion to Morganus. "I'm Numitor, commander of *Naiada*, and we're ready and waiting. So, if you'd come aboard with your party, we'll get under way."

"Well done," said Morganus. "A smart turn out at short notice."

"Thank you, honoured sir!" said Numitor the centurion, and Morganus looked at me.

"Is it worth waiting?" he said. "We could spot Blephyrix by his Gaulish accent."

"We need to be sure," I said. "We need someone who knows him."

"Well he'd better be quick!" said Morganus. "Centurion." he said, "we'll come aboard at once, then wait a bit."

So we marched down the navy wharf, with torches blazing on all sides, and myself in two cloaks, knowing how the wind blows cold over water. We went with boots pounding the wooden planks, and I felt the wonderful fascination that comes over me when I get close to a ship. This one was a liburnian: fastest type in the fleet, which could easily outpace a horseman over long distances. It was long and low and light, with bulwarks rising no more than five feet from the waterline. It had with a pair of eyes painted at the bow for the luck of the ship to see by, and the ship's name was painted at the stern: *Naiada*, the water nymph.

There were benches for forty oarsmen – twenty on each side – with one man to each oar. There was a small fighting platform at the bow for marines, and another bigger platform at the stern for the helmsman, commander and more marines. Amidships there was a single mast to bear sail for long-distance work, but this was being off-loaded for greater speed under oars, even as we marched along the wharf.

"Heave-*ho!* Heave-*ho!*" The crewmen struck the mast with Roman – or rather seamanly – efficiency, making easy shift of the labour, so that a company of shore-crewmen could lift up the big timber and carry it off for storage at a steady trot. It was most exhilarating to see such teamwork in action, even as the last few oarsmen took their places, and sat with oars raised, in tunics that left their arms bare, even on a cold night. They were big men with heavy muscles, but that was typical of naval oarsmen – all volunteers, all free men – who were chosen for strength and long limbs, all the better for pulling on the oars. They were the elite of the service and they knew it.

Then we went up the stern gangplank – which alarmingly had no hand rail – and crammed in behind Numitor the centurion, the helmsman, and marines. With myself, Morganus and the bodyguards, it was a squeeze.

"Clear gangplanks!" cried Numitor. "Let go fore! Let go aft! Stand by to shove off!"

"Aye, aye!" said the shore crew. Away went the gangplanks and securing lines, and the shore-crew took up long poles ready to push the ship clear of the wharf.

"Honoured sir," said Numitor. "Permission to pull away?"

"Well?" said Morganus, looking at me. "He's not here, is he?"

"Yes he is," I said, as I saw a man urgently running through the legionaries and dock people, and ducking past the torches.

"Hi!" he shouted. "Hi!" It was one of Scapula's shaven-heads. His baldness gleamed in the torchlight. It was Aetius of Athens. *He* would be able to recognise Blephyrix.

"Bring him aboard!" said Morganus. So Numitor bellowed orders, the stern gangplank thumped back into place, Aetius ran up it, slipped, staggered, and we seized him and pulled him to safety.

"You are late," I said.

"I had to show your message to the master," said Aetius, "to beg leave. And the master and mistress were asleep."

"Get going!" said Morganus to Numitor. "March! Make speed!"

"Aye, aye," said Numitor. "Shoremen push off! Oarsmen give way! Standard pace!"

Then it was pure magic – a magic of delight – especially at night, under stars and moon, and wispy clouds, and the torchlight bouncing off the river, and the oarsmen chanting. I loved it. The stroke was set by the port-side oarsman in the bow, a bearded veteran who sang in musical verse, extemporising each line, and the rest repeated.

"Pull for the ship, pull through the night!!
*"Pull, pull, pull through the night!"*
"Pull for the stars, shiny and bright!"
*"Pull, pull, shiny and bright!"*

Such poetry is weak when written down, but not when delivered by forty deep chests, in steady time, to the melodies of ancient sea chanties. Then, it becomes magnificent. Or perhaps I am a foolish landman in love with the sea.

The wharf and torchlight shrank behind us, the Thames's water hissed and frothed down the ship's sides. Then all of Londinium and its lights were fading behind, and we were pulling down-river towards the sea at cracking pace, and again there was exhilaration: the exhilaration of being the fastest thing on the water, or on land besides. The wind of our onrush was like that of a galloping horse. The sensation of speed was tremendous.

"Centurion." said Morganus.

"*Captain*, if you please, honoured sir, once we're under way." That was Numitor: cheeky and insolent, like all seamen.

"Captain, then," said Morganus.

"Aye, aye, honoured sir?"

"Can we catch them?"

"Can we catch a merchantman round ship," said Captain Numitor, "when there's barely a wind to blow?" He raised his voice and called, "Men of *Naiada*? Are you there?"

"Aye, aye!" cried the oarsmen.

"Can we catch a Gaulish wife with a fat belly?"

134

"Aye, aye!"

"I can't hear you! Can we catch her?"

"AYE, AYE!"

"There you are then, honoured sir," said Numitor. "It's what we're here for. Our main navy base is at Dubris, down south, but we keep a couple of libernians in sheds at Londinium with crews standing by, to go after anyone who's naughty, like ships that slip and run without paying their harbour taxes. And then – even with a good wind – we're three times faster, and *we* don't have to worry if the wind don't blow."

So: clank-clank! Clank-clank! *Naiada* charged down-river. The thirty-foot oars beat fore-and-aft in magnificent rhythm, the oarsman heaved, their chant rose over us, and occasionally geese and ducks rose squawking and flapping as we spoiled their sleep. The moon shone, the river gleamed, the shoreline was black dark against the sky, and we began to pass merchant ships making their way out on the tide, towards the Britannic ocean. They were all under sail, and heeled over, but making little way in a weak wind which at least spared my bones the cold.

"Is that the one, captain?" said Morganus as we bore down on the first ship

"Naaaah," said Numitor. "That's a south coast fisherman. That's not her."

"How can you tell?" said Morganus.

"By the rig," said Numitor. "*Good Wife Carata* spreads mains'l, artemon and fores'l."

"And this one doesn't have that rig?"

Numitor just laughed. As I have said, these mariners have no respect for anyone. Then he shouted an order. "Wake 'em up! Ge' 'em out of our way!"

A loud and urgent horn was blown in the bows of our ship: three great blasts, that caused the fisherman ship to pull aside.

"That's better!" said Numitor. "Show 'em what's what!"

The same happened again a number of times, as we passed more ships and the dawn came up slowly in the east. Twice we came alongside ships of the type we were chasing, and they were hailed and challenged.

"What ship?" cried Numitor, and each time the ship spilled wind from her sails, and heaved to, and replied and was not *Good Wife Carata*. So we pulled on past, as the light of day began to shine over the waters, and the shore was green not black.

"Captain," said Morganus, "what if we find her, and she won't stop? These merchant ships are higher than us, and strong built, and this ship doesn't have a ram."

"No!" said Numitor, "we're built for speed, not ramming."

"Then what will you do?"

"You wait and see," said Numitor, then stared hard ahead, "and if you're lucky you won't have to wait long, 'cos that looks like her! *Good Wife Carata!*" He took a breath, and bellowed orders. "Battle speed! Action stations! Stand by with hooks!"

Instantly, the oar-stroke picked up, the ship hurled forward, and the marines put down shields and took hold of two long poles with scythe blades at the tip that had been laid the length of the ship, between the oarsman. It took neat drill to do this under way, since the poles were so long and heavy as to need three men each, and each pole was made fast to the deck at its butt end, with a ring bolt and lashings.

"Ahhh!" said Morganus, "I've read about this in Caesar's book about the Gallic wars. This is how he beat the Veneti ships."

And indeed, it was fascinating. We closed fast on the big merchantman, with its bulging sails and foaming wake, and gulls

136

wheeling about. Heads were already peering over the high sides, looking down at us.

"Helmsman?" said Numitor.

"Aye, aye?"

"At my command. take us around and under, nice and smooth."

"Aye, aye!"

"Hook-men?"

"Aye, aye?"

"At my command, go for sheets, clewlines and bowlines!"

"Aye, aye!"

"Right then," said Numitor. "We'll at least give 'em the chance to behave." And he let out the most tremendous roar of "Ahoy, *Good Wife Carata!* Heave to!"

He yelled twice more, getting no reply, and we saw men in the rigging of the merchantman, busy at some task. "That's it, then!" he said, "they're trying to get more speed on her, so ... *Engage!*" he cried, and his men carried out the most wonderful manoeuvre. The helmsman brought us right round the bows of the merchantman, and under her heeled-over side, while the hook-men marines raised the scythe poles, and though one missed aim, the second hooked its blade firmly into one of the rigging lines of the big mainsail.

"Got you!" cried the hook-men, and the whole impetus of the two vessels sliding past each other bore on the sharp blade, and the rigging line parted, and the mainsail flapped empty, leaving *Good Wife Carata* wallowing helplessly. Then round we came again, under our helmsman's control, right round the stern of our victim, and then alongside, backing oars and slowing down.

"Stand by to board!" cried Numitor, and our oarsman raised oars to vertical, as the marines laid flat the hook-poles, heaved grappling lines of the side of *Good Wife Carata*, and pulled us close alongside. "You, stay put first javelin!" said Numitor. "You and your boys! You'd be in the drink, and drowned dead!"

"Aye, aye," said Morganus, because only the gods know how the marines in their armour, managed to get up the side of the big ship, and over the rail. But they did, led by Numitor. No doubt they had trained for it and knew where to put hands and feet. So up and over they went with a great cheer, and the sound of yelling and fighting … and then quiet, and Numitor leaning over the side.

"Scrambling nets!" he cried, "Heave 'em aboard!" Our oarsmen threw lines up to the big ship, and a heavy net was hauled up from the midships of our libernian. "Come on, first javelin! Come on you Greeks!" he said. "All done now: come aboard!"

So we went up: me, Morganus, the bodyguards and Aeitius. We found the big ship's crew in a clump, threatened by our marines with drawn swords. The Gaulish seamen were surly and angry, but unharmed except for superficial wounds and bruises.

"This here's the shipmaster," said Numitor. "He says it's all our fault!"

He stood next to a middle-aged mariner, well dressed and leather-faced, who immediately spouted Celtic and waved arms. Numitor grinned. "He says he thought we were pirates, and he says the ship owners will take us before the courts!" Numitor laughed and turned to Morganus. "But they all say that."

As he spoke, I was studying the shipmaster. His anger was under control, replaced by steady hatred, and he kept looking at a small man among the survivors, and the small man looked back and nodded. There was something going on, and I wished that I really could look inside heads.

"Do you want to take over?" said Morganus, seeing me staring, and I would have done so, but Aetius thought that Morganus meant *him*. After all, Aetius was a senior man, he was used to taking initiative, and he was here to identify Blephyrix.

"With your permission, honoured sir?" he said to Morganus. Then he spoke so well that I was content to let him continue. "Where is Blephyrix?" he said to the shipmaster. "We know he is aboard, and we charge you in the name of the emperor to produce him. Either that, or we impound this ship, and arrest you and your men."

Aetius spoke Latin, but the shipmaster understood and stared at Aetius in hatred, then glanced at a hatchway. A child could have read his expression, and Aetius certainly did.

"He's down here," said Aetius to Morganus. "Blephyrix is down there."

"Right!" said Numitor. He pointed at the hatchway and yelled orders at the Celtic crew. At first they did nothing, but our marines stamped foot, and pulled back swords to thrust. So the hatchway came off and a ladder was revealed. Then the shipmaster poured out more words, took the small man by the arm, and pointed to the ladder.

Numitor looked at Morganus. "He says the little bugger will show you the way, 'cos he's got keys for all the locks, and you won't find anything without him."

The little man came forward as the shipmaster spoke. He was all beckoning and polite and bowing. He was halfway down the ladder already, and he seemed harmless.

"Good," I said, and I would have gone first down the ladder. Indeed I *should* have gone first down the ladder, but it was the will of the gods that I did not, because Aetius was closer so he went first.

Then I stepped forward to take my turn, looked down and saw the gleam of a blade as the little man seized Aetius by the chin, jerked back his head and cut his throat.

# CHAPTER 14

There was a fierce and savage fight. The shipmaster and his men took up such weapons as they had – seaman's knives and belaying pins – and attacked us. But the bodyguards instantly stepped forward, and those four big men alone – with their swords and armour – killed or disabled half of *Good Wife Carata*'s crew. The marines easily dealt with the rest, while Numitor slid down the ladder and killed the small man who had murdered Aetius. Morganus drew steel but never used it. He likewise gave me his dirk, but I soon gave it back. Not one man of our party was even wounded.

Then we stood in our cheap victory, on the hideously rolling deck of a ship without a crew. Just three men – badly wounded – had survived of the ship's people, together with a boy who had gone aloft and stayed there, and below decks there was a small dog that they kept to chase the rats.

"What in the name of Jupiter Maximus were they trying to do?" said Morganus. "They had no chance, not with knives and bits of wood!"

But I was on my knees, looking at the dead. I turned them over, I pulled them apart, and I looked ... and every one of them had three dots on the left hand. Then I went down the ladder, in the hope that

Aeitius's killer might still have breath in him. But Numitor had run him through over and again. He was gone. He too had the three dots.

He also had tattoos on his body. I saw some of them at his neck and wrists, but I did not look closer, as I was feeling sick. In addition, every man of them had neck pouches with carvings of the three hooded figures. That made me think of the beliefs of seafarers.

"Where's the shrine?" I said to the captain.

"What shrine?' said Morganus.

"All ships have sacred shrines to the sea gods," I said.

"It'll be at the stern, by the rudders," said the captain.

So we went to look. "There!" said the captain, and he began to raise hands in front of a box on a pedestal. It was open at the front and roofed over. But he did not complete the gesture. "What's this?" he said. "This isn't Father Neptune!" Indeed, it was not. Fixed inside the shrine there was a stone slab incised with the three hooded figures: the Danuic trinity.

I looked at the slab and I looked at the dead all around us: the ship's crew killed in a hopeless, stupid fight.

"This is religious," I said. "Only religion does this."

"Quite right," said the captain, "False religion!" Then he raised hands. "Blessed be Father Neptune!" he said. "And a curse on all this shit!" He was offended, outraged. "My lads will follow the ways of the true gods," he said. "The sea gods! Bind up the wounded, be rid of the dead, clear up, clean up, and a prize crew to bring this ship to port."

"Aye, aye!" said his marines.

"What about Blephyrix?" said Morganus.

"Let's find him," I said.

So we did. He was hauled out of a little cabin under the stern and he blinked in the light. He was a broad, strong man and he did indeed have a purse of gold coins. Likewise he had the three spots and the carvings in a pouch. Then, as we stood on the rolling, heaving deck, and our marines threw dead men over the side, he tapped his three left-hand dots with the first three fingers of his right hand pinched together. Then he touched his brow and breast. He did it three times. I realised that this was the same ritual as had been performed by the father of the child I saved. It was part of the trinity faith.

Meanwhile it was part of the *sea* faith that all of *Good Wife Carata*'s crew went over the side, except the boy and the dog, since the wounded died even as bandages were applied. But at my insistence, Aetius was not thrown to the sea gods. As an Athenian, his patron goddess was the wise and blessed Athena: a powerful deity whom it was most dangerous to disrespect. So I argued that he should be taken ashore for burial under her rites, and Numitor readily agreed.

Meanwhile, I began to question Blephyrix, but only after Morganus and the bodyguards had searched him for knives. I was sweating with nausea but I did my best, with a challenge I hoped he would not expect.

"You got it wrong when you shaved him," I said, "you should have used wax!"

He struggled to understand, then gasped in recollection and reached for his neck pouch. He did that and said nothing. But his reaction told me that he knew about the shaving. Perhaps he had done it himself?

Unfortunately, that was all the questioning I could manage because the rolling and pitching had inflicted appalling sea-sickness upon me. Almost everyone suffered to some degree, so awful is the motion of a becalmed ship: everyone except Morganus and Numitor, that is. They both seemed immune.

Thus, I recall little of the voyage back to Londinium other than hanging over the side to vomit, because I could not throw off the nausea. Later, *Good Wife Carata* was brought in by six of the captain's men, while the ship's boy and Blephyrix were locked up awaiting my recovery. Later still, the small dog was adopted by the men of *Naiada*. They named him Morganus. These people have no respect.

I was fit for duty after a good sleep. For once, I did manage that. But Morganus thought it self-indulgence.

"Up at last?" he said, as I sat at breakfast in his house. He was fully armed and armoured, with the bodyguards behind him. "The world's been awake for hours."

"I was ill," I said. "Sea-sick."

"Huh!" he said.

"So were they," I said, pointing to the bodyguards.

"Yes," he said, "but they were up at dawn."

It was time to change the subject. "Where are Blephyrix and the boy?" I said.

"In the fort lock-up," he said, "with four men found with the three spots on their hands. I gave orders for an inspection. I'm pleased to say that no legionary had the spots, but four auxiliaries did."

"Any other news?" I said.

"Yes," he said. "Every fort and camp in the province is on a war footing, and I've had formal thanks – well, you have really – from Scapula, for bringing the body of Aetius ashore. He seems to have been fond of Aetius, and the family certainly were. Aetius had a family."

"I know," I said.

"I suppose you read that in his mind," he said, and I almost wished he was being sarcastic. But he was not.

"Shall we go to the lock-up?" I said. So we did. It was on the eastern side of the fort, brick-built, tile-roofed, with a dozen cells for defaulters. An elderly optio was in charge with five elderly legionaries:

re-enlisted veterans. He was waiting outside with his ring of keys, and his men all polished up for Morganus's visit. They saluted, and we entered. There were two rows of cells with oak doors and iron grills, and at the far end there was a day room for the optio and his men, with tables, chairs, cooking stove and a latrine beyond.

"Where are the prisoners?" said Morganus to the optio.

"Honoured sir," he said, "the man is in cell one, the boy in cell two, and the auxiliaries on the other side."

"Which do you want first?" said Morganus to me.

"Blephyrix," I said, "in there." I pointed to the day room.

Morganus and I went in and sat down. Morganus took off his helmet, the optio's men brought in Blephyrix and the bodyguards stood in front of the door. There was no way out for Blephyrix, who was stolid and calm: surprisingly calm for a man who should have been expecting a beating or a visit to the torturer's workshop. But he closed his eyes, tapped his three dots, and touched brow and breast as he sat down. So I threw out a challenge.

"You tied the loin cloth inside-out," I said. "That was stupid."

He frowned, then gaped in recollection.

"That's right," I said, "you took off his loin cloth to shave his buttocks, then put it back the wrong way round." I smiled. "I can see it inside your head. I am the Greek that reads minds."

He gasped and began to tremble.

"And who was it that helped you throw the body over the railings? Was it the tattooed man?"

Blephyrix cried out in anguish. "You are the Greek!" he said, "There's death on your head! Death to the Greek who reads minds!"

He jumped from his chair, looked round in desperation, saw the bodyguards, and threw himself on them, beating at them with his fists.

"Don't hurt him!" I yelled. "Just hold him!"

They did. They grabbed him, forced him back into his chair, and he fell into such dread that words poured out of him without my needing to ask. The words came in a stream and were much jumbled.

"The tattooed man was one of them, old power, deep power, new power. He said it was good to kill Zephyrix, and damnation on Rome, and Maligoterix says they're waiting in Gaul and beyond, and the trinity is with us, even women, even slaves, and all together, he has promised, he has promised."

To the best of my memory that is what he said, before staring at me in terrible fear, and lapsing into the Celtic speech. Nothing would shake him from that, so we had him thrown back into his cell, still chanting, and the Optio and his men staring in amazement. They were even more amazed when shouted orders.

"Don't lock him in yet!" I said, "Take his belt! Take boot laces! Anything he could use to hang himself! And anything else that's dangerous!"

"Yes, your worship!" said the optio, and I went back to the day room.

"You did right," said Morganus.

"I know," I said, because on past occasions we had seen religious fanatics kill themselves rather than betray their faith.

"Close the door," I said to the bodyguards.

"Yes, your worship," they said, and looked at Morganus.

"Do you want them in or out?" he said.

"In," I said, "they have a right to know." So they stayed.

"How did *you* know?" said Morganus, "about the tattooed man?"

"The druid?" I said, and all four of them shuddered. "That was easy. Did you see how *Good Wife Carata*'s shipmaster was nervous of him? And he killed Aetius and was ready to die afterwards: die on a Roman sword with no chance of escape." I fell silent and raised arms, "Blessed be the name of Apollo for sparing me," I said, "and blessed be the soul of Aetius, because the druid thought Aetius was the mind-reading Greek. He thought Aetius was *me*."

Morganus and the bodyguards made the bull sign. "Blessings in the name of Mithras," they said.

"And did you hear what Blephyrix said? *Old power, deep power?* And anyway, what was he saying when he went into Celtic?"

"A prayer," said Morganus, "it was all about oak trees and oak leaves."

"There you are then!" I said. "Druids! And did you hear that name– Maligoterix?"

"Yes," said Morganus. "This is bad."

"It is," I said.

We knew Maligoterix from previous troubles. We knew him well. We had met him and fought against his attempts to overthrow Roman rule. He was the high druid of all Britannia, and known to be hiding in the semi-independent tribal kingdom of the Regni tribe.

"What about the rest of them?" said Morganus. "The boy and the auxiliaries?"

"Yes," I said. "Bring them in, one at a time. Auxiliaries first."

What followed was interesting. The auxiliaries were in dread of punishment, and wondering what they had done wrong. They were Parthian archers, from the far east of the empire: a typical Roman recruitment, because whenever the Romans encounter military skills better than their own, they either copy them or recruit them: yet another reason why Rome rules the world.

The first man was typical of the rest: olive-skinned, hook-nosed, dark-eyed with long, black hair. He wore a mail shirt over a leather tunic, but his weapons had been taken away. He bowed to Morganus, putting palms to brow in respect, which gave me a nice view of the three spots on his left hand.

"Sit," said Morganus, "in that chair!"

The auxiliary bowed again, and sat straight-backed, bolt upright.

"Name and unit?" said Morganus.

"Rastag of Ithtar, honoured sir! Third century, fourth cohort, first sagitarii!"

Morganus looked at me and nodded. So I took over. Apart from reciting his rank, Rastag of Ithtar hardly spoke Latin, so I tried other languages and found that he spoke good Aramaic. So I used that language, first taking advantage of my reputation.

"Do you know who I am?" I said.

"You are the magic Greek," he said, and everything was easy after that, since he thought it impossible to deceive me. So I summarise his answers to my questions regarding why and how he bore the three dots on his hand.

" … my woman made me. I have a woman and two children…

… True faith, new faith, salvation for all …

… Daga the father, Danu the mother, Cernunnos the child …

… all the women believe; all have the three marks …

… the marks were made by a holy man …

… a man with tattoos …

… in the villages …

… everywhere …"

The other three auxiliaries said much the same, though I could speak Latin with them. Then, after some hours, when we were done with them, I asked for wine and cakes, but the optio brought beer and cold meat pies, which is all they had with the camp on high alert. So we made do – at least, the bodyguards did, and sat cheerfully munching and drinking, but politely separate from Morganus and myself.

"It is as we thought," I said. "It comes from their women."

"Yes," I said. "It's in the villages, everywhere. It must be widespread."

"I don't like the sound of holy men," he said. "Tattooed men?"

"Druids!" I said. "So what will you do with these auxiliaries?"

"Well," he said, "archers are scarce, they've done nothing that was forbidden, and we Romans think that honouring the gods is a private matter – apart from following druids, of course. But from now on, anyone found with the three dots will be flogged and expelled from the army in disgrace. And those four with dots can go to the surgeons and have them removed, and serve 'em right!"

Finally I spoke to the boy, or rather Morganus did, because the boy spoke only a Gaulish Celtic dialect which was difficult even for Morganus. The boy looked about ten or twelve, his name was Garos, he was barefoot, scrawny, exceedingly dirty, and his eyes flicked from one to another of us. He gaped in awe at the gleaming armour of the bodyguards and Morganus, and he picked his nose and ate the fruit, most disgustingly, until Morganus shouted at him to stop.

"The shipmaster was his uncle," said Morganus, after the boy had chattered at him in Celtic. "He was taken to sea after he'd begged his father, and the father asked the uncle."

The boy chattered again, whining and pleading. "And now he wants to be set free," said Morganus, "so he can go to sea again." Morganus looked at me. "I think he's younger that he looks. He's childish, and he doesn't properly understand what's happened."

But then the boy surprised us, as I took his left hand to search for spots under the dirt, dipping a corner of my cloak into a beer pot, then wiping hard, but finding nothing. He realised what I was doing and let out another long chatter.

"Oh?" said Morganus, "That's interesting! He says he'll get the sacred marks as soon as he is back home, because he'll soon be thirteen and a man. And …" Morganus struggled with translation, "he says the fort? Camp? Town? I don't quite know the word. He says it's in Gaul, and it is the birth mother? Womb? Something female."

He leaned forward and shook the boy by the shoulder and asked more questions. Then he turned to me. "This could be important, Greek," he said. "I think he's saying that the headquarters of this new faith, the place where it started, with the hooded figures and the three gods, it's in Gaul, and he knows where it is."

That was the beginning of a long series of questions, asked by me of the boy Garos, with Morganus translating as best he could, and both of us straining to keep Garos's mind on the subject in hand, from which he constantly wandered. We persevered until Garos got tired, and either could not, or would not, answer any more– not even when Morganus waved his vine-staff as a threat. Eventually, my judgement was that he had only a small memory, and that memory was now empty. So we gave up. But we took him out of the lock-up and gave him to the bodyguards to look after.

"Get him cleaned up," said Morganus, "and don't let him run. We're going to need him."


Later, in Morganus's house, we sat in the lamplight with some wine and discussed what we had learned from Garos.

"He's a Gaul, and he comes from Ambianum on the river Somme," said Morganus. "That's about ninety miles south of our Gaulish naval base at Gesoriacum."

"Can we get there?" I asked.

"To Gesoriacum, yes," he said. "Ships go there all the time, from Britannia's naval base at Dubris." He took a sip of wine. "What do you think of the rest of it? Did he make sense?"

"Yes," I said, "within his limits. He says it is a women's religion that they pass to the men. He says that holy men make the three marks, and they bless the triple images. He says everyone knows where the holy men come from, and he says he can find it: this fort, house, place? Whatever it is."

"What about druids?" said Morganus, "Was he hiding anything? What did you see inside his mind? I was too tired to argue what I could, and could not see. So I merely answered.

"He knows nothing about druids," I said, "not as such. But he was frightened of the man with tattoos."

"The one who killed Aethius?"

"Yes. Garos was frightened of him. He said that he was *old power*."

"*Old power*?" said Morganus, "Blephyrix talked about old power!"

"I know," I said. "It's very confusing. All mixed up. But I'm tired and it's late."

"We'll have to tell all this to Petros and the legate," he said. "In the morning."

So we did.

# CHAPTER 15

The headquarters of the Twentieth Legion's fort was its principia. It was strongly built in heavy Roman architecture, because Romans lack imagination to build any other way. So the principia stood within high walls, centred on a massive, multi-storey block, and was approached through a fortified gatehouse, beneath a statue of the emperor with the letters *LEG XX* picked out in gold leaf beneath his imperial majesty's feet.

On the evening of the day when Morganus and I interrogated Blephyrix, we were standing in the principia's assembly hall, with the legate Africanus and his legionary officers, plus officers of cavalry and auxiliaries, each unit with its note-takers. Also there were liaison officers from the other Britannic legions, and every soldier present was in battlefield kit, not parade armour.

At sunset large, multi-flame lamps were lit by orderlies, then hoisted up on lines to enable work to continue into the night. Such was the urgency of the occasion, such was Roman efficiency in the face of a vital need for late work, that all present had already listened to a report from Morganus of our investigations.

"I thank you, Leonius Morganus Fortis Victrix," said the legate

Africanus, when Morganus was done. "The army is grateful to you, for all that you, in your diligence, have learned."

He did not even mention me.

Then he went to a huge map of Britannia, which hung from hooks. The map showed towns and cities, roads and rivers, mountains and tribal areas, and icons representing formations of Roman troops. The icons were pinned to the map, so they could be moved as the troops moved. Also, the map showed the boundaries and capitals of the Celtic client kingdoms.

There were seven of these: semi-autonomous tribal states, ruled by their own laws under their own monarchs, each monarch living in a palace built to Roman standards of luxury. These kingdoms were encouraged by Rome, as a demonstration to the Celtic aristocracy of the excellent rewards for good behaviour, as opposed to the slaughter that would fall upon them if they rebelled. So the client kingdoms flourished, as long as they kept within strict borders and raised no armies. That was Rome's policy for the tribes, and it had worked since Boudicca. But now things were changing. So Africanus took up a long white rod, and pointed to the map.

"We are here," he said, "the Twentieth Legion, at Londinium with auxiliaries and cavalry." The pointer moved high up the map. "The Fourteenth Legion, with cavalry and auxiliaries, is here by the city of Deva on the river Dee, which is ten days' march from Londinium." The pointer moved on. "Further north, the Second Legion is at Eboracum, six days' march from Deva."

He paused and looked around. "And so to Maligoterix," he said, and there was angry murmuring. "Maligoterix," said Africanus, "high druid of all Britannia, safely hidden for many years … here!" The white rod tapped the tribal kingdom of the Regni, forty miles south of Londinium. "We are informed," he said, "*credibly* informed," and he gave me the ghost of a glance, "that Maligoterix is at the centre of a new rebellion, based on new gods, and which represents deadly peril, since it could unite all the tribes against us." He paused and looked around at us all. "I have, therefore," he said, "with the approval of his grace the governor …"

"Gods bless his grace!" cried everyone.

"Gods bless him!" said Africanus. "With his grace's approval I have applied direct to Rome for permission to enter the tribal kingdom of the Regni, to arrest Maligoterix."

This brought a great thundering stamping of feet, and a bellow of cheers. Africanus raised his hand for silence. "Blessings upon your enthusiasm," he said, "but be aware of the massive deployment of horse and foot, that shall be necessary to ensure Maligoterix does not escape, and be aware of the profound secrecy that will be needed in the deployment."

There was even more stamping and cheering, but I could see that Africanus was less enthusiastic than his officers. He was an old soldier, aware of the risks, and he would bear responsibility of any failure.

"Meanwhile," he said, "we are informed, that upstream of the machinations of Maligoterix, the home of the new gods is across the ocean in Gaul. We shall therefore send," and this time he looked straight at me, "an *investigator*, to deal with that phenomenon: a person whose cunning mind, swims in the ocean of strange gods."

I suppose that was praise, but it did not sound like it.

Africanus went on to give full details of his planned troop movements, then Morganus and I had a day and a night to prepare for a journey to Gaul. At dawn on the day of departure, the lady Morgana and her daughters brought out our luggage and food for the journey, and laid the bundles on the ground. Once again I was amazed to see Roman ladies do such servile work. But they did, in full view of the bodyguards, and a lightning carriage and driver waiting outside.

I noticed that the ship's boy Garos, from *Good Wife Carata*, was sitting in the carriage. He was clean, in a new tunic and cloak, and seemed awe-struck by everything around him.

The first century, first cohort were paraded in Morganus's honour, and they stamped to attention in a crash of arms as he and I emerged from the house. It was like everything Roman: it was formal, it was ceremonial, it was a parade, and the lady Morgana's farewell to her husband was in accordance with Roman *gravitas* and *dignitas*.

"Gods be with you, O lord-my-husband," she said, in a high clear voice. "Gods be with you as you go forth on your duties to Rome." She bowed, her daughters bowed, and all of them stone-faced, because Romans absolutely do not show emotion in public.

"Gods be with you, O lady-my-wife," said Morganus. "Gods be with this house, and with you and the children of our marriage." He bowed in return, equally un-smiling.

Then, the Roman-ness of the occasion was spoiled, and it was Morgana's fault as much as mine. She looked at me and, and once again I was her wayward son, and I could see her hands twitching to ensure my cloak was properly pinned. At least she did not do that. But she looked up at me, and blinked.

"You *will* take care," she said, "won't you? And you won't act alone?" She looked to Morganus. "He *will* take care, won't he?"

Then... I should not have said what I did. But I could not help myself, because I had been so lonely before I entered her house.

"I will take care," I said, "O mother-of-my-sisters." The result was floods of tears from Morgana and the girls, and enormous embarrassment for the onlookers.

So, later, as the high-speed carriage crossed a fort drawbridge, heading for the Great South Road, Morganus spoke to me. In fact he shouted at me, and the driver in front, the bodyguards behind us, had to pretend not to hear. At least the boy Garos could not understand.

"Well, that was a new one!" Morganus said, "I know you can't guard your tongue in other ways, but that was new. What will everyone think? My lady weeping and wailing in front of the men? Can't you act like a Roman? Just for once?"

"I'm not a gods-damned Roman," I said, "I'm a gods-damned Greek."

There would have been a considerable argument, but we heard a trumpet behind us. It blew in a distinct pattern.

"That's the recall," said Morganus, and he reached forward to clap the driver on the shoulder, but the driver was already reigning in and the lightning slid to a halt as a formation of richly-equipped cavalry galloped up, coming from the direction of Londinium.

"Governor's guard horsemen," said Morganus, "escorting Petros of Athens."

The horsemen rode up, stopped and saluted Morganus, while Petros came alongside the carriage. He looked very worried. He had trouble controlling his horse, because horses feel the sentiments of their riders, and are disturbed by them.

"I have caught you," he said– to me– then nodded to Morganus. "We must talk," he said, beckoned one of the mounted guardsman, handed him his reins, and dismounted. I could not help but notice that did so very neatly: he swung out of the saddle like a horseman.

Then he beckoned again, this time to both me and Morganus. "Come! Come! Come!" he said and walked along the road, until our conversation could be heard by nobody else.

I was cold. As ever, the Britannic wind despised me and plucked at my garments.

"Well?" said Morganus. "What is it? It must be urgent if you've chased after us."

But Petros looked at me. "I shall never know how you do it," he said, "but this time– please do *not* do it!"

"Do what?" said Morganus, then realised. "Oh," he said, "you mean ..."

"Get inside my head!" said Petros. "Now listen, because I am going to trust you with a secret that could see all three of us on a charge of high treason. Do you understand?"

"It's the druids," I said. "You talk to them, don't you?"

Morganus gasped. "Holy Mithras!" he said, and made the bull sign.

"You talk by pigeons," I said, and Morganus shook his head in amazement. So I suppose it seems clever of me. But it was not. The matter was so secret that Petros would not speak in front of others, for fear of high treason– which could only mean being found out in the crime of talking to the druids, which was a capital offence. It could only be that because Petros fiercely respected Roman law in all other matters, while this particular matter revolved around the druids. As for pigeons, the druids had used them since ancient times to carry messages, and Petros had obviously received some message that was urgent and secret. So I made my guess – which is all that it was – and if perhaps I perhaps I makes such guesses instantly and without conscious thought, then I leave it to others to define the nature of my guessing.

So Morganus thought of magic. But Petros merely sighed.

"How stupid of me!" he said. "You can't stop doing it, can you?"

"No," I said, "I can't."

"Then to save you the effort of looking," said Petros, "will you please concentrate on *what* I know, and now *how* I know it? Will you at least try to do that?"

"Yes," I said.

"So," he said, "Maligoterix is not necessarily our enemy."

"What?" said Morganus. "He's the high druid! Worst enemy of them all!"

"Please listen," said Petros. "He opposes this new religion of the trinity." He tapped his left hand with his right. "The three spots?" He raised a hand to his neck. "The three little figures in the pouch? Maligoterix hates all this. It is a rival to his power because it offers personal salvation without him and his druids."

"So what?" said Morganus. "Let 'em fight it out, and bad luck on all of them!"

"No!" said Petros. "We cannot stand back. The legate Africanus is convinced Maligoterix must be arrested and executed. He has written to Rome seeking permission to break the treaty with the Regni kingdom, and he has persuaded everyone who matters in Britannia to counter-sign the letter: the lord justice, the procurator, the consuls of the provincial council." He sighed. "And his grace the governor. Even I could not stop his grace from signing!"

"And so?" I said.

"Africanus will not move without approval from Rome," said Petros, "so his letter will go by imperial post. It will take about a week to reach Rome, it will be addressed to the emperor but it will be opened by the bureaucracy, and it will take another week for them to make a decision."

"A week?" I said. "As long as that?"

"Oh yes," said Morganus. "You don't know what they're like."

"Indeed," said Petros. "An entire host of precious and political persons must be protected before taking such a decision. It will take at least a week."

"At least," said Morganus.

"Then another week," said Petros, "for the reply to reach Africanus, then another week for Africanus to get his men in place." Petros looked at me. "You therefore have about a month, to prove to Africanus that he must not arrest Maligoterix."

"But why should we help Maligoterix?" said Morganus.

"So that he will defeat the trinity," said Petros, "and restore the status quo, which was at least stable. Remember that Maligoterix could never raise all the tribes in simultaneous rebellion, but this new religion may do precisely that, to our very great peril indeed!"

"Wait, wait," I said. "Petros? You said that I have a month to convince Africanus?"

"Yes."

"*Me?*"

"Yes, *you*."

"But how can I convince Africanus?" I said.

"Do you not know?" said Petros, genuinely puzzled.

"Know what?"

"That Africanus has the utmost respect for you. He believes that you have a gift of the gods: a gift of the very greatest value to Rome and the empire. He has the most profound respect for your opinions." Petros made a small depreciative gesture. "Though of course he could not show it. That would be beneath his dignity."

"Holy Apollo!" I said. "God of my fathers!" I was amazed beyond words.

"Ah!" said Petros and smirked. "Did you not see that in his head? Did your magic fail?"

"I've told you," I said. "I am not magic."

"With or without magic," said Petros, "you must go into Gaul, with this child you took from the ship." He looked at the lightning, where the boy was sitting with the bodyguards and the driver.

"Garos?" I said.

"Him!" said Petros. "Use him to find the home of the trinity religion, and decide whether or not it is something truly separate from druidism, and then return to Britannia– doing your very best to avoid being killed– and do all this before Africanus declares war on the Regni tribe and executes the man who may be our strongest ally."

Then Petros looked away. He looked at the officer commanding his escort. He beckoned and the man rode forward.

"Give!" said Petros, and the officer – a tribune and a knight – bowed in the saddle and handed Petros a leather satchel. Even in such a moment I marvelled of the power wielded by Petros, despite his being a slave– even if an imperial slave. "Here," said Petros, handing me the satchel. "Further documents signed by his grace, to ensure cooperation of all such persons as you might encounter. You will act in the emperor's name. Now go!"

So we did, and soon we were speeding down a ruler-straight Roman road, wrapped up against the dust and wind of our onrush. A legionary lightning is fast but not comfortable, nor is it silent because it creaks and groans, and the hooves and iron tyres make a great noise, and the driver is constantly urging on at the horses.

"*Go* on! *Go* on!"

Since our mission was urgent we had to have speed, but I did my best to comfort the horses when we stopped at the staging posts. I went to each one and promised best care, then made sure that they got it. Our journey was about eighty Roman miles, from Londinium to Dubris, which was the main port of the *Classis Britannicus* and surrounded by famous cliffs of white chalk which tell the incoming mariner that he is approaching Britannia. The port lies on an out-jutting peninsula, where savage Britannia reaches eastward towards the civilised world. Our intention was to run the whole journey in one go, changing horses at the ten-mile staging posts down the roads.

But the filthy Britannic weather – doubtless at the behest of the Britannic gods – decided that we should be delayed by such cold and heavy rain, that we gave up and spent the first night at one of the way-stations, found at twenty-mile intervals down the roads. They were called *mansiones* and were large establishments with accommodation, food, and most blessed baths where we could soak away the aches and cold of the journey.

So it was not until early the next day that we reached the great naval sea port, with its stone-built wharves, barracks, warehouses, and armories, and the smoke rising from dozens of chimneys including those of large manufactories of nautical gear of all kinds from anchors to oars, from pulley blocks to barrels.

It was exciting. It was so different from any city of the interior. It even smelt different. It smelt of tar, and seaweed and sawn timber. As we rode up to the defensive walls, we were on high ground with a fine view into the port and of the many and varied ship types at anchor or coming in on the tide. There was even a pair of triremes, coming in from sea duties. These were the biggest oared ships maintained by the Classis Britannicus: three banks of oars, heavy rams at the bow and rows of artillery machines.

Also, there were several libernians, such as we had been aboard so recently, shoals of small boats pulling in all directions, together with fishing boats and big, high-masted round ships of the merchant kind, except that they flew the banners of the imperial service. It was exciting, and the boy Garos was up on his feet chattering and pointing in delight– not that anyone could understand him, other than Morganus.

It was all so jolly and bright that I almost forgot the dread that was lurking at the bottom of my mind. It was fear of the sea-sickness, and it would not go away.

Then we were arriving at the main gateway, with the driver bawling out Morganus's name, and the guard turned out and the optio saluting, while another man sent to run for the centurion, and men peered down from the battlements of the walls and the towers of the gateway, and nudged one another and pointed out Morganus.

"May it please your victorious honour," said the optio, bowing. "May it please you to await a proper escort into the port, and to the principia and the legate?" He was enthralled at meeting Morganus, hero of the Roman army who was famous to every man that wore a sword.

"We shall wait," said Morganus. So we did, until a century of men marched up, led by a tribune, in his fancy muscled cuirass, and there was much more bowing and honorific words, and a gathering of the folk of the port as Morganus's name went up through the streets of Dubris.

In the end, we progressed through the town followed by the sort of cheering crowd that would have followed a champion gladiator or racing driver. Then we were received at the principia with much formality, much talking and much presentation of the port's officials to Morganus. As for myself, I did my best as a philosopher not to mind being ignored. At least I was inside the principia. The bodyguards, driver and the boy Garos had to wait outside.

Then we had to wait until a suitable ship was outbound for Gesoriacum, the *Classis Britannicus's* main port across the sea in Gaul. We were very well entertained and accommodated, but the wait was tedious, and I worried and worried about Allicanda. It was a bad time.

Finally, after two days, we were aboard a big, naval supply ship, *Saliens Tructa*, of 500 tons' burden, with two masts, three sails, a crew of twenty-five including marines, and three ships' boys who took Garos as one of their own, since they spoke the same Gaulish gibberish. They ran up and down the ship's rigging like a tribe of monkeys.

"Best thing for boys, your worship," said the helmsman to me as he watched them play. "They has to burn off the energy, you see? Like puppies. Elsewise they gets into mischief and you has to flog the arses off 'em."

I fear I said little in reply. The ship was making good speed under a steady blow, but she rolled heavily and her decks were canted over by the pressure of the sails on the masts. So it was hard for me to hang on, and the sea-sickness came back like a demon that has been dropped down a well to be got rid of, but which climbs out – chuckling and leering – then enfolds you in his foul embrace.

So I clung to the rail, I watched the evil grey waves heave up and down, I shivered in cold, and I tried to follow the advice that sea-sickness can be avoided by fixing the eye upon the horizon. Which it cannot. I tried and the method failed.

Morganus thought it was funny. Or perhaps he intended some chastisement for my parting words to the-lady-his-wife? In any case, he came up to me with the ship's captain and the pair of them smiling, and many of the ship's people looking on.

162

"How are you, Greek?" he said. "Oh dear, are you suffering? Is it the sea-sickness again? But never mind, just you look at what we've got here. Show him, captain!"

"Aye, aye," said the captain and held out a pan of warm, greasy fat. It steamed in the cold, it bulged in glistening lumps, and it moved as if alive under the ship's motion.

"You have to take a good gulp of this," said Morganus. "That's right, isn't it, captain?"

"Aye, aye!" said the captain.

"Then, if you can keep it down …"

The gods are kind in that I remember little of what happened next. But at least I survived, and eventually we did reach the blessed and beloved shore.

# CHAPTER 16

At least the voyage was short. In the words of the seafarers, we had *fair winds and a swift passage*. We were aboard *Saliens Tructa* for just a night and half a day before she was under reduced sail, and coming into the naval port of Gesoriacum, on the river Liane at the north-east extremity of Gaul. The ship was heading towards a Classis Britannicus warehouse to unload ingots of lead, tin and Britannic wool. The port itself was similar to Dubris. It was intensely busy, intensely full of ships and dock people, and near-identical in the design of its wharves and buildings– since Romans standardise everything that can be standardised. Even the sponge-sticks in the army latrines are the same everywhere.

So, finally, I was easing my way down a gangplank, struggling to throw off the nausea and convinced that my love of seafaring was a nonsensical affectation. Fortunately, since I followed Morganus – in armour and swan-crest helmet – nobody paid me any attention, and I was left to cherish my misery.

But I noticed the bowing and scraping, and the reaction of the dock officials and naval officers to the documents that Morganus presented, proving who he was– their delighted smiles, and the fawning attention of the staff of the dockyard's mansione, where we were given excellent accommodation.

I took no part in anything until dawn of the next day, having managed – by the grace of the gods – to sleep the night and doing so entirely without wine since my stomach was in rebellion.

But at least I managed breakfast.

"Ah," said Morganus as we sat at table, and the staff served hot porridge and fish sauce. "You're with us again, are you?"

"Yes," I said.

"Such courage in the face of affliction," he said. "You're almost Roman."

The bodyguards grinned, but I did not.

Later, as with all else, the principia of Gesoriacum proved almost identical to that of Dubris, and I thought the officers and officials near identical besides, at least in appearance, because a considerable number of them wanted to meet Morganus. So we were very well received and they were very helpful once we had got rid of the supernumeraries, and were speaking to only the port legate and his tribunes: five of them.

The legate's office was on the first floor, with big windows looking out over the port. The walls were lined with maps and a row of model ships was displayed on a side-table, all rigged with sails and oars. They were beautifully made, and must have been the legate's passion, because he kept looking at them, as if wanting us to admire them.

His name was Longinius – Marcus Publius Longinius. He was senatorial, young, fat and had a fine cluster of rings on his fingers. None the less, he was intelligent and anxious to oblige.

But I was surprised – as was Morganus – to see that none of these Roman soldiers were armoured. They wore swords with military belts, but over plain civilian clothes. There were no cuirasses or helmets.

It was only then that I recalled it had been the same on the quayside
yesterday. Nobody was in armour, except the sentries. Morganus and
the bodyguards stood out as exceptional, in their gleaming military
kit. We soon learned why, but first I explained the dangerous situa-
tion in Britannia, and Longinius was shocked.

"Druids?" he said, and his tribunes shook their heads. "I thought
you'd got rid of them in Britannia?"

I explained the truth, including our fears for the trinity religion,
and Morganus and I were surprised at his response.

"The trinity?" he said. "Dots on the hand?"

"Yes!" we said.

"What's wrong with that?" he said. "It's a native cult, like many
others. It's here in Gaul, and it's one of many native cults, and we
let the natives get on with their worship. That's the Roman way," he
said, and raised hands, "and may the grace of their gods be upon us!"

We all raised hands at that.

"So," I said, "if I understand you, honoured and noble sir, then
here in Gaul, there really are no druids, and the trinity religion is
perceived as harmless?"

"It *is* harmless," he said, "and it's none of our business as Romans!"

"So perhaps," I said, "it is the *combination* of druids and the trinity,
that threatens us in Britannia?"

"I wouldn't know," he said, "but it's plain fact that Britannia has
never yet been pacified, whereas Gaul was conquered by Caesar the
Great a hundred and fifty years ago, and Gaul has been a constitutional
province since the reign of the divine Augustus."

"Gods bless him!" they all said— and as they chanted this irritating
response, I thought of the blow beneath a knee which causes so
instinctive an urge to kick, that the owner of the leg is not aware of it.

But Longinius spoke on.

"Nobody even remembers when Gaul wasn't part of the empire," he said, and then he looked at Morganus, and gave a small bow even though – as a legate – he far out-ranked a first javelin. "And so, O hero of the legions," said Longinius, "while we respect with deepest admiration, the steel that you wear…" He paused, embarrassed. "With equal respect, I advise you that we wear no armour here in Gaul, unless on duty or attending a military parade."

Even I thought that strange. But then we discussed how best we might find and travel to the boy Garos's home, because we were still determined to investigate the trinity for ourselves, whatever Longinius said, and Longinius proved most helpful. He used one of his maps to show us the comprehensive network of roads which the Romans had built across the vast province of Gaul. He furthermore arranged a legionary lightning to take us to Ambianum, on the river Somme, at dawn the next day.

"It's Ambiani territory," said Longinius, "one of the biggest tribes. But they all behave themselves now." He smiled. "They don't have swords hidden in the house-thatch like your tribes in Britannia." His tribunes laughed at that.

So Morganus and the bodyguards took off their armour. But they packed it in the lightning with our baggage, in case of need. The lightning was like its Britannic equivalent, the horses were of the same Spanish breed, and the roads and mansiones were the same. The driver was different, though. He was not a taciturn legionary, but a Celtic Ambiani tribesman, born in the territory of our destination and chosen by Longinius to help us find our way. The driver spoke Latin, but was happiest chattering away to Garos, since both had the same mother tongue. After a very little of this, Morganus had Garos out of his rearmost seat, to cram beside the driver on the front perch. That way, they would not bother the rest of us.

So the driver was different and the countryside was, too. Superficially it was like Britannia: green hills, green plains and neat farmland. But here the hay stacks were round not square, the hedgerows were cut and laid in local style and the huts and houses – the native ones – were different. I was disturbed to find that this seemed foreign to me, when for years, in my longing for the Greek homeland, I had regarded all things Britannic as foreign. So it was not only the wearing of armour that I had come to think normal, or even homely.

We reached Ambianum in one day, after a hard drive with ten changes of horses. I know it was ten, because I counted them as I thanked the horses.

Ambianum was a small town on the banks of a huge and broad river. It had timber docks and wharves, and was enclosed in the remains of an ancient Celtic earthwork. It still had gates, but the fortifications had been allowed to decay; they were un-manned and were a further testimony to the peaceful nature of Gaul. But the gates were in the charge of a company of auxiliaries.

As ever, when Morganus arrived at any Roman city, town or camp, there was a turnout of the local military, bowing and smiling, and we were received in the principia and given use of the legionary baths, after which it was too late for anything other than sleep.

But the next day, we were entertained by the garrison in the town's basilica, with lavish food and drink. They even brought out the new first-born of the officer commanding, complete with his wife in best jewels – the lady looking slightly wan after the delivery – and with all prominent citizens and officers looking on, Morganus was asked to bless and name the infant. As with the small dog of *Good Wife Carata*, the boy was named Morganus, though here that name was chosen with respect.

"Must we do this?" I whispered to Morganus, as the infant was taken away bawling loudly.

His cries echoed back from the high ceiling, all the ladies said *ahhhhhh*, a line of dignitaries waited to be presented, and the garrison commander stood ready to introduce them.

"Yes!" said Morganus. "Tremendous insult to refuse. Unthinkable."

So it was not until dawn next day that we could search for Garos's village. Fortunately, that was not difficult. We boarded the lightning outside the principia, with fresh horses in harness and a guard of honour to see us off – all in armour, since this counted as a parade – the officers saluting with raised arms.

"Are you sure?" said Morganus to the driver. "Can you find it?"

"Yes, honoured sir!" said the driver, and looked at Garos, who grinned merrily and delivered a fluent stream of Celtic. "Him here," said the driver, "this lad, he says he can find it easy, and I think I know it anyway. It's a lake village. A big 'un. It's downriver from here, honoured sir, and we can do it there and back in a day."

So we set off with a crack of the whip and a rumble of hooves, and the garrison stamping and cheering. We went straight past the city gate guards and through the earthwork, and then we were on another straight Roman road, and for the first time I began to feel that perhaps Gaul was not quite as civilised as I had thought. The slow, shining river Somme was a vast wilderness of water. The land around was marshy. There were no farms or buildings. There were flocks of ducks, geese and swans. We even saw a fox dozing in a scrap of sunshine by the road's side.

But the driver knew his way. He took us down good roads, until finally we could see our destination and Garos reacted with hysterical delight. He shouted and pointed and laughed, until the driver obliged all the rest of us by cuffing him back-handed to make him stop. Garos stopped, but still grinned.

The road was on rising ground so we looked down on the river, where about two hundred yards from us, Gaulish engineering had contrived a large, perfectly round lake, with a village of houses in the centre. The lake was joined by a narrow canal to the Somme river, and about twenty thatch-and-timber round-houses stood on a timber platform raised up on tree trunks hammered into the lake bed. There was no way to the village other than by boat; there was a small jetty at the lakeside, and – in case further defences were needed – the village was enclosed by a tall palisade that must have had a fighting platform behind it, since I could see the heads and shoulders of people looking over it, towards us. Indeed, they pointed us out to one another.

Then, Garos was speaking again, though politely. Morganus understood.

"Let him go," he said to the driver, and summarised Garos's words for me. "The boy wants to run down and shout to them. To tell them we're friends, and that he's come home."

But Garos was already gone and running to the jetty, and yelling at the top of his voice.

"You'll have to go on foot from here, honoured sir," said the driver. "Can't get wheels and horses down there. Too soft."

"We'll go," said Morganus. "You stay here with the lightning. Are you armed?"

"I've got this, honoured sir," said the driver. He held up a cudgel.

"Only the army has swords, around here," he said. "It's against the law for anyone else. But nobody'll touch anything army."

Morganus nodded, and we all got down. At least Morganus and the bodyguards had swords: swords but no armour. It seemed strange.

We walked to the jetty, where Garos was still shouting, and we saw a wooden staircase being lowered from the village platform. Then two men and a woman came down the steps and into a boat, which pulled for the shore. The closer they got, the more Garos shouted. He shouted and pointed to the boat, and the woman waved back. She waved slowly and deliberately.

"Mam! Mam! Mam!" he cried, and even I knew what that meant. Then the boat was at the jetty, the men were making fast, and the woman clambered out of the boat and advanced upon us grim-faced. She was small, dark, and well dressed in tribal style, with elaborate embroidery on everything she wore, hair braided and a thick gold torc round her neck.

"Mam! Mam!" said Garos, in extremity of excitement, which ended as soon as the lady came up to him, and swung him a mighty clap around the face.

She was no bigger than him, but she was angry, and down he went, bawling like the infant at yesterday's name-giving as the lady leaned over him and poured out a stream of angry words, entirely ignoring the rest of us. She was a fine and shapely woman such as men admire, and are much amused by her anger so long as it is not directed at themselves.

The bodyguards laughed. Morganus grinned. Even I smiled.

"What's she saying?" I asked.

"Oh, dear me," said Morganus, "as best I can follow, he's a wicked boy, a stupid boy and he ran away. And his uncle– that's his father's brother, who's a seaman – drinks too much and lays with whores, and the boy was an idiot to go to the uncle." Morganus looked at me. "I think we can take it that she disapproves of Garos running away to sea."

When finally the woman was finished with Garos, she made him sit down, looking away from the rest of us. Then she came up to Morganus, me and the bodyguards.

She was younger that I had first thought. She had smooth skin and large eyes, with which she looked us up and down. To my surprise, she spoke first to me. She had good, clear Latin.

"I thank you," she said, with a small bow, then looked towards Garos. "The boy is a fool," she said, "but he is my only child and I thank you for bringing him home."

I bowed in return. "We are happy to have been of service, lady," I said, "and I ask your name, so that I might address you properly."

She stared me in the face and I saw that she liked me as a man. She liked me as women often do. It is a burden, like my gift of insight.

"I am Elantia," she said, "wife of Danos."

"I am Ikaros of Apollonis," I said.

"And who are the soldiers?" she said.

"I am Morganus Fortis Victrix," said Morganus, "of the Twentieth Legion, and these others are my men."

"The Twentieth?" she said. "From Britannia? Why are you here? Is there no work for you in that island?"

Morganus looked at me, smiled, and nodded gently towards her. So it was for me to answer that question. Truth is invincible and virtuous, and in this case I saw no harm in telling it. Also, looking carefully at Elantia, wife of Danos, I judged her an exceedingly clever woman who would find me out in a lie. So I told the truth.

"Lady Elantia," I said, "we are here to seek the fountain and source of the Danuic trinity, and to learn of its teachings."

"Why?" she said, with no expression that I could read.

"Because, in Britannia," I said, "the trinity has connection with the druidic faith, and the two are raising rebellion that Rome will meet with fire and the sword, such that countless thousands will die: countless thousands of Celtic folk who are brothers and sisters to the Celts of Gaul."

Her reaction was interesting. She considered my words, which in all modesty I thought well chosen. She closed her eyes in concentration and her lips moved as if she were reasoning with herself. It was like watching a skilled arithmetician flicking the counters of an abacus in deep calculation. Then she nodded, opened her eyes and looked at me.

"I will talk to *you*," she said, then looked at Morganus and the bodyguards. "But not them. Come with me. Come to my house."

"Oh, no!" said Morganus. "Not you, Greek. Not on your own."

"Then he will learn nothing," said Elantia. She turned away. "Up!" she said to Garos, and they walked to the boat, and got into it, and never looked back, and the oarsmen pulled for the village.

# CHAPTER 17

I ran down the jetty, calling her name.

"Elantia! Elantia!"

The oarsmen turned the boat and came back.

"Well" she said, and looked up at me.

"I will come," I said. "If you can tell me what I need to know."

"To show is better than to tell," she said. "But to show will take three days."

"Three days?" I said. "Why?"

"You will see when I show you," she said.

Then it was my turn to flick the abacus beads in calculation. "Will I be back here in three days?" I said.

"Yes," she said. "You will be back here at noon on the third day. I give oath in the name of the trinity. I give oath in the name of the father, the mother and the child." She tapped right hand on left three times, then on brow and breast: the first time I had seen a woman do that.

The argument that followed was short and fierce. Voices were raised.

"Listen to me, Greek!" said Morganus, with the bodyguards staring, "You may be clever, but you never watch your back, you're away in your thoughts half the time, and you're not safe on your own!"

"But we've come all this way!" I said. "Shall we give up now? This woman knows far more than she's saying."

"How do you know that?"

"It's my judgement!"

"Your judgement? You that nearly got yourself smashed under a barrel?"

"It's my judgement because ... because ... *I read her mind*. Isn't that what I do?"

That was unfair, because he believed I was magic, and I thereby won the argument at cost of considerable guilt. So I must admit that I was in the grip of fascination as often I am, when in course of investigation. I could not give up the pleasure of it, which is yet another burden on the soul of a philosopher. But I did wonder if I was right in taking this risk. Because if I was not returned safely in three days, when Morganus would return to collect me, then he would never, *ever* be forgiven by the-lady-his-wife.

But I got into the boat, the oarsmen pulled, and soon the boat bumped and rolled as we came under the dark shade of the great platform, with its dripping weeds, and I had to take care climbing the staircase that came down on ropes, with bearded faces looking down at me through a trapdoor and voices chattering in Gaulish.

The Lady Elantia went first, then me, then Garos and finally the oarsmen, and as I climbed the wet and slippery planks and came up into the light, the first thing I realised was that Elantia was one of the great ones of this place.

There were some dozens of people around the stair trap door, all well dressed, all well fed, and they bowed to Elantia. Men as well as women did this, including senior grey-beards who stood to the front, as tribal elders. They all bowed to Elantia, and asked questions about me, and she answered, and they all bowed again.

As they talked, I looked at the houses and the clutter of the place: goats tethered, chickens in coops, children peering from behind parents, wicker baskets of wet fish outside house doors, and grey wisps curling out of the smoke holes in the peaks of the conical roofs. All that and the sound of voices, and folk pointing at me. But there was no hostility, though many of the men leaned on the shafts of hunting spears. I wondered if these ranked as a weapons in civilised Gaul, where no swords were worn.

"Come!" said Elantia, finally. "My house is here, and we must talk."

In fact we did not enter the house. We sat outside, which – if weather permits – is the normal place of business for round-house folk who have no windows, and whose lamps, if they have any, are for night-time only, being expensive in terms of oil. So we sat outside the house of Elantia, which was the biggest in the village. I was given a stool, and a considerable number of men and women likewise brought stools and sat close, in confidence of their right to do so.

I noticed that, as with the Britannic tribes, these folk had characteristics in common. They were strongly built, with high brows, ears without lobes, and brown hair so pale as to be almost blond. The men had long beards, which they worked into plaits.

Elantia had a chair, not a stool, and it was brought out of her house by a servant girl who then, with polite muttering and low bows, took the bundle of clothes and other gear I had brought with me from the lightning. She took it inside the house.

Elantia sat so close that her knees touched mine, and looked hard at me with a stone-faced lack of expression that was impenetrable even to me. It was strange. It was not Greek or Roman, but something of their tribal culture was expressed in Elantia herself. She had an authority over men that I never saw in any other woman, in any other place, either before or since. She asked many questions of me, and the people looked from one to another of us as if following a ball game. Perhaps they understood Latin, I do not know. But they sighed and nodded, and whenever their faith was mentioned they tapped right hand on left, then on brow and breast. They did this synchronously, every hand moving as one. It was bizarre.

The questioning was prolonged and repetitive, so I merely summarise.

"What do want here?" she said.

"I want to learn about the trinity: your religious faith."

"Why?"

"Because your faith is causing rebellion in Britannia."

"No! The trinity brings salvation in the next life, and peace in this one."

"Not in Britannia!"

"I don't believe you!" she said. "The holy trinity teaches peace!"

"Not in Britannia," I said again.

The questioning continued in this manner for a long time. She repeated her questions, I repeated my answers, and I saw that, just as I was judging her and guessing her thoughts, she was doing the same to me. She did so, because just as I have always said, my gift is not magic but merely an extreme development of a talent that everyone has to some degree. Also, she was clever enough to cross-question me, to test for truth and hunt for lies.

Beyond even that, she questioned me as to myself, my duties in Britannia and my relationships with the people I cared for. She asked deep and personal questions, and I realised that she was inflicting upon me the very same process of inquisition as I was used to inflicting upon others. But I relaxed and accepted it, and I spoke at length. Superficially, I did so because it was necessary for the progress of my investigation.

But in truth before the gods, I said so very much of myself because it is delightfully warm and comfortable for a man to speak to a lovely woman, when she shows interest in himself and his worries: especially his worries.

Some hours later, I was sitting cross-legged on the floor of a round-house. It was night. It was dark, a fire was glowing in a stone hearth, everything smelt of wood smoke. Deep shadows were everywhere and the house was densely furnished, with half seen rabbits and water-fowl hanging from rafters, and pots and baskets on the ground in neat rows. I saw my own small bundle among them. But mainly I was conscious of Elantia leaning forward to give me a pottery drinking bowl.

"This is wine," she said. "I know that you like wine."

I nodded and took the bowl.

"This is my house," she said. "You are welcome and safe."

She smiled and I drank the wine. It was very good Gaulish wine.

"So you believe me?" I said.

"Yes," she said. "I found no deceit within you, and you spoke for so long that the people gave up and went to their houses. I have never known a man who talked so much." She saw that my bowl was empty and reached forward with a jug. "More?" she said.

She was very close to me, sitting cross-legged. I saw that she was dressed only in a thin tunic. She was very pleasing in face and form. I held out my bowl.

"Yes, please," I said. "Then you believe me about the druids?"

"Yes," she said. She filled my bowl, then frowned. "A great evil is moving in Britannia. A perversion of our faith." She tapped hands and touched brow and breast. "And now that I know *your* truth, you must know *mine*. Tomorrow I will take you up-river to the ring of stones, and you will see."

"Ring of stones?" I said. "Is that the centre of your faith?"

"It is, and you will see it tomorrow."

"Thank you," I said. I drank the wine, and thought a while. Then she placed a hand on mine. It felt pleasant.

"*My poor, sad man with so many troubles,*" she said, and studied my reaction to those words. "That is what Allicanda says of you," she said. "For the loss of your family, your city, your freedom, and because of Felemid."

I gasped. I was shocked that I had revealed so much.

"Allicanda loves you," she said, "and Morgana treats you as a son. You have the gift to enter the hearts of women, as well as their minds."

Such praise is not good for the self-discipline of a Stoic philosopher, but it was wonderfully pleasant to hear. It was thrilling.

She smiled. "Put down the bowl," she said.

I did, and she took both my hands and looked at me. "I like you," she said. "You stand tall among men; your manner is pleasing and your eyes are kind." She reached out and touched my cheek. "And you speak so often of the burdens that you bear."

"Do I?"

"Yes, you do. But now we are here together, the door is barred, my son is with his aunt, and Danos-my-husband is dead. He was old, and the gods took him three winters ago."

Then she stood, and pulled the tunic over her head and was naked.

"And in *this* house I do as please," she said. She said it without passion, as a statement of fact, and I felt that she was a women who did as she pleased in any place whatsoever. None the less, she was very lovely. Her limbs were slender, her waist was narrow, her hips were round and she glowed in the red light of the fire.

I was greatly aroused, and I stood and took her in my arms. But she looked at me and frowned. "Shall you not think of your burden?"

"Which one?" I said.

"The burden of being admired by women." She said it so seriously that for a moment I did not know that I was being mocked. Then she laughed and kissed me, and helped me take off my clothes.

There was a bed with a bear skin cover and a stuffed-grass palliasse. It should not have been as comfortable as a Roman bed of linen and soft wool, but in the company of Elantia it was pleasing beyond any words of mine. I had not enjoyed the physical company of a woman for a very long time, and so great a hunger brings fierce satisfaction in the relief of it, and the relief is wonderful.

Next morning, I was in a boat going up-river with Elantia. It was a large boat with six oarsmen, and a small company of youngsters – including Garos – who were to be received within the trinity. They wore their best clothes, and there were baskets of food and drink for the journey.

Elantia and I sat in the stern, which was the place of honour. As the boat left the village Elantia asked the question I had expected.

"And what shall you tell Allicanda?" she said.

"The truth," I said, "because I cannot lie, and will not lie."

"Yes," she said, "I saw that in you. But how will you bear the guilt?"

"I will place it among my other burdens," I said, and I prayed to Apollo that I could act out this cheap and tawdry response.

We were half a day in the boat; we passed shorelines of willows and reeds, the river flowed slowly, we saw a few other boats, some under sail, we stopped to eat once, and in the early afternoon, we sighted a hill with a ring of big stones at the top. They rose up twenty feet from the ground like the peaks of a crown, to form a structure such as was found throughout the Celtic world. I had myself seen Britannia's giant and monstrous example – the henge of stone that stands in an open plain, ninety miles west of Londinium.

This Gaulish example was far smaller, it had no horizontal cap stones, and the site was full of life, unlike the henge of stone, which is a place of fearful druidic power. Thus Roman law forbad Celts to enter it, while Romans themselves were nervous of it even in daylight, and went nowhere near it at night.

But here, things were different. There was a landing place on a beach near the hill with its stone ring, and many boats were moored, while crowds of people were moving around among a considerable village – a small town, in fact – of round-houses, and there was great, untidy cluster of open-front sheds where tradesmen bawled their wares. Everything from cloth to piglets was on sale, and there were rows of stalls offering every imaginable variety of carvings – some exquisite, some crude – of the three little figures of the trinity, and neck pouches to go with them, with craftsmen busy making more as ready stocks were bought up.

All this wealth of trade went on while holy men and women chanted and prayed, and beat drums in front of alters, and sacrificial animals were brought forward, washed and brushed and decked in garlands.

There were hundreds of people, present as entire families with children and old folk, and I thought of pilgrimage destinations like Delphi, home of the mystic Oracle, or Aquae Sulis, Britannia's hot-water city. There was exactly the same mixture here as there of crass commerce and profound religious devotion.

Then, as we came near the landing place, one of our oarsman

raised a pole with a wide cross-bar at the tip and three thick, fat rods sprouting from it – obviously a trinity sign– while another produced a horn and gave great triple blasts of sound. This caused a bustling on the shore, and people ran forward to help ground the boat, and women especially were calling out Elantia's name and kneeling and touching the hem of her robe as soon as she was out of the boat, while men bowed and tapped hand, breast and brow.

So, Elantia was an even greater person than I had guessed. I suppose that in Roman terms she was a chief priest. She was treated with deep respect, and was soon surrounded with men and women, all of them asking questions and looking at me, since – to them – I was so tall and so oddly dressed. But, as in the lake village there was no hostility and when Elantia had got them silent, she then pointed to me and explained me in their language, I was received with small bows and polite smiles.

After that, we were all the rest of the day in the place of the stone ring, and I followed Elantia as she moved in procession from one shrine to another, including one – a large one – where holy men and women wielded needles and ink to make the three dots on the hands of initiates. These included Garos, who yelped as he was jabbed, but then grinned and ran round with the rest, all waving their hands at each other. They seemed to take their faith very lightly and with joy rather than reverence.

At some of these shrines, Elantia was draped in robes and head-dresses which were appropriate to each rite, and were brought out by from chests in the houses. At each home– and they ranged from entwined branches to solid masonry – Elantia stood and preached, and the faithful chanted responses, and smiled.

Then, at night, campfires were lit and cooking pots hung over fires all across the hillside. Families sat together and raised tents, and there was singing of songs, dancing to flutes and much pleasant merrymaking. It was as different to bloodstained, violent Britannia as any place could possibly be, and I would have been most happy to stay there– except that Britannia kept creeping into my mind.

At least I was warm and comfortable, since Elantia was given a house – a big one – and we lay together in the firelight and talked. I asked about the origins of the trinity, and was told in such detail as would be wearisome to report in detail.

"First there was a holy vision," said Elantia, "given unto a virgin of the youngest clan of our tribe, who – while bathing in the river – saw three swans rising …"

There was very much more of this, in such words as are holy to the faithful, and ridiculous to the sceptic. But the bed was soft and Elantia was in my arms, and her skin against mine, so I was content to listen and give respect. Later, I asked how the trinity had reached Britannia.

"How can you ask?" she said, "when we live in this world of Roman roads? And the Roman peace, and of ships that sail to every part of the world? There aren't even pirates on the seas anymore. Your Roman navy has got rid of them!"

"I am not Roman," I said, "I am Greek."

"You talk like a Roman," she said. "You're as nosy as a Roman tax collector."

"*What?*" I said, and was insulted until I saw that she was smiling. So I smiled in return, knowing that we philosophers of Apollonis are so disciplined in logic that we are blind to humour. Hence the saying: *'don't tell an Apollonite a joke, because he'll explain it.'*

"So tell me," I said. "How do you spread word of your faith?"

"We send out messengers," she said. "Good women, faithful women, who will talk to other women."

"Women?" I said. 'You send women?"

"Of course. The faith spreads from woman to woman."

I nodded. I had guessed that. "Where do you send these women?" I said.

"Everywhere, not just to Britannia."

We talked a lot more until we were tired. Then: "Thank you," I said eventually.

"For what?" she said.

"For showing me the truth of your trinity," I said, "your holy trinity."

"And what will you do with this truth?"

"I will take it back to Britannia, where there is a different truth."

She said nothing, but caressed me in most gentle kindness. "I will be sorry if you go back," she said. "I have never heard anything good of Britannia."

I said nothing.

"So, why must you go back?" she said. "You are a slave under Rome, and Rome destroyed your city and your family. Why do you even think of going back?"

"Morganus will be at your village tomorrow," I said. "He will be waiting for me."

"I'll tell him that you drowned!" she said. "I'll say that a boat turned over, and your body was washed away. I'm not bound by truth as you are, and everyone here will say what I tell them, and we'll hide you. So hear my words, Ikaros of Apollonis! All day you have been saying that you could be happy here."

"Have I?" I said.

"Yes you have. So why don't you stay? Stay here with me!"

# CHAPTER 18

But I could not stay. Very much of what Elantia had said was true, but she was mistaken in one respect. Rome had indeed taken away my past life, but now– even if I could abandon Morganus and Morgana– I could never abandon Allicanda.

The next morning we returned by boat to the lake village, and just before noon of the day after, I said farewell to Elantia with all the village looking on.

Celts do not hide emotion, not even so powerful a creature as Elantia So her hair was unplaited in sorrow, she begged me to stay and she called on the village to witness that the intimate favours she had granted me were not those of lust, but of affection and esteem. Thus I knew that she cared for me. But I cannot help it if I am pleasing to women. It is the gods who made me that way. It is not my fault and it is indeed a burden.

Finally – in her generosity– Elantia gave benediction upon me.

"I bless you in the name of the father, the mother and the child," she said. "So tread carefully among those whom you choose as companions … rather than me."

Then she kissed me on both cheeks, and I climbed down the ladder into a boat and was rowed to the jetty.

A legionary lightning appeared a while later, with Morganus, the bodyguards and the driver. Morganus got down and walked along the jetty and embraced me.

"Holy Mithras!" he said, "Don't do that again, Greek. I haven't slept."

They were all relieved to see me, and on the journey back to Gesoriacum I told Morganus what I had learned.

After that we had to wait for a ship, and it was another four days until we reached Dubris, and Britannia. Such is the perversity of human nature, that I was pleased to see the great white cliffs. Or perhaps I was thanking the gods, who in their infinite wisdom and mercy had chosen to spare me the worst of sea-sickness on the return voyage? They spared the worst, though I suffered enough to complete the abolition of my love of seafaring.

With delays for weather, and waiting for a lightning, we finally arrived back at the Twentieth Legion's fort three weeks after we had left. We found Londinium full of anticipation of the governor's races at the stadium, and we reported to the principia of the fort. There we found that the legate Africanus had taken the field, with five cohorts of legionaries, plus a greater number of auxiliaries and a wing of one thousand Batavian cavalry.

We learned this from the camp prefect, Secundus Casca Turilius. In theory he was third in command of the Twentieth, after the legate and senior tribune, but Turilius was a caretaker, not a fighting soldier. He received us in his office, and was typical of camp prefects in being an elderly super-veteran: shrivelled, infirm and bald.

"Africanus marched three days ago, with the cavalry," he said. "The infantry went two weeks before, to join men of the Second and Fourteenth, to surround the Regni kingdom and await orders. He left you this."

Turilius waved a finger, and a clerk passed a scroll to Morganus.

"It's for you," he said, "you and your Greek." He sucked at his teeth. "It's all good!" he said. "They moved so fast in Rome, that Africanus got his written permission four days ago, to enter the Regni kingdom, and arrest that scum of a druid!"

Then, Turilius looked at me. "Give *him* the other one," he said, and the clerk gave me a scroll. It was elaborate and bore the governor's seals. Turilius looked at them and frowned. "Is that really for *him*?" he said.

I was becoming irritated with Turilius. But the clerk spoke up.

"Yes, honoured sir," he said, "the message is for Ikaros of Apollonis, the reader of minds, upon whose good judgement the governor relies."

The clerk looked at me with a minute smile. He was Greek.

Then we went to Morganus's house, where Morgana and the girls were waiting at the door. They kept Roman dignity outside the house, but once we were inside, Morgana instantly challenged Morganus.

"Did he behave?" she said, looking from me him. "Did he stay with you?"

"Yes, lady-my-wife," said Morganus, and for once I allowed a lie. Then, even with the bodyguards looking on, there was Roman delight and Roman tears at our safe return.

So it was some while before Morganus and I could open the message-scrolls given us by Turilius's clerk. We went into the garden to do this, since it was private and there was rare Britannic sunshine. We sat on a bench, broke seals and read.

"Africanus wants *you*," said Morganus, looking at the scroll. "It's addressed to me, as ever, but he wants you with him when they take Maligoterix." Morganus looked at me. "Maligoterix is high druid and Africanus is nervous of what he might do … with magic … he's nervous even with an army behind him."

"Does he say that?" I said.

"Not in plain words, but he's nervous. Who wouldn't be? This is Britannia and the gods of Rome are stretched thin here." He made the bull sign. "Even the Lord Mithras!" He looked at the scroll again. "Africanus says he'll do his duty alone if he must, but he'd prefer to have you there. He says we're to join him at once. He says he'll wait until the kalends of next month – that's a week from now – then he'll go in and take the druid anyway."

I sighed. Nobody would believe that my 'mind-reading' was done without magic. That was bad enough, but now even a hardened old soldier like Africanus thought I was a talisman against druidic powers. How, in the name of the gods, was I supposed to live up to that?

It would not be only Maligoterix who was in hiding among the Regni. There would be a host of druids, gathered in for sanctuary against Rome, and I had no idea what they might contrive together. Perhaps they really did command mystic forces? I was worried and I was distracted, lost in my thoughts.

"Greek!" said Morganus, nudging me. "What does yours say?"

I looked at the scroll. "It's from Petros," I said. "In the name of his grace the governor, and please don't say *gods save his grace*." Morganus frowned.

"Just tell me what he says."

"We must go to Petros at once, on our return from Gaul. We must go before all other duties without exception. He stresses that heavily."

"Is that all?"

"Yes."

"He doesn't say why?"

"No."

So we went to find out. We went with only the bodyguards, to avoid delay in turning out an escort. We left the fort, marched through the east gates of the city, and on to Government House.

For once, there were no formalities. The officer of the governor's guard took us past his sentries, through the great building, and to Petros's office.

There was a deep rumble of voices inside, since the room was full of men. The model of the racing stadium was still there, and the six shaven-heads were here and there, among tables covered with scrolls and tablets. They stabbed fingers at various documents, in loud discussion with tradesmen, who made notes.

I saw Petros arguing with a tall, fat man dressed in elaborate robes, with a crown of laurel leaves on his head, and acolytes at his elbow who nodded at his every word.

"Ah!" said Petros, as we entered. "Most urgent business, your reverence," he said. Then he bowed and turned his back on the fat man, leaving him outraged and furious, as Petros pushed through, took my arm and walked out of the office. Morganus and the bodyguards followed.

"That was the pontifex of the college of augurs," said Petros. "Those who examine the entrails of beasts to predict the future." He looked at me. "They are respected by some but not others. Thus it is said that when two augurs meet unexpectedly on the street, they cannot help but burst out laughing."

Morganus smiled. He liked that.

"The pontifex thinks that he has a central role in the coming races," said Petros, "while I do *not*, and the races are of overwhelming importance to his grace's promotion. They must not frail, and this druidic business comes at the worst of all times. There are senators coming from Rome, to judge how well his grace manages the races … and Britannia."

Then he stopped, found a door and opened it without least regard for doing it himself. "In here," he said. We went in and found an office with scribes at work. "Out!" said Petros, and they ran.

Then Petros looked at the bodyguards. "Outside, lads," said Morganus, and they saluted, left and closed the door.

I looked at Petros, He had aged. The worry on his shoulders was enormous. He drew breath, and turned to me.

"First, what of the trinity cult? What did you find out in Gaul?"

I told him, and he did not know what to make of it.

"Harmless?" he said. "The cult is harmless?"

"In Gaul, certainly," I said.

"But this is Britannia," he said, "and here there is great danger." He looked at me. "Now listen, and do not trouble to look into my mind, because I shall tell you everything." He paused as a horse does before a jump. Then: "Know this!" he said. "Know that I am in regular communication with the high druid, Maligoterix. We correspond by pigeons and we do this to feel the pulse of each other's power. It is a political process, whereby each side manoeuvres to avoid total war in Britannia. Do you understand?"

"To *avoid* total war?" I said. "I thought that was what Maligoterix wanted."

"You are wrong," he said. "He believes that whatever the outcome of total war, Rome would abandon all restraint, and kill him and all remaining druids, thereby extinguishing his faith forever. I have assured him that he is entirely correct in this belief, and he therefore says that he does not want total war."

"Do you believe him?" I said.

"No," he said. "Maligoterix is infinitely cunning and may be deceiving me."

"So what *does* he want?" I said, "And what does he say about the trinity cult? Are they not entwined? The trinity and the druids?"

"I do not know," he said. "He will not discuss the trinity and I do not read minds."

"Ah," I said. "You want me to meet Maligoterix?"

"Yes," he said. "And in time, I will explain how this can be done. But first I want to you meet Felemid the merchant."

"Why?"

"Because Maligoterix mentioned him, as an example of a powerful Celt who … *might be brought from the dark into the light* … Those were his words."

My heart jumped, and my expression must have shown it.

"No!" said Petros, "We cannot arrest him. Felemid is a citizen of the broad stripe, and Roman law applies. Could you even *imagine* going to court on the testimony of a druid? Written on a parchment strip? Taken from a pigeon's leg?"

"Impossible," I said. "What do you expect to learn from Felemid?"

"Anything that might bear on what Maligoterix is saying."

"Especially about the trinity cult?"

"Especially about *anything!* Anything at all. You are the mind-reader. Go and read Felemid's mind! You have every imaginable authority to do it, long since given to you by myself. I am informed that he has left the city. Go and find him! Go and question him! Do it now! I have a thousand other things to do and his grace's promotion comes first."

So, Morganus and I went to Felemid's house to ask after him. We took directions from a doorkeeper at Government House and set off. It was a long walk from Government House, and we passed several quite excellent wine shops. But I could feel Morganus's eyes burning into the back of my head even as I looked. The streets were even more full than usual, with rural people – arrived for the coming races – wandering around, gaping at the huge buildings. And there were street vendors yelling loudly, with stalls set up on street corners, offering little plaster models, in lurid colours, of racing chariots and busts representing famous drivers. The street-crowds on the Via Principalis were so thick that we marched with two bodyguards ahead and two behind so that Morganus and I were not jostled.

Felemid's house was huge: a whole city block rising to four levels, and with the usual three entrances at the front: a citizen entrance, a trade entrance and a slave entrance. The citizen entrance, in the centre, dwarfed the others. It had a pair of oaken gates between granite pillars under a marble pediment of sculpture, depicting the conquest of Britannia by Emperor Claudius. A host of brass trimmings was burnished like gold, and the effect was rich, but garish, so I could see that no Greek had been involved in the design. The other doors were small, plain and functional.

So the house was very grand, and a slave in a tunic of the house stood at the door to save citizen visitors the trouble of knocking, which he did with his knuckles, while going up and down in repeated obeisance. The doors opened, and a doorkeeper with well-dressed hair emerged in a full length robe. He took one look at Morganus, bowed low, and clapped hands to summon others.

"May I know your pleasure, O great and victorious sir?" he asked, as more slaves emerged: six of them, with the look of farm boys. They were suntanned and muscular, and while they were respectful, they did not have the abysmal servility of household slaves, bred up to a lifetime of pleasing their masters. None the less, they stood in line and bowed to Morganus.

"I am Leonius Morganus Felix Victrix," said Morganus to the doorkeeper, "and I need to see your master. I need to see him at once. So where is he?"

"O great and victorious sir," said the doorkeeper, "my master is gone away, but if you would honour the house by entering, then full explanation will be given by my superiors."

So we went in, and were led to the atrium— the business centre of a Roman house. It was large and gaudy, and crammed with gilded statues, urns and vases and silken drapes. In Roman style, the atrium was open to the sky at the centre, where the roof was shaped to run rain water into bronze spouts in the shape of dolphins, sending a dozen little streams into a rectangular pool below. The pool – like the atrium itself – was formed of marble blocks, and the pool was full of priceless red fish brought from China.

I thought of the lamprey pool in Scapula's house, and much preferred this one, even if the purity of the marble was spoiled by the cramming and jamming of ornaments around it, almost hiding its edges. Or perhaps I am a snob?

Someone had run ahead of us, because as we entered the atrium, three more slaves stood waiting and bowing. The one in the centre was a man in middle years, expensively dressed. On either side stood a serving girl holding a golden tray: one with a wine flask and goblets, one with neat little cakes. I was fascinated to see the skill with which the girls could bow, and yet spill nothing from their trays. And I was pleased to see the wine flask. But then I looked around, and listened, and even before the senior slave spoke, I noted the absence of any sounds of life from within the house, and guessed that the dozen or so slaves in the atrium might be the only life in the house, when normally there might be hundreds of slaves in the home of so rich a man as Felemid.

"O most honoured and victorious sir," said the senior slave, "by whose military trappings I see you to be the …"

"Enough!" said Morganus. "Who are you and where is your master?"

The man gulped and stopped dead in his formulaic utterances.

"Ah … Ah … I am Banovix of Alpes, honoured sir. I am assistant major domus, and my master? He is gone to his properties in the north."

"Not to his villa?" said Morganus "Are you sure he hasn't gone there?"

"No, victorious sir," said Banovix. "He has gone north."

Morganus looked at me and nodded: the sign for me to take over.

"Why has he left Londinium?" I asked. "Your master is consul of the provincial senate, and the governor's races are coming."

Banovix looked at me, calculated my status, and replied. "Your worship," he said, fastidious in his choice of title, "a conjunction of events has occurred. Thus my master has urgent business in the north, at the same time as a noble senator is coming from Rome to attend the races, bringing a large retinue of followers. Therefore my master – in his patriotic generosity – has offered this house as accommodation for the noble senator, for the duration of his time in Londinium, and free of all cost."

"When did your master leave?" I said. "And where are the slaves of the household?"

Banovix bowed again. "Your worship, the master and his chosen slaves departed yesterday leaving only we few and a house guard." He looked at the farm boys. "The rest are on loan to friends of the master."

Those last words stabbed. They hurt. They hurt with great pain.

*On loan? On loan to friends of the master?*

I hated Felemid. I wanted to kill him. I feared that he had already done as he threatened. I was in such fear that I could not ask the question which filled my mind like a monster. So I asked around it.

"Of the slaves," I said, "who went with your master? Who was sold? And who is on loan to other masters?"

Banovix shuffled in awkwardness. "With regret, your worship," he said, "I do not know, at least not in full."

"Is there no list?" I said. "Are there no records? Slaves are valuable property, especially exotics. Look at me! Surely you know!"

Banovix wrung his hands in fear. I suppose I was a figure of terror, with Morganus and the bodyguards behind me.

"All records went with the master and the accountants," he said. "The master is very strict with records. He guards them carefully. He keeps them close."

"But surely you know what he did with the exotics?" I said. "Doesn't your master have some special Greek boys? Surely you know where they are?"

"Yes, yes!" said Banovix. "The Greek boys went with the master. I am sure of that."

Then I fell silent. Morganus looked at me, puzzled. Everyone looked at me. So I took a breath and gathered my courage, and asked the question.

"Where is the exotic Allicanda?" I said. "You must know about her. She'd be worth millions if ever she came up for sale. What about her? Where is she?"

He gasped, he raised hands in supplication and he fell to his knees. So I imagine that the look on my face was ugly, and he probably feared for his life.

"Your worship," he said, "most honoured sir." He grovelled before me. "I swear by all the gods and goddesses ... I swear on my eyes and limbs ... I swear on everything sacred ... that I truly do not know where she is."

# CHAPTER 19

There was a battle at the first mansione on the Great North Road. It was a savage battle with many killed on each side.

Morganus and I were there, acting on best judgement– which meant guesswork. We knew that Felemid and a retinue of slaves were ahead of us, and we judged – guessed – that he would take the Great North Road and not go across country. We likewise judged – hoped – that he would take Allicanda with him. Morganus at least was sure of that. We talked as we set out, mounted, from the legionary fort, with the bodyguards and an escort of legionary cavalry. It had to be legionaries because all the Batavians had gone with Africanus, which was a pity since Batavians were miraculous horsemen, while legionaries were merely efficient.

We took the military road that ran through green Britannia. Morganus and I rode side-by-side, with hooves rumbling, equipment jingling, and the standard-bearer in front. At least the sun was shining. But I was sunk in misery, because we had to go at the trot, not the gallop, to spare the horses in case the chase was a long one.

Eventually, Morganus leaned towards me.

"He won't have done that vile thing to her," he said. "Because he was saving that as a threat, or as revenge if we moved against him, and we haven't done that because we were in Gaul."

"But he might see that as a move against him," I said.

"How could he?" said Morganus.

"I don't know," I said, "he just might."

"Listen, Greek," he said, "I won't tell you to cheer up, or to face your front, or anything like that, because I know how afraid you are. I'd be the same if it was my lady or my girls. But just leave it to Sylvanus and his lads to go round those – places – to see if she's in one of them, and take her out, if she is."

The pain came again. It came in waves and wrenched my insides. I never knew that worry could inflict muscular spasms. But it did, and there was much indeed to worry about. Thus we could not even concentrate entirely on finding Felemid and Allicanda, because soon we would have to turn around and go back the way we had come, to be with Africanus before he went into the Regni kingdom. I could see how a multitude of worries turn a man grey, as they had done to Petros of Athens.

But the gods were kind in one respect, because we found Felemid at the first mansione, which we reached as the sun was setting. Like all the Britannic mansiones it was fortified with high walls, and leased to contractors who paid a fee to the provincial treasury for the right to sell their services to travellers. So the stations were run for profit and guarded by auxiliaries, who were cheaper than legionaries but notoriously unfit, since they lived fat and easy with no route marches or heavy drill.

We rode forward, towards the main gates, just as torches were lit and the gates were about to be closed for the night. But not on that night. Not with our cavalry centurion yelling out Morganus's name.

"Give honour! Give honour to Leonius Morganus Fortis Victris!"

That brought the auxiliaries running, it swung open the gates, and brought out the mansione officials and clerks, holding lanterns. It also brought out the wineshop girls, the ostlers and the cooks. So the courtyard was full of horses and people. It was a standard mansione courtyard, surrounded by buildings including a bath house, stables and an accommodation block. But also there was a line of heavy wagons with hooped-over canvas hoods, and even some tents set up beside them The wagons and tents were full of people, who looked out, peering and respectful in the manner of slaves. They were Felemid's slaves, the chosen ones that had gone with him. They bobbed and bowed in the torchlight and shadows, but made no chatter. They kept looking at the accommodation block, which was on two levels with a line of windows and a tiled roof.

Then Morganus shouted at the mansione officials. "Is Felemid here? Gentius Civilis Felemidus? Consul of the Britannic Council. Is he here?"

"Yes, honoured sir," said the senior-most official, and the others nodded and looked at the accommodation block. "We have the privilege of his presence, and we…"

But Morganus shouted again. "Centurion, place your men!" He pointed at the accommodation block. "Guards on all doors! Guards on the main gates!" Then he dismounted. "You," he said to the bodyguards, "with me!" Then he looked at me. "Well," he said. "Are you coming?"

I was out of the saddle and beside him as he marched forward. But then we stopped.

We stopped because there was Felemid. There he was, the man himself.

He came out of the accommodation block with two men beside him holding torches. They were two of the knife-men we had seen at his villa. Felemid was in a travelling cloak and boots, and he smiled and came close.

"Honoured Morganus!" he said. "Worshipful Ikaros! It is always a pleasure to see you, but why are you here? Is there some urgent matter?" He looked around. "There is a dining place over there." He shrugged. "The wine is not good, but it *is* wine, and perhaps we could talk in there?" He smiled again. "Out of the night cold."

Morganus looked at me. "All yours," he said.

"Where is Allicanda?" I cried. Indeed, I yelled it into his face, and in my anger I uttered such words as betrayed the Stoic discipline of my upbringing. "You piece of filth!" I said. "I'll have your life if you've done anything with her!"

I stepped forward. I wanted to choke him, throttle him. But Morganus grabbed my arm.

"Steady, Greek," he said. "If she's here, she's safe."

"Of course she is here!" said Felemid. "If I might speak to my followers, I shall send for her."

He smiled again and said something softly and rapidly to his knife-men. He said it in Celtic, they nodded, and one ran off towards the block.

Morganus frowned for a second, as he struggled with Felemid's words. Then:

"Stop him!" said Morganus, to the bodyguards, pointing at the knife-man who had run off, "two of you get him! Two stand fast."

He saved his life, and probably mine too, with that order, because there was great confusion in the half-light, as Felemid himself ran off, and two of the bodyguards chased the first knife-man.

But the other knife-man drew steel and came at Morganus, in a professional killer's crouch with blade held low and the left hand forward in defence. He moved slippery fast, caught Morganus by surprise, knocked him down and drew back the knife to stab him. I tried to block the blade, but was knocked sideways as one of the bodyguards charged, hit the knife-man with a heavy shoulder, threw him staggering back; then the bodyguard chopped with his sword. The knife-man grunted as his right hand was half-severed, and his knife fell to the ground.

But, incredibly, the knife-man knelt with easy grace, snatched the knife with his *left* hand, leapt up, spun round and stabbed the bodyguard precisely under the cheek-guard of his helmet, plunging his blade in a death stroke into the blood vessels of the throat. Then the other bodyguard was on him, and running a sword through the knife-man's body. The knife-man grunted again, but as the bodyguard pulled out his sword for a second stroke, the knife-man struck, again aiming at under the cheek guard and *again* inflicting a death wound.

Then, as the two bodyguards staggered and fell. Morganus was up, and thrusting sword into the knife-man. I did the same with a sword dropped by one of the bodyguards. It was the first time I had held a sword since the days of my freedom in Apollonis, and a great anger was still upon me, so in the absence of Felemid, I poured out my fury in repeated strokes. I stabbed even as the knife-man fell to the ground.

"Greek!" cried Morganus. "Leave him! He's done! There's more coming!"

He was right. The battle was only beginning. It was confused, and dark, with slaves howling and officials shouting and the bar girls screaming, and horses rearing in terror, and torches falling to the ground, and a body of men – the main strength of Felemid's knife-men – running out of the accommodation block. Even in the dimness I saw that they had shields as well as the big knives. They had round bucklers.

"To me!" cried Morganus. "Standard-bearer to me! Form up on the standard!"

That should have brought order from chaos, and the legionary cavalrymen and mansione auxiliaries tried to obey. But the knife-men were among them, stabbing and butting with shields, and legionaries and auxiliaries were going down. Then, one of the knife-man yelled a command and they charged, all together at the trot, directly towards the cavalry standard and Morganus in his swan-crest helmet. They came in a line with shields raised. They did not clump together shoulder-to-shoulder, but came on with a careful pace between each man, giving themselves room to fight. They were fearfully efficient.

"For Rome and the gods of Rome!" cried Morganus.

"For Rome and the gods of Rome!" cried our legionaries and auxiliaries, but there was fear in the shout, and the knife-men were breaking through our lines, and it then came to sword strokes even for me, even for Morganus, and even for the two remaining bodyguards. We all fought to exhaustion, and we fought because there was nowhere to run, and no relief coming.

So we fought hard, and finally we won. But we won only by weight of numbers, since the auxiliaries were unfit, while our cavalrymen were trained to fight mounted, not on foot. Thus later, when we counted the dead, we found that there had been only sixteen of the knife-men, against over fifty of us, including Morganus, the bodyguards and myself. Also our men, apart from me, had the huge advantage of body armour, while the knife-men had only their shields. None the less, they had killed thirty-two of us, leaving none merely wounded, since they finished every man that went down, such was their skill at arms. Then they fought to the last and none would have survived, because our men took revenge by methodically stabbing any of the knife-men who showed signs of life when the battle was done.

But Morganus stopped them.

"Don't kill 'em!" he cried. "I want prisoners for questioning!"

So the killing ended, and we stood, shaking with effort. But Morganus picked up one of the round shields the knife-men had used,.

"Look at this, Greek!" he said. "This is a gladiator's shield, and that's totally illegal outside the arena. Seriously illegal! Anyone using this beyond the games gets crucified or thrown to the beasts!"

I looked and saw the gaudy decoration. "Gladiators?" I said. "That explains why they fought so well. We saw them at Felemid's villa, didn't we?"

"Yes," he said. Then he cursed: "Jupiter Maximus, Father of gods! Where is he?" He shouted, as loud as he could, "Where's Felemid? Who's seen him?"

There was silence. Nobody knew.

"Guard the gates," he cried. "Nobody gets out."

"Good," I said, "let's look for him. And let's look for Allicanda!"

"Of course," he said. "Of course we will, but we've got sacred duty first: duty to the fallen."

I nodded. He was right, even though I was burning inside to find Allicanda – if she was even here. But men had died, their spirits were wandering loose, and the gods would be watching.

"All ranks give respect!" cried Morganus. So the legionaries and auxiliaries gathered our dead and laid them in a straight row, with the two bodyguards to the right of the line, in the place of honour. Then they laid out the dead knife-men in another row, at the feet of the Roman dead, and they dragged the three surviving gladiators to one side, under guard. When they were done, and with the horde of slaves gaping and looking, Morganus raised his voice again.

"Form ranks!" he cried. "Off helmets!"

So the Romans stood bareheaded in their lines and chanted the responses to an army prayer as Morganus declaimed it. Then they all made the bull sign as Morganus gave a further prayer, this time to Mithras the soldiers' god.

I stood in respectful silence during the army prayer, as I did not know the responses. But during the prayer to Mithras, I thought it proper to raise arms and ask blessing upon the lost, in the name of Apollo. It is only a short prayer, and I spoke softly so as not to offend Mithras.

Finally, Morganus approached the two fallen bodyguards, knelt beside them, and raised each man's right hand and kissed it.

"Farewell my bulldogs," he said. "You'll be laid to rest in full armour, with swords at your sides. Those are my orders, and may the gods take you safe to the next world."

Then he got up, and looked at me. He was a veteran, used to losing comrades, but I could see his sorrow at the death of two exceptionally fine men, who had volunteered to be in his personal service. None the less he was Roman, so he put on his helmet and straightened his back.

"Go on, Greek," he said, "go and look for her. I'll get on with the rest."

I turned to go, but our cavalry centurion stepped forward.

"Honoured sir! Worshipful sir!" he said. "Them three won't last long," he pointed to the remaining three gladiators. "In case you want anything done with them?"

So I ran towards the three dying men, who lay on the stone sets of the courtyard. "Bring lights! Quickly!" I shouted … and then I stopped.

Allicanda was running towards me. She was safe, safe, safe! She ran towards me and I to her, and I seized her and swung her off her feet.

"Oh my lady! Oh my lady!"

"Ikaros! Ikaros! Ikaros!" she cried.

It was joy beyond relief. It was heaven. It was wonderful. I kissed her lips, her brow, her hair, her hands, and she laughed wonderfully, and I saw that her joy was as great as mine, and I think that everyone must have gaped at us, and I saw Morganus smile. But the centurion shouted again.

"Worshipful sir," he said, "one of them's gone and the others are going."

I heard him and could not resist turning away, to look where he stood holding up a torch over the last of the gladiators. If the gods have blessed me with a clever mind, they have also cursed me with a sense of inquiry that others think obsessive.

"I'll be quick," I said to Allicanda. "Very quick." And I kissed her and ran to the centurion. Then I looked, saw, and made a decision.

I ran towards the mansione officials. "Who is a clerk?" I said. They blinked, and they looked at one among them. I grabbed his arm. "Where is your desk?"

"In there," he said, pointing to one of the buildings. So I ran towards it, dragging him after me. Soon, I came back and knelt beside the gladiators. I calmed myself, and spoke gently.

"I am of the faith," I said, and held out my left hand to show the three black spots, while hoping that they understood Latin. They were bleeding to death, they were not fully conscious, and one merely groaned, but the other looked at me. He was the one who had yelled commands to the rest. He was a big man, taller than the rest and had yellow hair like a German. He tried to move his right hand, even as he lay on his back, but he could not manage it, so I helped him. I cradled his head in my arm, raised him up and touched his fingers three times to his left hand, then to his brow, then to his breast. He sighed in contentment, and smiled at me, and we spoke for the few moments that remained until the light left his eyes and the soul left his body. After that, I stood and faced Morganus and Allicanda.

"First of all, the tribes are raising armies. They're taking men from the villages, arming them and sending them north, across country. And Felemid will be gone," I said. "He had a horse waiting by the east gate in case he needed to run."

"Centurion!" cried Morganus.

"Honoured sir?"

"Send gallopers up the road: chase him!"

"Yes, honoured sir!" The centurion ran off, and Morganus looked at me.

"Go on," he said, "what else did you find out?"

I looked down at the gladiators. "These were his bodyguards," I said. "Chosen men: exceptional men and very expensive, because Felemid is afraid the province is heading for fire and sword. And now he is going north to be safe. He's heading for the Briganti kingdom." I looked at Morganus. "Is that a client state?"

"Yes," he said, "a client state under tribal law, with its own ruler: King Brax."

"Well," I said, "according to that gladiator – the yellow-haired gladiator – King Brax is a convert to the trinity, and so was yellow-hair. I saw the dots on his hand and I did this," I held out my left hand to show my own three dots. "It's ink," I said, "so I could pretend to be like him. So he would talk to me."

Morganus shook his head in admiration. "Were they all in the trinity?" he said.

"No," I said, "just yellow-hair and one other."

"Greek," he said, "you did well, but there's much more to be done. We've got to clear up, bury the dead, look after all these slaves in the wagons, and then get on the road to join Africanus. So I'll deal with that, while *you* look after this lady." He looked at Allicanda. "You just take her into the canteen and share a flask."

Then, even though she was a slave and he was a Roman citizen of great rank, he bowed to her. "Madam," he said, "you will be treated with high esteem. You will be escorted to the fort of the Twentieth Legion, where you will stay in my house, protected by my family, who will make you most welcome."

"You are very kind," she said. "I thank you, honoured sir."

"I can do no less," he said, "for the beloved lady of my brother."

She bowed to him and then looked at me. "There," she said. "Why can't you speak like *that*, Ikaros of Apollonis?"

I wondered if I was being mocked. But she smiled, and we did go to the canteen, where wine was served, and I got rid of the canteen staff so that I could sit and hold her close.

"What happened to you?" I said. "First of all, did he ... Felemid ... did he ..."

"No!" she said. "I was never given to the whore-masters. I think that he said it to hurt you, to punish you because you would not do what he wanted. So perhaps he never even meant it."

Perhaps. But the mere thought of it shuddered me with horror and I held her closer still, and she held me and I never touched the wine, because I did not need it. Thus we sat a while, in deep contentment, with all the bustle and shouting of Morganus's work coming from outside.

But then I began to say the wrong things.

"You're mine now," I said. "Felemid is guilty of high treason, his property will be seized by the state, and I can buy you. I easily have enough money."

She stiffened. "You will *buy* me, as a slave?" she said. "Buy me? As a *thing*?"

"Forgive me," I said, "I never meant that, and I am in dread of what might happen to us. There could be a war coming. There might be total war between the tribes and the Romans."

She sighed and relaxed a little. "I know," she said. "Felemid spoke about it. He said that he wanted to move to Rome, and had prepared, but it was time to get away from Londinium to a place of safety: the Briganti client state. He said we'd be safe there."

"He said this to you?"

"No, to his Greek boys– and they spoke to me." She shrugged. "They like me."

That made me wonder. It made me foolishly jealous. "How much do they like you?" I said, which in retrospect was an extremely dangerous thing to say because of the response that it prompted.

"And how much do women like *you*?" she said. She said that and I cursed and damned myself a thousand times for leading myself into such a trap. I cursed and damned and could not look into her eyes. So I looked down. I looked down … and she instantly guessed.

"You've been with someone," she said, and I could not lie to her. So I spoke of Elantia.

"She was a good woman," I said, "a decent and honourable woman."

It was true, but I was mad to say it. So Allicanda moved away from me, and I could not bear the expression on her face. She was betrayed, and I had betrayed her.

"A good woman?" she said. "Was she better than me?"

I said nothing. I could think of nothing to say.

She shook my arm. "I asked if she was better than me."

I did not answer, because there was a renewed shouting of orders, and a movement of men, wheels and horses, and Morganus came in with the two surviving bodyguards and the cavalry centurion. He looked at us and frowned. He could see the trouble between us. Anybody could have seen it. But there were things to be done.

"Greetings, lady," he said, then looked at me. "You were right, Greek. Felemid had a horse by the east gate and he's gone, and now we must join Africanus, while this officer…" he looked at the centurion, "this officer and his men will escort the lady Allicanda to the fort."

She nodded at Morganus, but she did not look at me.

Morganus and I spoke later as we rode through the night, with half of the surviving cavalrymen. We were so tired that it was hard to keep our saddles, and it was dark and we had to trust the horses to follow the road. But the need was urgent. At least we had fresh horses from the mansione stables.

"We'll have to forget Felemid for the moment," said Morganus. "If he's in the Briganti client state, he's under their laws and we can't touch him." He thought about that. "Unless, of course, Africanus has permission to go into *any* client state." He looked at me. "*Has* he got that? I can't remember."

"No," I said. "It's only the Regni state, and that's a pity because I'm sure Felemid knows a lot. About the trinity, druids– everything."

"Maligoterix will know more," said Morganus. "He's the centre of all this, and Africanus will go after him once he's got *you* with him."

I groaned at that. "I'm not a magic shield," I said. "I don't know what the druids can do if there are lots of them. How am I supposed to protect a whole Roman army?"

"I don't know," he said. "Just stop grumbling and do what you can. You're always grumbling and muttering." He was weary and annoyed. "And why don't you watch what you say to Allicanda? You should thank the gods for that woman. She's gorgeous, beautiful. No wonder she's an exotic. You don't know how lucky you are."

"Yes. I do," I said.

"Then what, in the name of holy Mithras did you say to her? She wouldn't speak to you when we left. She just turned her back."

Great sorrow fell upon me as I remembered that. Then I must have muttered about Elantia and Morganus heard me.

"The girl at the lake village?" he said. "You've already told me about her. You said it made you guilty."

"I never said that!"

"Yes, you did!" Then he turned in the saddle and looked at me and cursed. "Pluto, god of the underworld!" he said. "You didn't tell Allicanda about *her,* did you?"

I said nothing. We rode on. A horse stumbled and whinnied, behind us in the dark. The moon came out. The road and the countryside was black.

Morganus sighed. "Greek," he said, "you're the cleverest man I've ever met in all my travels. You may well be the cleverest man in all the world. But sometimes you are gods-damned stupid!"

# CHAPTER 20

We rode down the Great North Road towards Londinium and the Twentieth's fort. There, since we were falling from the saddle with exhaustion, we slept for some hours because otherwise we should have been incapable of any further action. Our plan was then to report to Petros before pressing on down the Great South Road towards the Regni kingdom and Africanus.

In the event, we sent a written report to Petros, since we were assured that Londinium was bursting with people come for the governor's races, such that Petros would be tearing his hair with preparations and organisation. I wrote the report and Morganus signed it, suggesting that Petros – acting in the name of the governor – might ask permission from Rome to enter the Briganti kingdom. Soon after, four of us – just two bodyguards now –were on the seats of a lightning, with the driver thrashing the poor horses to get speed out of them.

With stops to change teams, it took us six hours to reach Noviomagus Reginorum, the nearest town to the palace of King Cogidubnus III – ruler of the Regni tribe – where Maligoterix was hiding. Noviomagus was a *civitatis capital*: a Roman device to turn free tribesmen into regulated townsfolk. There was one for each tribe, intended as centres of government. But most were empty, weed-grown failures, since the tribesmen would not live in them. However, Noviomagus was an actual grid pattern, well populated town, since the Regni had long since accepted Roman ways ... or so it seemed.

We left the lightning in Noviomagus, at the town's garrison fort, and took horses, since although there was a good Roman road to Cogidubnus's palace, we would have to cross country to find Africanus's camp. We were given directions by the garrison, but in fact Africanus found us first – or rather, his Batavian cavalry did – as our horses plodded across a vast green plain of rolling hills that ran to the horizon on all sides. The view was magnificent, the weather fine, and for once even I was pleased to be in Britannia. And then:

"Here they come," said Morganus as a company of horse came over one of the hills. "He'll have scouts out in all directions." He smiled. "You can trust Africanus for that!"

I was once an officer of horse, so I watched in approval as the Batavians came on in fine style: fifteen troopers, five abreast behind their dragon standard and centurion, all going a steady trot. They were magnificent horsemen, their formation-keeping was splendid and I admired them.

Then they were alongside of us and reining in, and the troopers lowering lances in respect and their officer throwing out his arm in salute. To us, he was a new face: a smiling youngster whom we had not met before. But he recognised Morganus by the crest on his helmet.

"Hail to the swan feathers!" he said. "Do I have the honour of addressing Leonius Morganus Fortis Victrix, Father of the Twentieth, Chief Priest and Hero of the Roman Army?"

"I am Morganus," said Morganus, and then ... true amazement followed, because the centurion looked at me.

"And do I have the pleasure to address Ikaros of Apollonis?" he said. "The Greek who is famous for his love of horses? And who rides so well that he must surely have Batavian blood in his veins?"

His men cheered and waved their lances, and I blushed because I never knew I had such reputation, and I was never so flattered in all my life.

"All hail to Morganus! All hail to his follower Ikaros!" cried the officer, turning to his men. "All …"

"*HAIL!*" cried his men in a great, barking shout.

"All …"

"*HAIL!*"

"All …"

"*HAIL!*"

It was a joyful moment, and I forgave the youngster for reducing me to the rank of *follower*. After all, he could have said *slave*. Or perhaps I am too sensitive in these matters.

Then we were taken the few miles to the entrenched and palisaded camp, well placed on rising ground, where Africanus's expeditionary force was based: some nine thousand legionaries and auxiliaries, a thousand Batavians, and even a siege train of engineers and artillerymen. It was a very large camp, where everything stood in regulated Roman lines, with Roman right angles, and everything was in its standard and proper place, so anybody could find anything without even thinking– because every other Roman camp in all the world was laid out on exactly the same plan.

We rode in through the *portus principalis* – the main gate – with legionaries saluting, and found an organised cacophony of noise with men drilling everywhere. I had never before seen a Roman field camp on active service and I was amazed at the force, vigour and relentless nature of training that was under way. It was an army where not one man was allowed to lounge at ease or do anything that was not purposeful.

We passed a century of legionaries – six ranks of ten men – practising at the stabbing posts: six-foot wooden pillars embedded into the ground. One rank leapt forward, shields leading, slammed shields into posts, and stabbed the post repeatedly with wooden practice swords.

"Ugh! Ugh! Ugh!" they chanted, then they wheeled about, ran back through the ranks to the rear of the formation, and the next rank came forward. "Ugh! Ugh! Ugh!" They kept right on doing that, rank after rank, again and again, over and over. They were already dripping with sweat, their centurion bellowing and waving his vine staff to keep them at it.

Other centuries were trotting round the inside perimeter of the entrenchments, heavily laden in full marching kit, chanting as they went. Others – with full armour and shields – were labouring over a practice run of purpose-made ditches and ponds, and obstacles that could not be climbed except through teamwork. Still others were running races in six-man teams, and each team carrying a tree trunk on their shoulders.

All of this exercise was incessant, and some of the men looked as if they were ready to drop, and yet they did not.

Morganus saw me looking.

"That's the way we do it, Greek," he said, "and that's why it's only the *first* charge of barbarians that's dangerous. They get tired after that and the battle goes to those who don't get tired. It's no good being a gymnasium beast, with big muscles for heavy weights, because it's stamina that counts. You have to come back again and again, and never give up. And then there's *that!*"

He pointed across the camp to the field kitchens, where stove chimneys were smoking and food cooking. We could even smell it. "Him that feeds well, fights well!" he said. "We train the men to exhaustion, and then fill their bellies right up!" He nodded. "That's the Roman way."

It was. It was indeed. Who knows that better than an Apollonite officer who saw his city destroyed by the Roman army?

We were taken straight to the principia, which was a huge tent within its own separate entrenchments, and guarded by men who did a brief spell at this duty before being sent to run, jump and train, and be replaced by others fresh from training. In a Roman field camp there were no idle guardsmen in polished armour and immaculate boots.

Morganus, the bodyguards and I dismounted and found Africanus was waiting for us. He was standing outside the big tent with his staff officers: his tribunes, senior centurions and cavalry commanders, and the specialists: artillery, transport, medics and the rest. There were nearly twenty of them, and I was astonished to see Africanus smile! The aged, wrinkled, scarred old face, with its milky eyes, actually smiled at me. So I got the smile, but Morganus got the formal welcome.

"You are most welcome, first javelin!" said Africanus, and clasped hands with Morganus.

"Ready to do duty, honoured and noble sir!" said Morganus. "Myself and my comrade."

Africanus led us into the tent, where there were camp tables set up and documents laid out –absolutely no cakes and wine – and a series of blackened boards, each a yard square, set up on easels. They were covered in writing and diagrams in white chalk. Africanus went to these, and his officers clustered around us, all holding their helmets in their hands.

"First, tell us what you learned in Gaul," said Africanus.

"My comrade will speak for us," said Morganus, and Africanus nodded approval. Another gracious gesture. So I gave my report. I gave it in full. Then, when I was done:

"It's the druids, then," said Africanus, and a shudder went round this cluster of elite soldiers. "The druids and this gods-forsaken trinity?"

"Yes, honoured and noble sir," I said.

"So," said Africanus, "the sooner the better, for us to cut into this Regni tumour, find Maligoterix … and run a sword through him!"

That brought cheers, then Africanus pointed to the blackened boards. "See here!" he said. "This is how it will be done. See where our cavalry are placed entirely around the Regni king's palace? That's where Maligoterix is hiding, and with so many horsemen, I have made sure that neither he nor anyone else has been in or out since we made camp here. My patrols are everywhere, night and day." He moved to another board. "See here! Infantry placements once we go forward. We've seen no sign of formed bodies of Celtic foot, so our legionaries and auxiliaries are mainly a precaution. But I will have them ready if needed."

He paused, and looked at me. "And so we come to the special nature of this expedition." He looked at me and said nothing more, and I was astounded to see doubt in his face.

Looking around I saw that it was the same for all present, and I realised two things in that instant. First, that all these officers of the all-conquering, world-dominating, super-fit, superbly-equipped Roman army were afraid of the druids. Second, that it was my job to deal with their fear. So I did my best.

"Honoured and noble sir," I said to Africanus, "may I speak plainly of the druids?"

"You may, and you must," he said.

So I looked around at the assembled officers.

"Know then," I said, "that the druids have great powers." That was a bad start. Most of them – including Africanus – shuddered and made the bull sign. "But," I said, "his honour the first javelin," I bowed to Morganus, "his honour and I have met Maligoterix and we have the measure of his powers and we know how they can be opposed."

That was better. I got an appreciative murmur for that.

"So," I said, "the druids have been the spiritual power of the Britannic Celts since ancient times. They have such power among the Celts, that they can make and break kingdoms, start wars, and even stand between armies to *stop* wars. Their power to do this comes from two main sources. They know what everyone is doing because they have spies everywhere."

"Even now?" said Africanus. "Even under Rome?"

"Yes, honoured and noble sir," I said. "Even now! And they send this knowledge up and down the land, tied to the legs of pigeons. So even with Roman roads and the imperial post, the druids talk to each other faster than we can."

"Does that mean that Maligoterix knows we are here?" said Africanus.

"Honoured and noble sir," I said, "he will have known before you first set out!"

There was another murmur at that. A murmur of fear.

"You said they had two sources of power," said Africanus. "What is the second?"

"That is a personal power that seems like magic, but is not," I said.

"Hmm …" said Morganus, in doubt, and unfortunately everyone heard him.

"It is *not* magic!" I said. "It is what we of Apollonis called hypnotism. We used it to treat illness of the mind and to dull the pain of surgery. It is the ability to cast a person into a trance, and place suggestions into that person's mind. We used it beneficially, but the druids use it to make a man, or woman, do anything they choose. Even things that are evil."

"So it *is* magic," said Africanus.

"Yes," said Morganus, and I chose not to argue, since argument was doomed to fail. Also, Morganus spoke on, "It is magic but my Greek comrade can defeat it."

"Ah!" said everyone,

"How?" said Africanus, "How do you defeat magic?"

"By recognising that it exists," I said. "And by treating the druids with extreme care. Thus, no man should ever be alone with a druid. Not ever! Maligoterix himself is fearfully dangerous, because he is tremendously adept at hypnotism. So, there should always be several men facing each druid. Four or five at least. This is most important."

Africanus nodded and looked at his officers. "Let this be given as an order to all ranks!" he said.

"Yes, honoured and noble sir!" they said.

"Good," I said. "But there is another defence, and the army must know it."

"Which is?" said Africanus.

"It is this," I said. "Hypnotism works best on those who do not know that it exists. I works badly, if at all, on a man who is warned and who fights it."

"Yes!" said Morganus. "The Greek can fight it. I've seen him do it. They can't bend his mind to their will."

"So," I said, "any man who even suspects that the druids are attempting to use hypnotism, should defend himself by reciting anything that is powerful and good."

"The army battle anthem works," said Morganus.

"Ah!" said Africanus. "Well done, Greek! You have given us a drill. It shall be proclaimed through the ranks."

He smiled, Morganus smiled, they all smiled. They smiled because they were Roman, and a Roman is happy when he has a drill and does not have to think. That was good– but perhaps too good, because then I had to disagree with Africanus.

"I shall, of course, lead the vanguard," he said. "I am not too old to mount a horse, so I shall ride with the Batavians and be first to face these supernatural enemies– these druids!"

There was foot drumming and cheering at that from all the officers.

I chose my words carefully. "Most noble sir," I said. "It is, of course, a matter of honour that no general asks his men to face a peril he would not face himself."

"But?" said Africanus. "I see that the word *but* is approaching."

"*But*, sir," I said, "if – even with all precautions – the druidic power proves irresistible, then we must not allow them to seize control of our commander-in-chief! Let me go forward in your name, because I have faced the druids before and won, and even if I do fall under their power then you will still be able to form other plans, whereas if they control *you*, then all is lost."

That was plain sense, and Africanus had the intelligence to agree. Morganus and I would go with the vanguard, and I was given charge of the document sent from Rome, giving him permission to enter the Regni kingdom. It came in a waterproof leather case with a shoulder sling.

On the very next day, Africanus made his move against the palace of Cogidubnus III. First, before the cavalry could move, the legionaries and auxiliaries had to get into place. They were off at dawn with standards raised, and I saw them go with in their thousands, with nailed boots beating the ground in synchronous rhythm: crunch! Crunch! Crunch! They roared out their marching songs and looked cheerful. But I had doubts, and on the day after when the cavalry moved, I spoke of them to Morganus as we rode out with the column of two hundred Batavians who were to lead the advance. In fact, he spoke before I did.

"Why are you looking glum?" said Morganus. "It's a lovely day, you're on a horse, and we're going to catch Maligoterix. At last!"

"I'm worried about hypnotism," I said.

"Why?" he said. "Every man in the army's been given your drill."

"But will it work?" I said. "I'm not sure it will work for everyone. That's why I warned Africanus."

"Oh, you and your misery," he said, then as we came over a hill, "Ah, just look at that!"

It was the Regni palace. It was some miles off, it was enormous, it was exceedingly beautiful and it stunned our eyes. It had the same awesome dignity as the Parthenon of Athens and it positively shouted Greek design. It was even clad in white marble, doubtless imported at ferocious expense. At the very centre, there was a line of eight fluted columns on top of a flight of broad stairs, beneath a massive portico enclosing sculptures of Celtic deities. That much at least was Britannic, not Mediterranean. With the centre piece, and wings to left and right, the palace was easily two hundred yards across.

It was beautiful, and yet there was even more, because the palace stood beside a river with a harbour – a pretend harbour of marble nymphs and tritons – with little pleasure craft ready for boating. Beyond that, the entire landscape had been worked into a garden, with obelisks, manicured trees and exotic shrubs. Every contrived and elegant feature was in harmony with every other contrived and elegant feature. So perhaps it was just a trifle excessive? But beautiful, none the less.

"That's what you get when you're rich," said Morganus. "The Regni kings have tin, copper, corn and cattle. But it's also what you get when you sell your soul." He waved a hand at the palace. "This is what you get when you're the empire's best boy, and do what the empire tells you. This lot – the Regni – were Romanised before ever we set boot on beach. They'd been trading with us since the time of Caesar the Great, and we'd been sending engineers and builders to make palaces like this." He smiled. "Palaces! And Greeks like you to design them."

Meanwhile, our column deployed into a series of lines, two ranks deep, spread out to deal with any attack that might come out of the palace. The senior officer cantered up beside Morganus, and saluted.

"Honoured sir?" he said, "I'm told that we can expect horsemen to come forward, and that there'll be some guards in there." He pointed at the palace, "Is that right, honoured sir? I know you've been here before."

Morganus nodded. "Yes," he said. "You should have no trouble with them. The client states are not allowed armies: only a small company of horsemen and a house guard." He looked round. "And if there was an army – an illegal army – we'd have seen it by now." He looked round again. "In fact where are they, Greek?" he said. "We're supposed to be facing a tribal rebellion, and this is tribal heartland. So where are their men?"

"Gone north?" I said. "That's what the yellow-haired gladiator said."

"Who knows?" he said, and turned to the officer. "You can expect a dozen or so riders. But that's it. Nothing more."

And he was right. Soon after, a company of horsemen appeared from behind the palace and advanced at the trot. Our commander ordered a halt, and we waited with our horses tossing heads and shuffling hoofs, and the riders patting their necks. We outnumbered these Celtic horsemen so greatly that there was no cause for fear.

So the horsemen came forward in loose formation. They were Celts to the bone– bare-chested, with tattoos, long moustaches and heavy jewellery– and they were well mounted, and armed with swords and spears. The leader came forward and addressed us. He delivered a most strange and disturbing speech. It was strange, because he and his men were afraid and ashamed: I saw that in their faces. Also, while they looked at Morganus, none of them would look at me, and the speech was disturbing because we had arrived without warning, and therefore he should have known nothing about us: not who we were, nor what we wanted.

But: "My master gives greeting!" he said. "The great Lord Cogidubnus welcomes Leonius Morganus Fortis Victrix – spear of the Twentieth Legion, who is under the command of Nonius Julius Sabinus Africanus!"

Then he forced himself to look at me, before swiftly turning away.

"My master also welcomes Ikaros of Apollonis, who sees within the minds of men, and whose own mind cannot be bent to the will of others. Thus my master gives welcome and proclaims that every door in his house is open to you, so that you might seek the fabled person whom you have come to find, and thereby learn … that the fabled person is not here."

# CHAPTER 21

None the less, we searched for *the fabled person*. The Celtic horsemen led us to the main entrance and there they stopped, not dismounting but simply sitting in their saddles, looking round at the Batavians and making no further move. Once again, I thought they seemed embarrassed, even ashamed.

"Come on!" said Morganus. "There's the main door. Let's go in."

So we did, together with a great number of Batavians, who Morganus sent in all directions to open every door and look inside.

"Groups of five, remember?" cried Morganus. "Nobody goes alone! And if you find a druid, then grab him, gag him so he can't speak, and send for me!"

The Batavians ran off, making a great noise, opening and slamming doors, and shouting to one another, and pointing out the wonders they saw, since the palace was full of wonders, with vast rooms, echoing ceilings, wall-paintings, marble floors and granite columns.

I stress that there was not the slightest opposition from the house folk – dozens and dozens of them – and not even from the small corps of Celtic guardsmen, with their fancy armour and swords. These guardsmen stood still, looking at the ground or the ceiling and keeping their hands away from their weapons. But as with the horsemen, there was an oddity of behaviour towards me. Everyone cringed away from me, and clung together and would not meet my eye.

"What is it, Greek?" said Morganus. "Are they afraid of you?"

"Yes," I said. "I think someone has warned them about me. Someone who knows about me."

"You mean your mind-reading?" he said.

"Yes," I said, and I was pierced with the irony that someone – Maligoterix, perhaps – had given exactly the same warnings about me, as I had given about him! In a perverse form, this was as great a compliment as the Batavians praising me as a horseman.

"Enough of this," said Morganus, and grabbed one of the house slaves. "Where's your master?" he said. "Take us to him." He looked at me, then back at the slave. "Tell me, or I'll give you to the Greek!"

Perhaps he was joking, but he was pulling on a mighty lever in that respect, and the slaves fawned and bowed and ushered us forward, and led us to the audience chamber where his majesty was waiting for us with his councillors and chosen ones. There was a considerable number of them, all elaborately dressed, and even at this dire time they were edging forward like the minions that they were, ever seeking to be closest to the king, and to be his most favoured subject.

The audience chamber was an odd mixture of the Roman and the Celtic. Morganus, the bodyguards and I stood beneath a coffered, masonry dome with a round oculus in the top to admit light. This was standard Roman architecture, yet the walls were lined with whole trunks of oak trees, still with their bark, and still bearing boughs with faded brown leaves. Also, while the floor was tiled with a black-and-white check of Roman tiles, the tiles were thickly strewn with rushes.

The king himself – the great lord, Cogidubnus III – stood up from his throne as we entered, and tried to be bold. But he was as frightened as the rest, and was a deeply unimpressive man. He was clumsy, tall and lean, with long hair, a thin beard and a multitude of jewellery: three neck rings, plus bracelets on his arms, and many brooches on his tunics. He had layers of tunics, all differently-coloured and the outer ones slashed to show the colours of those beneath. All this and a Celtic longsword, in a scabbard that clattered with gold chains.

He stood with his councillors around him, staring just over my head to avoid looking me in the eye. He stood and trembled and said nothing.

"Go on, Greek," said Morganus. "This one really is all yours!"

It was indeed, and perhaps I was inspired by the gods, because so much seemed obvious that my words flowed without effort.

"Your majesty," I said, "why do you not ask why we are here, when Roman troops are forbidden to enter your kingdom? Do you not want to see our legal permission?"

Africanus's document was slung over my shoulder in its case, so I patted it. He blinked, and his followers stirred and mumbled to each other. But none of them spoke. So it was time for a serious challenge.

"You do not ask," I said, "because you already know everything."

Then I moved close to Cogidubnus. I moved very close, since Celts do not keep distance, like Greeks or Romans, but stand almost nose-to-nose. "And since you know all about me," I said, "you know that I can see into your mind."

He shivered and clutched at his supporters for comfort.

"I will therefore tell you what has happened, here in your palace." I paused for effect, then spoke. "Maligoterix has been here but is gone. Maligoterix speaks to all the druids of Britannia using pigeons. His spies have warned him – and he warned you – that I am coming with

Morganus and Africanus, and he commanded you to say nothing to me, on pain of damnation in the next world."

He gasped at that, and tapped right hand on left, then brow and breast. All of his councillors did the same. So I performed a piece of theatre.

"But," I said, and placed a finger on his brow, causing a united gasp of horror from the councillors at so outrageous a familiarity towards one of royal blood. "But, you cannot hide what is in your head. Thus I see that you have raised a great army and sent it north, while your house guard and cavalry are ashamed because you told them not to fight, in order to hide your warlike plans."

I paused again, to check that I was correct, and saw Cogidubnus nod slightly.

"Finally," I said, "we come to the greatest secret of all. Where is Maligoterix?"

He trembled. He was in fear of damnation: him and all his councillors.

"Ah!" I said. "I see it written in your mind that Maligoterix has gone north to the realm of King Brax of Brigantia, where your army has also gone, and where he supposes himself to be safe."

Cogidubnus groaned and fell to his knees.

"I did not speak," he said. "I call witness by the holy trinity that I did not speak!" He turned to his followers. "Bear witness!" he said. "The words were stolen from my head by this Greek. You all saw that! I said nothing! It is not my fault!"

There was much more of this. There was hand-wringing, grovelling and tears on all sides. It was embarrassing to see. But that is the power of religion, when driven into the human mind by priests and dogma. Men tremble in fear of their religions. They kill and die for their religions. They do so especially when they believe that only *their* beliefs are true, while all the rest are false.

What nonsense this is. Does Apollo care if occasionally I pray to Athena? Or Athena if I pray to Apollo? Who knows?

Meanwhile, Cogidubnus wallowed in his misery, now profoundly believing that I worked magic. Even Morganus was looking at me awestruck, and that was painful to see in a friend. The two bodyguards were the same, and they all three made the bull sign as I turned to go, and led them out of the audience chamber. Then, outside the palace on the steps, with the Batavians around us and the horses waiting, Morganus spoke.

"What now, Greek?" he said. He always said that when our investigations uncovered something. But the awestruck look was still there.

"I did it by reason and logic," I said, trying to explain, "and it was only a guess that Maligoterix has gone to Brigantia. Believe me. Please believe me."

"If you say so," he said, but he made the bull sign again. "So, what now?"

"We tell Africanus that this entire expedition is wasted," I said, "and that it is time to ask Rome for another legion if Rome wants to keep Britannia."

"Is it that bad?" he said.

"Yes," I said, "if every other client state is behaving like this one."

"We'll have to tell the governor," he said. "I mean Petros. It's serious politics to ask for another legion."

He frowned and shook his head. He shook his head– and so did Africanus, when we reported to him in the field camp.

"Another legion?" he said, as we stood in the principia tent with his senior officers. "If we can't hold the province with three legions, what will they think of us in Rome?"

He sighed, and all his officers looked at one another in fear for their careers.

"On the other hand," said Africanus, "if we lose Britannia, what would our enemies think *outside* the empire? What would the Germans and Parthians think? They'd see it as weakness, and they'd be right, and then gods save us!"

Everyone agreed and Africanus continued. "This is too big for one man," he said. "I want to see Petros, the chief justice and the fiscal procurator. Those three and the consul of the provincial senate."

"Consul?" I said. "That would be Felemid."

"Bah!" he said. "Then whoever is his gods-damned deputy! Meanwhile, I'm going to Londinium."

He turned to his officers. "I want horses saddled to get us to the nearest road, and a lightning waiting there with full cavalry escort. Get it done! Do it now! Then strike camp and march the army back to the fort, at full pace."

"Yes, noble and honoured sir!" They saluted, and stamped.

"You're coming with me, Greek," said Africanus. "You and Morganus."

We were on the road before noon, with Batavians riding before and behind the lightning, and just three of us on the bench seats behind the driver: Africanus, Morganus, and me. The two bodyguards were left behind to lighten the load for greater speed. We made excellent time, with best available horses, and were approaching Londinium well before dusk, with limbs aching from the journey. Africanus suffered the most and a litter had to be improvised, to carry him from the Twentieth's fort to Government House. But legionaries are good at such matters, and message-runners were sent ahead to warn Petros and the others, and summon them to a discussion of imminent peril to the entire province.

Finally, well past sunset, we were sitting round a table in Petros's office with the dark banished by clusters of lamps. Petros headed the table, since he represented the governor, while Africanus and the chief justice sat to his right and left. Next down the table came Scapula the fiscal procurator, then Morganus, and then me and finally the co-consul of the provincial senate: a young Celtic billionaire who was so nervous of being in such exalted company that he said nothing throughout the entire meeting.

I told them everything, and a furious argument followed, led by Gaius Julius Domitius, the chief justice whom Morganus and I had met on other cases. He was a senatorial nobleman, quite young for his high position, exceedingly clever and a formidable lawyer. But he was a horrible little man— quite literally little, since he was short, with stumpy fingers and a large head – with a ferocious prejudice against Greeks. His disklike of me was only equalled by my dislike of him.

"All this this is merely rumour and innuendo," he said, "depending on the word of a Greek slave." He waved a hand at me. "Are we really going to risk our posts and our future on his word alone?"

"Yes!" said Africanus. "Because he is gifted with great powers. Magic powers."

"Magic?" said Domitius, sneering. "Roman law takes no account of magic."

"Then it should!" said Morganus. "I've seen what he can do, and it's real. He knows what men are thinking."

"Yes," said Scapula, "I've seen him do it."

"So, what am I thinking?" said Domitius, looking at me.

"You are *attempting* to think that I am a fraud," I said, "but you know that I am not, and this truth makes you angry with yourself."

It was an arrow shot in the dark, but it hit the target. Domitius gabbled and spluttered. He went red in the face and clenched fists such that Morganus and Petros laughed at him. But that did not stop him.

"Listen to me," he said. "In the name of his grace the governor…" He raised his eyebrows, seeking a response.

"Gods bless his grace," we all said.

"So!" said Domitius, "Let us consider the … *limitations* … of his grace." He stared at Africanus, Petros and Scapula. "And let us remember that because of these limitations, we four are – in effect – the real governor of Britannia. Thus, his career is our career. We are bound to him, and we are bound to each other." He looked round at all of us. "Does anyone disagree?"

There was silence, and Domitius continued. "Therefore, if we ask for another legion, at a time when the governor is about to receive a great promotion, then Rome will believe that we want another legion, so that his grace can go beyond that great promotion *to march on Rome and declare himself emperor!*"

"Never!" said Morganus.

"Rubbish!" said Petros.

"Nonsense!" said Scapula.

That is what they *said*, but they were unsure. I saw it in their eyes.

"Gentlemen," said Domitius. "Since the time of Augustus – Rome's first emperor – *seven* emperors have been murdered by the army and *three* forced into suicide by the army."

We fell silent, thinking about that.

"Rome knows its own history," said Domitius, "so we dare not ask for another legion, because we'd be asking for our own executions."

"But what if we don't ask," I said, "and we lose Britannia? Will Rome forgive us for that?"

"We will not lose Britannia," said Domitius. "Three legions is the biggest army in the empire, Africanus is a skilled commander, and in any case I do not believe the threat is real."

The argument went on, with Domitius winning every step. He was a powerful advocate, using every rhetorical device from flattery to mockery, so that even I was beginning to wonder if I was wrong. After all, I do not really work not magic, and I do not really read minds. I merely draw conclusions based on evidence.

Then we were interrupted. There was a polite knock at the door, and one of Petros's shaven-heads entered, and bowed low. With such deep secrets under discussion, even these closest advisors had been excluded, but now one of them was here.

"I beg forgiveness, most noble, honourable, and worshipful sirs," he said, and bowed again. "But a matter has arisen which is of uttermost urgency, and which cannot be resolved without the participation of my master, the honourable Petros of Athens." He looked at Petros. "A message," he said. Just those two words, but Petros stood up at once.

"Noble Domitius," he said, "I ask that you chair the meeting while I attend to this matter." Domitius frowned massively.

"What is it?" he said, suspicious of political deceit.

"Something urgent, but small," said Petros. "But as I go, noble Domitius, I state that I am now of your opinion, being convinced by your arguments."

"Ah!" said Domitius. "No fourth legion?"

"No fourth legion," said Petros, and Domitius smiled.

"Then go about your business, honourable Petros," he said.

"I shall, noble sir," said Petros, "though I shall need the assistance of Ikaros of Apollonis."

"Oh?" said Domitius. "Must someone's mind be read?" He laughed at his own joke, then fell serious. "Take who you like, so long as there will be no fourth legion."

Petros bowed and left the room, followed by me and the shaven-head. Once the door was closed, Petros spoke.

"A message?" he said.

"A pigeon," said the shaven-head. Petros looked at me.

"I want you to see this," he said. "which, like much else, is illegal."

"What is it?" I said.

"Come and see," he said.

Petros led the way up flights of stairs, to the roof of Government House in the cold night, with a damp Britannic wind. There was a fine view over night-time Londinium, with a black bulk of buildings, a few lights, the encircling walls, and the wild, wet wasteland of Britannia beyond. I shivered, having brought no cloak because nobody had told me that I should need one. There was a walkway all around the pitched, tiled roof, and I instantly recognised what we were heading for. It was something forbidden by law. Forbidden because of its associations.

"You've got a pigeon loft!" I said.

"Of course," he said. "How else should I converse by pigeon post?"

"Converse with druids?"

"Who else?"

The pigeon loft was a large wooden shed, lit with lanterns, and with cages for many of the grey birds that kept up a constant, soft noise. Alongside there was another shed, where the pigeon keepers lived. There were two of them, a man and a woman, both Celts in rough garments. They bowed as we approached.

"Can you trust them?" I said to Petros, speaking Greek for privacy.

"Don't bother with Greek," he said, "they know only Celtic, they are illiterate, and I have my own ways to enforce trust."

I looked at him, and he gave a smile that was not quite pleasant. He turned to the shaven-head. "Show me!" he said, and the shaven-head revealed a talent by speaking to the two pigeon-keepers in Celtic. Thus the woman went into the loft-shed and came out with a most tiny and neat little cylinder of brass, with a cap on one end and a leather thong attached. The woman bowed and offered it to Petros.

"It came during the day, master," said the shaven-head, "but I have only just seen it, being constantly at work on the governor's races, and of course the pigeon-keepers cannot read. But as soon as I saw it, I went to you."

"Good!" said Petros, and drew off the cap and pulled a tiny scroll from the cylinder. "Light!" he said, and the shaven-head fetched a lantern.

Petros unrolled the scroll, which was inscribed with a line of minute characters. It was code: a vital precaution, because communication with druids brought death under Roman law. Petros looked at the scroll, then took a deep breath and closed his eyes in contemplation such that I thought of Elantia, because he was calculating his next move as if working an abacus.

"So," he said finally, "you must both go." He looked at me. "*You* must go because you can resist druidic powers and have powers of your own, and Morganus must go, because Domitius will believe his testimony. Domitius and any court in the Roman world."

"Go?" I said. "Go where?"

He looked at me again, and I saw how he strained under the burden of his duties. Thus he held up the tiny scroll in disbelief.

"By all the gods of Athens and Rome," he said. "This is from Maligoterix himself! He fears for his life and is appealing to me for help."

# CHAPTER 22

A week later, with the governor's races already under way and Londinium thinking of nothing else, Morganus and I were on horseback, going across country, high up along a ridge of hills. We were following an ancient track that wandered in slow, Celtic whirls that could never be disciplined into straight lines, not even by Roman engineering.

We wore hooded riding cloaks over plain, dull clothes – even Morganus – because for this duty there could be no helmets, no armour and no military weapons. Nor could there be any bodyguards. There was just the pair of us, with a pack horse tethered behind, bringing food, a tent and other essentials, and we each had the largest belt-knife that could not be construed as a sword.

But we were not alone, because we rode behind a Celtic guide. He was a Parisi, one of the tribe to the north west of Briganti territory, and supposedly hostile to the Briganti. Without him we should have had no idea where we were, or where we were going. So I could not help worrying.

"Can we trust him?" I said to Morganus, as the guide signalled us to stop, and rode to the crest of a hill to check his directions.

"You've said that before," said Morganus. "You keep saying that, and you keep giving the same answer. You say that Petros *has ways of controlling people*, and Petros found us that guide."

I nodded. It was true. But then the wind found me as always it does in Britannia, and I wrapped the cloak closer. Why is Britannia always so cold?

"What about the extra legion?" I said. "Do you think Domitius was right?"

Morganus nodded. "Yes I do," he said. Then he made a rare admission for a proud Roman soldier. "Our history's rotten with civil wars," he said. "They know that in Rome and they'll never trust us with four legions." He looked at me. "Meanwhile – right here and now – can we trust Maligoterix? He hates us from the depth of his soul."

"According to Petros, we don't have to trust him," I said. "Petros says everything has been arranged. He was three days sending pigeons to-and-fro with messages."

"Yes," said Morganus, "but what was in the messages? Did he show you?"

"Yes," I said, "he explained the code, and I followed it … *most* of it."

"Not all?"

"There wasn't time, and if we cannot trust Petros, we are lost in any case whatsoever."

Then the guide came trotting up towards us. His name was Flambrox and he rode well. He was a mature man, with the Parisi features of broad chest and high cheekbones. He was well dressed in in Celtic style, with baggy plaid garments, hair bound in a horse tail behind his head, and clean-shaven except for moustaches. Best of all, he did not have three dots on his left hand, being devout to the faith of his ancestors and offering prayers before making fire, eating, or lying down to sleep.

He came forward, touched brow in salute and spoke to Morganus.

"Your honour," he said, "the way is clear." He spoke well because he had learned good Latin, and he spoke to Morganus because he had also learned to ignore slaves on first greeting. It was annoying.

"Good," said Morganus. "Where do we camp tonight? The sun's low."

"There's a place just ahead, your honour," he said. "It's nearby."

Later, as he had since our journey began, Flambrox raised tents, cooked food and served it. Also he attended to the horses, which he did well, so I approved of that at least. There was wine to drink, the fire was warm and we sat in our cloaks and talked as the night came, stars shone, and all of dark, black Britannia enclosed us.

"Flambrox," I said, "tell me about this path along the hills. You say it is ancient?"

He touched brow to Morganus, then spoke to me. "Your worship," he said, "in our speech this is *Fond Fawory Drogren,* the Great Way of the North. The land was crossed by such paths long before the Romans. The paths follow ground that stays firm in the rains. All the people, in all the tribes, use them for trade and for sacred duties, because the paths are gifts of mother earth."

"Do the druids use them?" I said, and Flambrox raised hands like a Roman and declaimed a prayer. Morganus and I looked at him as the fire crackled and the shadows twisted on his face. No decent man interrupts a prayer, so we waited until he was done. Then:

"Your worship," he said, "we do not name those of whom you speak. But yes, those high folk use them. They know every path and stone."

"I see," said Morganus. "So, what about this meeting place you're taking us to. Will they know about it?"

"Yes, your honour," said Flambrox. "It's a place chosen by tradition. It was built by holy mother earth as a place for meetings between men who can't trust each other, not even after blood oaths and exchange of hostages."

"Shall we reach it at the agreed time?" I said.

"Yes, your worship," said Flambrox, "if the weather holds, and the gods spare us, then we shall be there on the day after tomorrow."

The weather held, the gods were kind, and two dawns later we were riding towards the holy place, with the pack horse trotting behind. We halted a few miles from it and Flambrox spoke.

"There, your honour," he said. "It's exactly as I said."

It was indeed. We were already on high ground since the Fond Fawory Drogren sat entirely along the mountain range that runs from south to north of the Britannic island, such that it is called the backbone of Britannia. We were up in wind-blown isolation, on a stony roof over the world, while the soil all round was so poor as to support only thin grass. There were no shrubs, trees or boulders: nothing to provide hiding for an ambush.

"That's the meeting place, your honour," said Flambrox, pointing. "Did I speak well of it, or did I not?"

"You spoke well," said Morganus, and indeed he did. The meeting place was a great rock, fifty feet high, that could be climbed only on the side next to the path. It was vertical on all other sides and its flat peak was visible at great distance, as was the path itself. Thus rival parties could see each other approach, and check that all things were as previously agreed. Which indeed they were.

"Look, your honour!" said Flambrox. "Here they come!"

Three horsemen were approaching the rock from the north. They were at first like black insects on a white page. But soon we saw them as men on horses.

"One of us, and one of them, is supposed to meet on the rock," I said. "That was agreed between Petros and Maligoterix."

"And is that Maligoterix?" said Morganus. "The one in white?"

"I think so," I said. "We'll see soon enough."

Morganus turned to Flambrox. "You stay here," he said, and Flambrox tapped his brow as Morganus and I rode forward. Then, as agreed and well out of bow-shot of the rock, we dismounted and I gave Morganus the reins of my horse.

"They're doing the same," he said. "Just the one in white is coming forward on foot."

"Morganus," I said, "in case of betrayal, I ask that fondest regards be given to my lady and to your family."

"Huh!" he said. "That's easy for you to say. But what do *I* say to the lady-my-wife?"

I think he was using humour in the face of danger, but as I have said, we Apollonites are slow in humour. Then he clasped my hand.

"Gods be with you, Greek," he said.

"And with you," I said, then I walked forward, and I saw that the man walking towards me was indeed Maligoterix. I had met him before and he was an easy man to recognise. He was tall, fit and strong but with no colour in his body. His hair was white, his skin was white, his eyes were pink, and he wore a white cloak over white robes. His face was profound with intelligence. He was confident, arrogant and dominating. He was master of many languages and I knew from past experience that he had exactly the same gift of 'mind-reading' as I had. He was exceedingly, profoundly dangerous.

We both stopped, each about twenty feet from the rock on our own side. Then Maligoterix pointed to the rock, and for the first time I saw that steps had been carved so that it could be climbed. The steps were deep worn, and they were very wide, so that suspicious men could climb without being close to each other.

At the top, there was a flat platform about twenty yards wide. By mutual consent, Maligoterix and I approached each other, the mountains and plains of Britannia stretching out below us. As ever, I felt the chill of the wind.

Maligoterix saw that and spoke to me in Greek.

"I see you shivering," he said, "the engineer with his mechanisms …" He paused and smiled. "I see you now I always see you … I see you flattered by Batavian horsemen … I see you dreading Felemid's plans for a slave girl … I see you breathe life into a drowned child … I see you speak to Allicanda … You are a fool with words … a fool … a fool … a fool …"

I went rigid with fright, but it was not because he knew so much. That was impressive, but he knew so much only because he had spies everywhere. What shocked me was how close I had come to defeat in the first instants of our meeting. It was only the slow-paced delivery of his last words that alerted me, because he was pretending to attack with personal knowledge, to hide the real attack. He was deceiving me: *me*, Ikaros of Apollonis! Ikaros of Apollonis who had warned others of this very danger!

*He was trying to hypnotise me and he had very nearly succeeded!*

I gasped and fell back a pace.

"Well done, little engineer," he said. "You avoided that trap, but there are many others, because you know nothing with your machines and science. What do you know of the real powers?"

It was time to hit back. So I did my best, even knowing that Maligoterix was my equal in all matters of intellect. But I could make use of that.

"You read minds," I said, "just as I do, so you will know that I speak the truth."

"Because truth is not only virtuous but invincible?" he said, and almost threw me over with his knowledge of myself. But I breathed deep and carried on.

"Yes," I said, "so listen well, druid, because these are your thoughts. You pretend to despise engineering because you are afraid of it. You are likewise afraid of what you have done to the trinity – the teaching of Gaulish women – because you cannot control it, and it has caused such division within your people that you fear for your life."

He gasped and ground his teeth.

"And worst of all," I said, "you know that you are risking damnation of your soul, by asking for help from Rome."

Those last words hit like an artillery bolt. In all my career I was never so gods-gifted in revealing a truth that a man was hiding from himself, and Maligoterix threw the temper-tantrum of an infant. He foamed at the mouth. He stamped and raged and stabbed finger into my chest. He screamed every insult of the languages he knew.

"Tape worm! Dung eater! Copulator of pigs! Cannibal of children!"

All that, and more. But he made no attempt to deny what I had said.

Then he became calm again, and stared at me, fully under control, because a Celt who foams at the mouth is no less dangerous than a Roman who shows no emotion. To prove that, he stabbed again.

"So," he said, "what now, Greek?"

Once more I almost fell, because he said that in Latin, with an excellent imitation of Morganus's voice. But I thought of Morganus and pressed on.

"We must stop competing," I said. "Competition between us is vanity, because we are here to solve a problem. Do you agree?"

"Yes," he said, after a long pause.

"Then what is the problem?" I said.

"Rome knows that already."

"You do not want total war,"

"That is true."

"Then how can Rome help you?"

He suffered agonies with that question, because he despised Rome so utterly. Then he stepped even closer, with his pink eyes staring.

"It is true that we cannot lie to each other," he said, "because we both detect lies."

"And so?" I said.

"So listen to the truth," he said. "Yes, the trinity came to us from Gaul. It was brought by women, and the common people loved it because it offered peace and salvation. Also it bound together the tribes in a manner which I could never achieve. Thus I saw its power, and I took it, and consumed it." He showed me his left hand. "Look," he said, and I saw the three spots.

"You consumed it?" I said. "What does that mean?"

"It means that I sent druidic lore-masters to study its teachings and then combine these teachings with truth."

"*Your* truth?" I said.

"There is no other!"

"What about the women from Gaul?" I said. "Did they not argue against your truth?"

"Of course!" he said. "And of course, I dealt with them. I dealt with them before all the people." He smiled. "It took three whole days. Shall I tell you what we did to them?"

"No," I said, "because your cruelty failed. You do not control the trinity, and now you are in fear of your life. So what went wrong?"

He frowned, and paused greatly before replying.

"There was a division among the elect," he said. "Some of the highest believe that our trinity demands total war against Rome and a rising of all the tribes."

"They do, but you do not," I said.

"I do not," he said, "since Rome would take opportunity to extinguish the truth absolutely. There would be no more client states where we could take refuge." He seized my arm. "Do not misunderstand me," he said. "I do not want to hide forever, but so long as there are client states, the truth can be kept alive and better days may come. But some of the elect do not – will not – see this, because they believe the tribes can extinguish Rome."

"And you are outnumbered among the elect," I said.

"Greatly," he said. "To the degree that I must pretend to support total war, or face death. That is why I ordered the skinnings outside Londinium and other places."

"So that was your work?" I said.

"Yes. And I caused the rumour of skinnings to be spread among the soldiers."

"And was it you that ordered me killed? Smashed under the barrel in the docks?"

"The barrel?" he said. "Dropped by Denmultid the Writer? Yes, I ordered that. I ordered you dead in many ways, by many hands, because you are a persistent irritant and there were things I wanted kept from you." He shrugged. "You escaped Denmultid only because he was grateful for his child's life."

"Gods bless him!" I said. "What about Zephyrix the Thousander? Was he killed on your orders?"

Maligoterix shook his head. "Not entirely. Blephyrix the slave hated Zephyrix, so Blephyrix was encouraged towards the act, and caused to do it in such manner as would wound the Roman soul." He smiled. "They do so much love their racing drivers."

"I see," I said. "And now I ask again: what do you want from Rome?"

"I want a great demonstration of Rome's power," he said. "You have perhaps half a year to do this, because it will take us that long to raise all the tribes and arm them. So before then, I want Roman boots to march from end to end of Britannia, to prove to the elect that a rising will fail."

He leaned so close that his breath was in my face. "I want another legion," he said. "I want Rome to send another legion, as proof that Rome will never give up Britannia."

# CHAPTER 23

It was bizarre beyond imagination. Standing together on the meeting rock, with all Britannia below us, Maligoterix and I became allies. We did so, even though for both of us, such alliance was a mixture of treason, profanity and betrayal. But we each wanted the same thing. We wanted a fourth legion sent to Britannia, and when I explained Roman doubts in this matter, he was swift in understanding Roman politics and swift with arguments to change the Roman mind. Furthermore, he amazed me with his knowledge of the greater world.

"The Germanic kings are constantly waiting to lead their folk across the Rhine," he said, "and they will do so on the instant that Rome stumbles."

"How can you know that?" I said.

"Because I have personal communication with them."

"Do you?" I said, and he pitied my lack of understanding.

"Do you think that pigeons fly only to Londinium?" he said. "And that ships do not sail? And ambassadors are not sent out?"

"You send ambassadors?" I said.

"Of course!" he said. "And it is not just the Germans who are watching and waiting. Think of the Greek city-states, the Parthians, the Sasanians and the Egyptians.'

"Do you talk to them all?" I said, and he laughed and came so close I could feel the warmth of his body.

"Rome thinks it is secure," he said, "because Rome has conquered everyone. But all the conquered people are waiting their time. And remember that Rome took Britannia mainly as a demonstration of power. So if Rome loses Britannia the world will see that Rome is not invincible, and the whole empire will fall apart!"

"But isn't that exactly what you want?" I said.

"Yes!" he said. "But not if the Romans take revenge by the extinction of the druidic faith."

I nodded. I understood, and therefore and between us – a Celt who hated Rome and a Greek enslaved by Rome – we planned a course of action to save the Roman Empire.

Three days later, with Flambrox left behind, Morganus and I were in the client kingdom of Brigantia, in sight of the palace of King Brax: a modest and shabby reflection of the palace of Cogidubnus. Or at least, that is how it seemed by moonlight, since we were smuggled in at night.

"That's all they get, this far north," said Morganus looking at the so-called palace. "The kings aren't so loyal up here, and can't be trusted. So they get brick instead of marble."

We rode through wooded country, with an escort of Brigantian horsemen under the command of a young druid, Lossigi, who was faithful to Maligoterix. Lossigi was small and thin, so he stretched himself up, and raised chin for extra height, when facing tall men such as myself or Morganus. His horsemen had mail shirts, helmets and swords, and Morganus looked at them. "I suppose they're King Brax's men," he said, "from his house guard."

"You are wrong, Roman," said Lossigi, riding close behind. "The king's riders are elsewhere. Those around us are simply free men who ignore the laws of the occupying power."

Morganus turned in the saddle and stared at Lossigi. He said nothing then, but later, we were given a squalid little hovel for the night, in a squalid little village, and we talked.

"I'll strangle that druid," said Morganus. "I'll twist his neck."

"He doesn't like us," I said, "nor his present duty."

"Yes," said Morganus, "so I suppose it's stupid to wonder if we can trust him?"

"If they wanted to skin us," I said, "they'd have done it by now." Then I raised arms and muttered a prayer, in case the gods were listening to such dreadful words.

We were kept guarded in the hovel all the next day, and let out only at night. The boredom was appalling, and the fear of treachery even worse. We were given no food and only water to drink. Then Lossigi came for us, and we ducked out through the low doorway and found armed men with torches standing around the druid in the dark, and the village empty of people.

"Come," said Lossigi, "and you shall see many wonders."

We followed, and were led out of the village, towards a great glow of light seen above the woods, and hearing a vast concourse of voices, and that most barbaric of all sounds: the beating of drums, in deep rhythm. Then we were up on a ridge, looking down on vast numbers of men and torches, and gleaming blades raised in the night, and druids in white, running among the masses and howling and calling. The noise was tremendous.

"See!" said Lossigi, shouting to be heard. "And this assembly of thousands is only one of many that are planned, and all brought together by the trinity of true faith." He looked at Morganus. "See, Roman," he said. "See and be afraid!"

Morganus said nothing, and there was a great stirring among the masses as a procession came forward, with drums pounding, cymbals clashing and horns blowing: a procession of men led by a group with long robes over Celtic arms and amour.

"That's King Brax," said Morganus, pointing to the leader. "I've seen him before. He comes to Londinium for the emperor's birthday parade."

The king and his elite were followed by many dozens of men holding hurdles on their shoulders and druids riding the hurdles. The druids raised voices in a chant as they tapped right hands to left, then tapped brow and breast. The chant was taken up by the multitudes, and they began to sway, and then kneel, and then rise, over and over again.

But the ceremony was only beginning. The drums changed rhythm, the horns blared, and a great pyramid was formed of hurdles, with men yelling and screaming, yet acting together to clamber on to the first level of hurdles, and raise more hurdles to a second, smaller level, then another, and another.

Finally – by teamwork that the legions would envy – one man was raised up in the middle of the pyramid: raised up and up, until he stood alone on the topmost hurdle, looking down on all others. The man was Maligoterix, and the vast gathering bowed low – even the king – and fell silent as he raised his arms high and began to sing. He sang, and paused for responses, which were roared out like thunder by the crowd. When the song was done, he made a great speech in a high voice that all could hear. As with the song, it was in Celtic that I could not follow, but I saw Morganus frown and make the bull sign.

He looked at me. "It's fire and the sword," he said. " It's not nice. They won't just kill us quickly. Not if they can help it. It's not nice."

"Yes," said Lossigi, standing close and listening. "So learn and be afraid." He looked at me. "Because none will be spared." Soon after that, he insisted that we should leave. "You have seen enough," he said, "and it is not proper for heathens to see more."

"Heathens?" said Morganus, when we were shut up in the hovel again, cross-legged at a miserable fire. "*Heathens?* I'm a Roman and you're a Greek!"

"He hates us," I said. "He hates us."

There was some bread and native beer in the hovel, so I chewed some bread. It was coarse and full of grit, and the beer was even worse: it smelt bad. But we were thirsty.

"What did you think of it?" I said. "What we saw?"

"If that gathering really was just one of many," he said, "then they've got the numbers– vast numbers. They won't have our discipline and gear, but they've got the numbers. That's bad." He paused. "And I'd like to know where they got the weapons. I saw thousands of swords. They couldn't have made that many, in Britannia, in secret. They've come from outside Britannia."

"From the Germans? Or Parthians?" I said. "I told you what Maligoterix said about them. He said he talks to them. Perhaps he trades with them?"

"But they'd want payment in gold, surely?"

"Probably," I said. "Where did they get the gold?"

"Let's talk in the morning," he said, "I'm very tired."

I felt the same. I was tired, and feeling sick and dizzy.

\* \* \*

They had drugged us. It must have been in the beer. So I woke up long after dawn. I woke up with a headache, still feeling sick and dizzy, and was horrified to find that Morganus was gone. I got to my feet, pushed through the skin-covered door and met several Celts who levelled spears at me, and chattered in Celtic while one ran off, then came back with Lossigi, who strutted like a fighting cock and looked at me as if I were made of dung.

"Did you sleep well?" he said.

"Where is Morganus?" I said.

"In safe keeping," he said. "So come with me."

"Where?"

"To see his holy druidic reverence the high druid."

"Maligoterix?"

"Yes. And he will explain about Morganus. Come with me: *now!*"

He gestured to the men with spears, and they shouted and prodded with sharp points so that I had no choice but to follow. They marched me towards the palace of King Brax which, in daylight, I could see was quite close. I could likewise see that there was a whole town – no, a city – of tents and encampments around the palace, and thousands of young Celtic warriors with their furs and plaids and tattoos, and their faces displaying the features of many different tribes. They peered at me as I passed, and every one of them was fully armed.

The palace was more miserable in daylight than in darkness: brown brick, wooden pillars, thatched roof, and hounds running around unchecked.

There was a house guard at the gates, with Celtic horned helmets, oval shields and long hair. They grovelled low as Lossigi approached, and threw open the main doors and backed out of our way. Thus I was taken through the palace, into the presence of King Brax and his courtiers, with spearpoints prodding my back.

I should have noticed, first of all, the shabby dirtiness of the audience chamber as compared with that of Cogidubnus. No dome, no tiled floor. I should have noticed that, except that something – *someone* – stood out like the sun in the sky.

Felemid!

He was standing next to King Brax on his throne. He smiled at me, and bowed, and smiled again. He smiled in ease and comfort, here in this strange place where I was surrounded by enemies. At least, I thought that they were enemies– until Lossigi spoke.

"Majesty," he said. "I bring Ikaros of Apollonis, to hear your royal words."

King Brax nodded and looked at me. He was old, fat, and over-dressed as Celts often were. But he spoke Latin, and he had intelligence and cunning too, which is not surprising since no man remains king of a Celtic kingdom unless he is clever and cunning. So he listened to courtiers who whispered into his ear, then raised a hand to Felemid, who likewise whispered in his ear. Then King Brax spoke to me.

"The high ones have brought you to me," he said, nodding towards Lossigi, "so that I might show my true loyalty."

He said that with a smirk so small that only my gift perceived it. I saw that, and I saw vast deceit in his face.

Then he turned to Felemid. "I therefore ask you, Gentius Civilis Felemidus," he said, "to explain the importance of your contribution to the great affairs in which we are involved."

Felemid bowed to him, then spoke to me.

"My poor, dear Greek," he said. "You were so worried for Allicanda." He smiled. "And you were right to be worried, because I had the whore-masters lined up and waiting." He waved a hand, as if brushing away a fly. "But that doesn't matter. Rome is doomed in this province. I saw that long ago, and I have therefore adopted the true faith…" he touched hands and tapped brow and breast, "and I have given my gold to the high ones, so that they can buy food and arms for the coming struggle." He leered at me in self-satisfaction. "You had your chance to join me, but you never did, and more fool you."

He bowed to King Brax and stood back.

"Thank you, Gentius Civilis Felemidus," said the King. "And now I ask Lossigi to add further words."

Lossigi stepped forward and spoke directly to Felemid. He spoke in a series of short, brutal statements.

"You are a liar and deceiver!" he said. "You seek favour with the Romans and you give them gold. You wear their toga, yet you adopted our faith. But you did so only as political expedient, and you gave us *all* your gold when we threatened you with a Roman death sentence for speaking to us. You would long since have left Britannia for the city of Rome, except that we have your gold."

"Quite so," said King Brax. He pointed to Felemid, and the two courtiers behind him seized his arms, while King Brax looked at me. "This man is a traitor to Rome," he said, "and I shall now demonstrate my own true loyalty."

He struggled out of his chair, assisted by courtiers. He held out a hand, he was given a knife, and he approached Felemid.

"No! No!" said Felemid, and turned to me. "Help me!" he said. "You can do anything. You are magic … *help me, because I love you.*"

Those last words were profoundly disturbing. I had often wondered exactly what Felemid wanted from me, but never guessed it was that. It did explain why he tried so hard to get me into his service, and I felt a surge of pity for a man who – for years – I had wished dead, and damned across the river Styx.

Meanwhile, King Brax made an ugly job of it, because Felemid wriggled and screamed and fought, and King Brax was afflicted with arthritis of the hands. But he hacked away at the neck until blood spurted everywhere and Felemid throttled and choked, and finally became limp and fell, and was a corpse on the beaten-earth floor.

Then, King Brax handed the knife to a courtier, and turned to me impassive and steady, even if covered in blood. He was a king, after all.

"There," he said, "It is done. Note that well, Ikaros of Apollonis. So, go back to your masters in Londinium, and tell them of it when they think of abolishing the client kingdoms: especially mine!" He turned to Lossigi. "Now take this Greek to Maligoterix, to hear the rest."

So the spears prodded, Lossigi strutted, and I was taken to a vastly superior place. I was taken to a suite of rooms that were clean, with walls plastered and painted in elaborate native style, depicting trees, and flowers and animals.

We came to a set of double doors, with two druids on guard. Lossigi bowed to them. They bowed to him and opened the doors without speaking, I was admitted, but not Lossigi or the spear carriers, and Maligoterix was waiting for me.

He stood in the middle of a large room, bright lit with glazed windows and a flagstone floor. The walls were lined with oak trunks, still with their bark. It was like the audience chamber of Cogidubnus, but pale, cold and ascetic. There was no furniture of any kind, nor any ornament.

"Where is Morganus?" I said. "What have you done with him?"

"You must understand that I am obliged to take great care," he said.

"Where is Morganus?"

"I am balancing one need against another."

251

"Where is he?"

"Alive and safe," he said. "For the moment."

"What does that mean, by all the gods?"

"It means a near disaster," he said, "since I cannot entirely trust Lossigi because, like King Brax, he is attempting to please everyone."

"So you know about King Brax?" I said.

"Of course!" he said, "I know about him, and Felemid, and many others who are wondering which side will win. It is always like that when two great powers are opposed and men think first of themselves. Surely you know that! Are you not the Greek that reads minds?"

"So what has happened to Morganus?" I said.

"He has been taken hostage. He was …"

"Taken in the night? After we had been drugged?"

"Yes," he said. "Because Lossigi insists that he must be held hostage, and I dare not oppose that. There are factions competing here, and I must be careful."

"But you still want to stop the rising?" I said. "You still want another legion sent to Britannia?"

"Of course," he said. "I want that or some other great demonstration of Roman power. You must persuade Petros, Africanus and Domitius to bring another legion, or the province is lost. So, go back to Londinium and tell them what you have seen here."

"They won't believe me," I said. "I rank too low in Roman eyes. We need Morganus to tell them. They will believe him."

"He cannot go. He must stay here."

"But I cannot persuade them without him."

"You *must* persuade them," he said, "or they will kill Morganus. They will skin him alive and send him home with his face untouched, so that he can be recognised."

# CHAPTER 24

I was given Flambrox as a guide, because he had not been left behind at the meeting rock. The druids had taken him and kept him. We were given horses, and an escort of horsemen to see us safe out of Brigantia, and on to a Roman road. Then it was some days of travel, stopping at the mansiones, to reach Londinium.

On the journey I worried till I was sick. What might be done to Morganus? What should I tell Morgana and the girls? What of my stupid words to Allicanda? Could I trust Maligoterix? Could I persuade Petros and the rest to summon a fourth legion?

It was a bad time: a very bad time. But in the end we were in sight of Londinium, and we saw the smoke of many hearth fires, the tiled roofs, the fortifications and the fortress of the Twentieth nearby. So we rode to the city's north gate, crossed the drawbridge and were met by a guard of auxiliaries.

Looking through the gates, I saw that the streets were empty. The city was quiet. So much the better, since it was my intention to go to Government House. But the auxiliary centurion spoke first and I found that I had more reputation that I had thought.

"I give you good day, your worship," he said, "because I see that you are Ikaros of Apollonis."

"Yes," I said, but he frowned.

"Then where's the big man?" he said, "You're always with him. Where's his honour Morganus?"

"In Brigantia," I said.

"Is he all right?"

"I must see Petros of Athens," I said. "It is most urgent."

"Of course, your worship," he said, "but is the big man safe?"

"I must see Petros at once!" I said, and I regret that I was brutal, in the pain of my worries. "Take me to him or I'll have you flogged!"

The centurion blinked in fright. "Yes your worship," he said. "His honour Petros is at the stadium for the races. He left word you should be taken straight to him – you and the big man – so I'll call out an escort to get you straight there. Yes, your worship. Yes."

"At once!" I said, and turned to Flambrox. "Farewell, and the gods be with you," I said and clasped his hand. "Where will you go now?"

"Gods be with you, your worship," he said. "I'll go to the fort. I've got pay coming. Petros said they'll pay me, and give me a bed."

Then there was much yelling of orders, a troop of Batavians rode out and I was taken to the racing stadium at the gallop. As we rode, I realised that the city was empty because the stadium was full. There were great crowds of people even outside it, and a great host of market stalls, and hawkers and sellers of food and drink, and trinkets, and a huge roaring of voices bursting from the stadium and making the very hills shake.

The Batavians got me through all that and to the main gates of the stadium, with regulars from the Twentieth on duty and another centurion, who also recognised me and asked the same question.

"Where's the big man?" he said, as I dismounted, "You're his Greek, aren't you? So where's our first javelin?"

"Get me to Petros," I said, "or you'll never see the big man again!"

That hit harder than the threat of flogging, and the centurion personally escorted me into the stadium, which was crammed with a vast number of people. A race was in full flood, with folk screaming and standing and waving, and the dust rising as the chariots tore round the course, with whips cracking, hooves pounding and trumpets blaring from the spina. The noise was colossal and speech impossible. Then, the noise dimmed as we went through brick-lined tunnels to stairs leading up to the governor's box, a complex of seating and dining for the elite of the province, entirely walled off from the common herd. It was raised up to give a perfect view of the track, and men of the governor's guard were on duty, but the centurion pushed past all of them.

"Fall back!" he said. "Orders from Petros, orders from Africanus!"

Then we were standing between a line of guardsmen, at the entrance of the box looking down at the raked seating. I saw the governor and his wife and son, right at the front. I saw Africanus, Domitius and Scapula beside them, and behind them there were two whole rows of senatorial noblemen in purple-striped togas: men I did not recognise, men from Rome. I saw them, and ladies in jewels and perfume. I saw slaves standing with food, drink, ewers, basins and towels, and I saw Petros of Athens– who could not sit with the nobility, since he was a slave. But he had a small, private box to one side, and was attended in luxury by his own slaves.

The centurion gave me a small bow and ran down a flight of steps to Petros's box. He spoke to Petros, he pointed, Petros looked at me then leapt up, bowed towards the governor and ran up the stairs.

"Where's Morganus?" he said.

"Where can we talk?" I said.

He nodded, beckoned and ran off. I followed, and he ran down tunnels and corridors to a small room with windows facing out of the stadium. It was a cashier's office with a strong-box. There was a guard on the door but nobody inside.

"What's happened?" he said, and I told him everything as briefly as I could. His reaction was to sink into a chair with his head in his hands. He sat a while then looked at me.

"We'll never get the fourth legion now," he said.

"Why?" I said.

"Because the races have been a complete success," he said. "There are senators here from Rome, sent to investigate how well the province has been governed. They are greatly impressed, and will report back, and the governor's promotion is therefore assured ... unless we ask for another legion, which will prove that *nothing* is well in Britannia. It would be total disaster. We'd be finished. We'd be in fear of our lives. That's how Rome works. Believe me."

"But I've told you what's happening in the north," I said. "There's a real threat to the province. Maligoterix has made a monster that he cannot control."

"So we're damned either way," he said. He sat quietly among all the roaring and yelling of the stadium. He could see no way forward.

*He* could not, but perhaps I could. It was my own last words that gave me the idea, especially the word monster.

"Petros," I said, "Maligoterix wants another legion marching up and down Britannia. He wants that or *some other demonstration of Roman power*."

"Meaning what?" he said.

"Let me think," I said. "Because the druids are nervous of Greek science: *very* nervous. I know that now. It's a power that they don't understand."

256

"And so?" he said.

"So," I said, "if we could show them something to frighten them – really frighten them – then Maligoterix might be able to stop the rebellion."

"Are you sure he wants to?"

"Yes! So we must help him. We need a demonstration to him, and to the druids."

"What about the Celtic tribes? Countless thousands of them, up in arms?"

"They don't matter. The druids control them."

"So, what do you propose?"

It was my turn to stop and think. I looked round to see if there was any wine in the room, but there was not. So I sat down.

"First," I said, "we still have some months to prepare, before the druids muster all their forces."

"So what will we do? What do you want from me?"

"I need some way to persuade a group of druids to come to a demonstration in a place of our choosing, but without them being afraid of treachery."

"Is that all?" he said, in sarcasm.

"No," I said, "I shall need a special place to work: a forge with tools. I shall need that and number of items: boilers, cisterns, pipes and valves. That, and some men. Perhaps five of them? I shall need men who are skilled in metal work. They must work in secrecy so they must be men that we can trust."

"That, at least I can promise," he said.

"I know," I said. "You have ways to enforce trust." He nodded. "One more thing," I said. "Months ago you sent me to investigate a cargo of naphtha that came into the docks in a ship. Is any of it left?

I hope so, because it is the most indispensable item of all. Without it, nothing can be done."

"I'll find out," he said. "And is there anything else?"

"Yes," I said, "I ask that the Lady Morgana should be told only that Morganus is on service in the north. She is an army wife, so she will understand that. But don't tell her what they are threatening to do to him."

"Why not speak to her yourself?" he said.

"No," I said. "I am clumsy with words when speaking to those I esteem."

"Ah," he said, "that reminds me. Allicanda the exotic has been sequestered as property of the empire, along with all of Felemid's goods. But the empire surely owes you some reward ... so do you want her? As a gift? Free of charge?"

There are times when decisions are too hard to bear. There are times when work brings greater comfort than wine. So I work. I work hard, and by this means I ease the pain, or at least push it to the deep of my mind.

In this respect Petros was helpful and efficient. I was given everything that I needed including the entire ship-load of naphtha. It was almost untouched because nobody wanted it, since it was proven useless in all its exotic purposes. Petros also found me a workshop and craftsmen, and I began work instantly. I worked till exhausted and so did the craftsmen. Then shortly after the ceremony of the closing of the governor's races, Petros provided something more, and insisted that I must stop work to see it.

So I had to bathe, wear clean robes and stand among a company of the province's leading men and women on the steps of Government

House, to mark the departure of Teutonius and his family. They were off to take the sacred waters at the great baths of Aquae Sulis, where – by the unfathomable workings of the gods – fresh, hot water surges from the deep of the earth. Since Teutonius was skies-high in popularity after the races, the streets were full of merry people and decorated with flowers and banners. The streets were decorated all the way to the gate from which Teutonius would take the road to Aquae Sulis. It was a holiday for the entire city, and the fountains ran with wine.

I stood some rows behind Petros, since many civic dignitaries out-ranked me. I stood with Petros's shaven-heads. But I saw the pontifex of augurs and his robed attendants, as they opened a hare on an altar in front of Government House. The senior shaven-head whispered to me as he did so.

"Fear not," he said, "my master has spoken to the pontifex, regarding the omens."

"The omens are good!" cried the pontifex, to cheers from the crowd. Thus Teutonius, Secunda and the child went down the steps, followed by their slaves and attendants, to a line of carriages, enclosed by the governor's foot guard and cavalry. Teutonius's people climbed aboard and the procession set off, to cheers and a fanfare of bugles.

Later, Petros spoke to me, alone and privately in his office.

"Teutonius and his family will stay in Aquae Sulis," he said. "They will stay there until I tell them to return."

"Will they?" I said."

"Yes," he said, "Teutonius knows only what I tell him, he is ignorant of danger, and I have withdrawn all the carriages ... Now! What of your part? Have you found a place for your demonstration?"

"I have," I said. "A lake with a small island."

"How did you find it?"

"I asked Flambrox, the guide. He is a great geographer of Britannia."

"Will Maligoterix be able to find it?"

"Yes. Flambrox says it is famous in Celtic mythology," I said. "It is called Innisin Lin, and is sacred to the water nymph Innis."

Petros nodded. "I have exchanged initial messages with Maligoterix," he said, "so I need only name the place." He rubbed his palms over his brow and sighed. "Forgive me," he said, "I have a headache."

"Who would not?" I said.

"So!" he said, "Maligoterix and his druids will occupy the island. Teutonius and his family will stay in Aquae Sulis. Then we withdraw our troops from Aquae Sulis, while Maligoterix withdraws his armed men from Innisin Lin."

We sat a while in silence, thinking of the appalling, hideous, colossal risk that we were taking, then Petros spoke. "I hope that Maligoterix understands the extent of what we are doing."

"We are offering Teutonius, and his wife and son," I said, "as hostages against Roman treachery. We are offering Teutonius, who is soon to become governor of Italia, and who is the current darling of Rome and just one step from being emperor."

"Well," he said, "they can kill us only once, if things go wrong."

He looked at me and I saw how grey he had become in these few months, and how lined was his face.

"This thing you are building," he said. "Will it work?"


My dreams were full of it. As ever, they were bad dreams: bad and confused. Even in the night I could not escape from the heavy labour: the clanging and banging, and sawing, and lifting.

I dreamed of labour, and mistakes, and repairs, and alterations and improvisations and injuries, and diagrams thrown away in disgust. I dreamed of the explosions and fire that killed three men, burned and gutted the first workshop such that another had to be found.

Yet I myself was unharmed. Perhaps the gods were with me? Perhaps I was doing right after all?

Most of all, I dreamed of the bronze distillation cylinder. It came of three separate hot water boilers, cut and soldered together, to stand the height of two men. It was studded with valves, sprouted with copper pipes, packed with metallic innards and resting on a charcoal furnace. It was vitally important but constantly failing to deliver the liquids. There had to be two separate liquids, each very different from the other.

The cylinder was a monster, but not the final monster. That came later, when we achieved manufacture of the two liquids – one in flasks, one in lead-lined barrels. After that, the building of the final monster was less of a task. It was merely complex, tedious and horribly dangerous.

It was the first and second building of the final monster that caused the explosions: two of them.

So the monster that went to Innisin Lin was a much-modified third attempt, with improvements and safety devices that I hoped would make it safe, at least for the users.


Flambrox was my guide again. Our train of wagons could easily follow the Great North Road, but we needed him to find Innisin Lin. He rode beside me followed by our train of wagons, bearing flasks and barrels and trained men. There were ten big wagons, and the main load was barrels, except for one wagon that carried the monster.

"We come off the road here, your worship," said Flambrox. "It's firm going. It's one of the ancient paths. It'll take the wagons."

I looked round, and as ever with Roman roads, the ground was cleared for a hundred yards on either side, to prevent ambush. But beyond that there was oak forest too dense to see through, except for the path, which was narrow and entirely enclosed in trees.

"That's it," said Flambrox, "but there can't be any danger, not on the road and not here because … *they* … wouldn't allow it."

He was right. We were under druidic protection. It was bizarre beyond belief.

"Lead on," I said. So we followed the path, and some hours later we came to a great clearing, with a lake and island exactly as Flambrox had said. The island was in the middle of the lake and quite small, a few hundred yards across. More important was the fact the druids were already there by the lakeside: a line of tents and men in white robes – about twenty of them – standing in front of the tents, and the foremost was Maligoterix.

I rode forward and dismounted as the wagons rumbled forward and stopped, and I saw the fear on the faces of all my people. They were terrified of the druids, but that could not be helped.

Maligoterix and I approached each other, but made no greeting. No gods were invoked, no hands were clasped, no gifts exchanged. But each of us was satisfied to see the other, since that meant that our plans were working. So our conversation was brief and without preamble.

"Have you brought it?" said Maligoterix.

"Yes," I said, and looked at the druids behind him. "And are these the men …"

"The elect!" he said, in sharp correction.

"The elect," I said. "All of them? Enough for our purpose?"

"Yes," he said and looked at the wagons. "Can it be done tonight?"

"No," I said. "We must make preparations on the island."

"There are boats for that," he said. "We will show you. But first I will show you something else."

He waved a hand towards a tent in the druids' camp. A druid raised the tent flap and three men walked out. Two held swords to the third, who was in chains. He was Morganus. He was unshaven and filthy, but very much alive. I ran towards him. I could not help myself. I threw arms around him.

"Hello, Greek," he said, and raised his manacled hands. "Sorry about these, or I'd have come home sooner." He looked at his chained feet. "And these, too," he said. I supposed him to be joking. But I turned around.

"Maligoterix!" I cried, but I need not have bothered. He was close behind. "Get rid of the irons!" I said. "Get rid of them, or nothing else happens here!"

It was an empty threat, but it worked. Maligoterix gave orders, and the chains were struck off.

"I need a bath," said Morganus, "and some food."

"What happened?" I said to Morganus. "How are you safe? I thought … I thought they…"

I could not say it.

"Thought they'd skin me?" he said.

"Yes," I said.

"They didn't dare," he said, and looked at Maligoterix, who stared at me with hatred in his pink eyes.

"He was not spared for kindness," he said. "He was spared because I know his reputation. If we inflicted such a death upon him, then every legion in Britannia would turn on us. Even legions in Gaul would come. They would act without orders. They would slaughter and burn all in the client kingdoms, and that is exactly what I seek to avoid."

"They why did you threaten to do that to him?" I said.

"To skin him alive?" said Maligoterix. "That was political: a threat to put urgency into your efforts to persuade Petros and the others." He looked at the wagons. "But now you are here with your device, the objective is achieved, and I await your demonstration."

That night, and all the next day we got everything across to the island, while some of my men made camp ashore, as far from the druids as possible. Then, in the full dark of the next night, we gathered on the island, by torchlight: Maligoterix and his elect, myself and my trained men. So everyone and everything was ready.

The machine was ready.

It steamed and hissed.

It was the Chimera reborn.

# CHAPTER 25

The Chimera rested on its turntable: its reservoir, furnace, boiler, pipes and spouts in copper and bronze. It was a thing of mechanistic devilry: cunning, shining and grim. It stood waiting with its crew, while others of my men were ready with barrels.

The druids stood apart. They stood together in groups and they were mostly old. They were men with lifetimes of learning in the occult arts, and in languages, ceremonies and rituals. They were old, but they stood straight. They were men of great pride and great power. But they deferred to Maligoterix. They bowed heads to him, and they muttered about him to one another as he stood before them with arms folded.

I wondered what feats of druidic politics he had performed over the years, to reach pre-eminence over these learned and gifted men.

But now it was my duty to help him in his latest feat of politics. So I stood by the machine, holding a wine flask and a waxed taper. Morganus stood beside me, holding aloft a torch. It was time for the demonstration of power. It was also the time for words, since I could see that the druids were hanging back. So I raised my voice.

"Come forward!" I cried. "Because there are no secrets here. There is no magic. Only science. But science is very great, and what you shall see, here tonight, can be done anywhere in Britannia."

They looked at each other and frowned and shook their heads.

"Come," said Maligoterix, "let us see what this Greek can do."

So they advanced, staring at the Chimera, and the men operating it. As for myself, I was attempting to proclaim the triumph of science, but it was very hard. There were few torches, many shadows, and the druids were stroking their beards, and their white gowns rustling. I saw their faces and my gift told me of their deep intelligence and wisdom, which was their kind of wisdom and not my own. Thus, my courage faltered. After all, we were in the depths of wild Britannia, where the gods of Greece and Rome might not rule, and there was only one of me, over twenty of them, and I knew how dangerous druids could be.

But then the gods were kind and my gift saved me, because I could see in the druids' faces – even in Maligoterix's face – a precise reflection of my own fears. They really, truly were disturbed by Greek knowledge and by Greek science. They were as nervous of me as I was of them, and it was time to show them that they were right to be nervous.

So I began my demonstration. I took a gulp from the wine flask, lit my taper from Morganus's torch, and spat hard into the night, towards the small flame.

There was a great *whoosh* of flame: brilliant, dazzling and bright. The druids gasped and staggered back, seeing the impossible as I truly breathed fire. I took another gulp, spat again, and breathed another huge gout of flame. Even Morganus would never, ever again believe that I did not work magic– and the druids were horrified.

But this was only the beginning. I called out commands to the Chimera crew. I called out and they responded.

"Furnace man ready?"

"Ready!"

"Safety valve clear?"

"Clear!"

"Aimed at the lake?"

"Aimed!"

"Hose men ready?"

"Ready!"

I looked at the druids, and saw them huddled in groups, wondering if I was uttering an incantation, and if so what could it mean? Then:

"Shoot!" I cried, and a thick jet of liquid shot out to fall on the surface of the lake. It was the working of the Chimera: the furnace heating a reservoir of fire liquid, building pressure that drove out a fierce stream at the turn of a valve.

The druids cried in amazement, noting the power of the jet. But that was nothing. I took another gulp from the wine flask, and spat through the burning taper ... and the Chimera jet was ignited, and became liquid flame that terrified all who saw it, so fierce and bright as it was, and with such a blast of heat, and horror of horrors to the druids, as the flames fell upon the lake, they kept right on burning as they floated on the water.

Yet there was more to come.

"Tip!" I cried to the men with the barrels and they heaved and strained, and the barrel contents splashed, and then one after another, the barrels went over and foul, stinking fire liquid gushed over the lake surface, met the inferno delivered by the Chimera, and then ... and then ... the night was blasted with vast sheets of lurid flame and a huge, roaring sound like that of an angry volcano.

We all backed away. We ran, tripped and clambered up to get into the middle of the island away from the blinding flames and roaring heat. We held up hands and arms to shield our faces. We got behind trees, some hid behind others. A pure terror of burning was upon us.

Then a hideous, unplanned, climax as – true to the despicable nature of the Chimera and despite my supposed improvements – the roaring flames on the lake were eclipsed as this Chimera, like all its ancestors, betrayed its builders in a colossal explosion.

Thus fire and fragments flew in all directions. We were deafened, blinded and wounded, and for every man of us: druid, Roman or Greek. It felt like the end of the world: the end of all things.

# EPILOGUE

Except that it was not the end of all things. Not quite, though for me it very nearly was. It was very nearly a journey across the Styx with Charon the boat man, but instead, it was a journey down the Great North Road in one of the wagons that had carried our gear to Innisin Lin. My memory of the next few weeks is unclear. I recall being in the wagon, wrapped in blankets, and bandaged around my chest. I recall sleeping a lot, and feeling much pain. I also recall some of my conversations with Morganus.

"What happened?" I said, the first time he came to me.

"Your machine turned into thunder and lightning," he said.

"Yes, but what happened with the druids?"

"They ran. They took boats ashore, and mounted up and fled. They left their tents and everything. They rode off in panic."

"Yes," I said. "Pouring the barrels was an excess. I did not realise how great a fire they would produce." I frowned. "So the machine exploded and the demonstration failed."

"No! No! No!" he said. "You put the fear of all the gods into the druids. They ran off in terror of you – and Rome!"

Then, later– or perhaps it was before?– I remember my wound

being dressed. One of my craftsman did it. He did it with Morganus helping, and Morganus was worried.

"It's gone into his chest," he said.

"Yes," said the other. "See here, there's a wound where it went in."

"A bit of metal?" said Morganus. "From when the machine burst?"

"Don't know," said the other. "Can't see it. But the Greek gentleman's lucky, because five were killed outright. Five of us and three druids."

Then I remember coughing a lot, and drinking a lot of wine on the journey, which dulled the pain. I remember the wagon pulling up outside the legionary hospital in the fort, where I was bathed, and my wound dressed, and my case discussed.

"Can we remove it?"

"Not if it's in the lung."

"If it's in the lung, he's finished anyway."

"He's a surgeon himself, isn't he?"

"Yes. Trained in Apollonis."

"Surgeon and engineer too! He actually built the thing."

"Why did he call it Chimera?"

"Don't you know? Chimera was the mythical monster that breathed fire!"

"Oh yes. Of course. So what happened to it? The machine?"

"Smashed, ruined, nothing left of it."

I recall the operating table, the instruments, and the orderlies holding me while the surgeons worked. I am alive only because of their skill. They were Greeks, so I should not be surprised. Nor should I be surprised that the wound turned bad, as some wounds do for no reason known to science. This led me to a further depth of illness, fever and distress. And all that time I was cared for in Morganus's house. I was cared for partly by Morgana and the girls, but mostly by someone else who lived in the house.

Also, Morganus spoke to me often.

"No word from Maligoterix," he said on one occasion. "I've spoken to Petros. No more pigeons, no more messages."

"What's happening with the tribes?" I said.

"Nothing. No great muster of armies, and no more skinnings outside our towns." He smiled and patted my shoulder. "You did it, Greek. You frightened them off."

"What about Maligoterix?" I said.

"We don't know. But we think he's got what he wants. No tribal uprising. No total war."

"So, he has escaped?"

"If you call living forever in a client state 'escaped' then yes, he has." Then he hesitated. "That thing, the Chimera, it was the weapon you spoke of, wasn't it?"

"Yes."

"Was it Greek science? Only that? Or something more?"

I made the effort. I made the effort to dispel the existence of *something more*.

"Naphtha is a mixture," I said. "It can be divided into lamp oil, which is harmless, and fire liquid, which is dreadfully dangerous. The liquid I spat out, to make flame, was lamp oil, and the Chimera was filled with fire liquid."

He thought about that.

"You made these liquids in your workshop, didn't you?"

"Yes. Using a device called a still."

"Did you know that your workmen have smashed it?"

"I told them to do that, so that there shall be no more distillation of naphtha."

"Good!" he said.

Some weeks later, Londinium was in great celebration for the final confirmation that Teutonius was to be made governor of Italia. There were parades, and marches, and bulls were sacrificed in the Temple of Jupiter with thousands in attendance.

There was also a lesser ceremony in the great hall of Government House. It was, none the less, an important ceremony for me, with Morganus standing by in full dress armour, with an escort of the first century, first cohort, likewise in full dress, and of course there were four bodyguards again, since every man in Britannia's legions volunteered, and two were chosen to stand with the two who had survived all our adventures.

Teutonius, his wife and child were on the rostrum, attended by Domitius the lord justice, Scapula the fiscal procurator, representatives of the provincial council, and Petros standing discretely at Teutonius's elbow as Teutonius handed me the document.

"Ikaros the Greek!" he cried. "Your services to Rome are famous. You have saved the province, and perhaps even the empire itself." He looked round the hall, and there was a great drumming of feet in applause, and loud cheers from the soldiers. "It is therefore my pleasure, to present you with this instrument of manumission, which not only grants the honour of full Roman citizenship…" He looked around again, to more drumming and cheers. "It grants not only citizenship, but awards you a great sum from the public purse, and raises you to the rank of knight!"

This time, the hall shook with cheering and stamping, as the lady

Secunda herself handed me a purple-striped knightly toga, all neatly folded and bound with golden cords.

Petros found words to congratulate me later on.

"You have what they will never give me," he said.

"Freedom?" I said. "Surely you can arrange that for yourself?"

"Perhaps," he said. "But I am content as I am."

My gift showed me that he was *not* content, and I saw his envy. But I bore the burden of my gift, just as Petros bore his own burden.

None the less, it was a great moment, even if a greater moment followed some days after, because the person who had cared for me during my recovery was Allicanda, now granted her full freedom. She had sat by me and spoken to me, over many days. I think that there were many conversations when I was not fully myself. But in the end, my wound healed, and though I was weak, I was fit to sit on a bench in the lady Morgana's garden, with Allicanda beside me. So perhaps my memory of that particular conversation was a synthesis of many

"Are you cold?" she said.

"No," I said, not wishing to complain, but I wrapped my cloak closer, and she smiled.

"You are always cold," she said. "You always complain of the cold."

"I do not!" I said. "I never complain."

This time, she laughed aloud. "And you are a fool with words."

"Am I?"

"Yes. And you are a fool with truth."

"But truth is ..."

"Virtuous, except when it is cruel."

I thought of that, and I watched a robin bouncing round the garden between the flowers. I thought very carefully of what was true.

"I love you," I said. "You are my princess, my sweetheart and my darling. You are all the world and there can be no other."

"And I love you," she said, "you silly man with all your worries."

She embraced me so tightly that my wound hurt. But I did not mind.

So the greater ceremony was our marriage in the basilica. Morganus stood as her father, *in loco parentis,* as the Romans say.

Afterwards there was a formal dinner, a formal reclining-dinner, which only citizens and their wives may attend, and during the dinner, the lady Morgana spoke to me.

"You are a free man," she said. "You have a wife, and you're rich, and I know that you long for your homeland and the sunshine. So, what will you do now? Where will you go?"

I was filled with emotion to see that she feared I might go away. Over her shoulder I could see that Morganus felt the same. So did his girls. So I answered.

"I shall practise surgery and engineering," I said, "And I shall write books and …"

But the-lady-my-wife interrupted.

"The-lord-my-husband is sometimes clumsy with words," she said, to much laughter, "because he neglects to say that – before all else – we shall take a house in Londinium: a house near the fortress of the Twentieth Legion, so that he may be close to his family."

Which we did, to the great contentment of us all.

John Drake,
Cheshire,
England.

July 2022

AVE ATQUE VALE

# AFTERWORD

### *Greek Fire*

A machine that pumps inflammable liquid, like the Chimera of this book, is not a fantasy but an actual device known to historians as 'Greek fire'. It was used by Byzantine civilisation from about 600 BC to the early middle ages, mounted on warships to project flaming liquid on to the decks of the enemy. The liquid burned even on water, and the weapon was not just the ancestor of the modern flame thrower, but the very same thing.

Historians argue as to the exact nature of Greek fire, but since it was developed in the middle east, where mineral oils seeps out of the ground as naphtha (crude oil), it is my contention that the Byzantines learned to distil crude oil to produce what we call petrol for the weapon, and also paraffin for lamps, or for fire-breathing as practised by modern street artists.

Likewise, note that Roman plumbing, valves and cisterns were highly sophisticated. So anyone who knew how to do it, could have used this technology to make a still, to extract petrol and paraffin from crude oil.

### *Modern names for Roman Towns in Britannia and Gaul*

I have used Roman names for a number of towns that now have different names. I will let you guess which modern city used to be Londinium, but

Amibianum is now Amiens,

Aquae Sulis is now Bath,

Deva is now Chester,

Dubris is now Dover,

Eboracum is now York,

Gesoriacum is now Boulogne,

Isca Dumnoniorum is now Exeter,

Lindum is now Lincoln,

Lugavalium is now Carlisle, and

Noviomagus Reginorum is now Chichester.

### *Why do I make Londinium so big and splendid?*

First, because the Romans were easily capable of architecture which even now, impresses in size and complexity. If you don't believe me, go and stand in the Pantheon in Rome and look up at what is still the biggest unsupported concrete dome in the world: a marvel of design and technology. Similarly, the basilica of Londinium was one of the biggest in the Roman Empire and if little of it survives, that is because the peoples who came after the Romans – Saxons, Normans, medieval monks and others – saw Roman buildings as a free gift of squared, dressed masonry, ready to be pillaged. So, goodbye basilica, hallo Saxon church and Norman castle.

Second, I am describing everything through the eyes of Ikaros of Apollonis, who lived 1,900 years ago and never saw modern London. He never saw the Shard, the Gherkin or Oxford Street. So to him, everything Roman was indeed enormous and splendid.

Anyway, I write fiction. So what do you want: smallness and squalor?

### *Why do my books present such favourable aspects of Roman civilisation?*

What about the ruthless conquest, the crazy emperors and the blood-stained arenas? My answer is Monty Python's answer: aqueducts, sanitation, roads, law, wine, walking the streets in safety, irrigation, education, medicine, the baths, and of course… "they brought peace".

Equally of course, the peoples they conquered didn't want any of this. Not if it came at the price of their freedom, and this is something that I do stress in my books. So, the Romans inflicted civilisation upon the unwilling by the use of the world's first fully professional army, and they didn't do it out of kind concern but for selfish Roman reasons. Then, having grabbed land in all directions, they found themselves – perhaps to their surprise – to be in possession of an empire. Which behaviour, in terms of land-grabbing by military force, was exactly what was done in other times by the Arabs, Greeks, Mughals, Turks, Chinese, Russians, Americans, Genghis Kahn, Aztecs, Incas, and of course the British.

As a final *of course,* the fact that this behaviour was once common does not make it acceptable in the twenty-first century. But my Londinium books are not set in the twenty-first century. They are set in the first century AD, thus I argue that our rules don't apply. But if you cannot accept that argument, then you should read the vast literature of books dedicated to the iniquities of the Roman Empire. Try, for instance:

*The Twelve Caesars* by Suetonius, published c. 120 AD

*Barbarians* by Terry Jones and Alan Ereia, published 2006 AD

Each of these well-written, entertaining and scholarly works gives Roman civilisation a bloody good hiding. They put the boot in. They do it something fierce. So there you are. There are all sorts of viewpoints.

### In conclusion and finally ... I am a fraud

You must be an intelligent person or you would not have read this far. Thus you will have guessed that I am a fraud. I admire the Romans so much that I am totally on their side. But I am not a complete idiot, so I close with my admission that I recognise how different they were from us. They were not ourselves, dressed in togas, and in random order, here are some of the things the Romans believed in:

- Slavery,
- The empire,
- Respect for the gods,
- Service to the city and state,
- Ghosts,
- Patronage,
- Bribes,
- Signs and omens,
- Luck,
- Curses,
- Hierarchy and subordination, and
- Gravitas and dignitas (for the upper classes, anyway)

And in random order, here are some of the things the Romans did *not* believe in:

- Democracy,
- Human rights,

- Health and safety,
- Equality of the sexes,
- One almighty God (nor atheism either),
- Technical progress (everything had already been invented by the Greeks), and
- *Any* idea that *anyone* was better than them (except the Greeks).

Lightning Source UK Ltd.
Milton Keynes UK
UKHW041211031222
413256UK00001B/111